*HE WAS ABOUT TO BECOME THE
NEXT RECIPIENT OF AN
ARTIFICIAL HEART. . . .*

The thought was incredible! He, Ernest P. Freeman,
would be known to the world within in few short
days. And the heart that had been his companion all
his life would be torn from its foundation, disconnected and tossed aside so that it would never be
of use to him again. What would they do with it once
it had been removed? Throw it in an incinerator?
Bury it? Certainly it deserved more than that. It had
been part of him, formed at the time of his conception. Would this mechanical replica be as efficient a
servant? Could it really take on the overwhelming
responsibility of keeping him alive? Had he made
the right decision, or was he only taking a risky gamble? And the one thought that was the most disturbing came in the echo of Dr. Sloan's original words of
warning—once he agreed, there was no turning
back.

Also by Linda Brieno:

BRAIN DEAD

PACEMAKER

LINDA BRIENO

LEISURE BOOKS ❧ NEW YORK CITY

A LEISURE BOOK

Published by

Dorchester Publishing Co., Inc.
6 East 39th Street
New York, NY 10016

Printed in the United States of America

To my son,
Michael

ACKNOWLEDGMENTS

To Jane Thornton, my editor, for helping to shape a hill into a mountain. To Roger, my husband, for inspiring the idea and assisting as it was followed through. To Veronica, Theresa, and Connie, who listened patiently as each chapter was developed. To Kathie and Fred Giese, for taking the time to share many ideas of their own. To Melvin R. Weber, my father, who spent many hours discussing philosophical thoughts. To Olga Stegal, both my mother and my greatest cheering section from the South. To those who have died so others may live.

PACEMAKER

1

Ernest P. Freeman was the son of Timothy and Katherine Freeman, a couple born and bred from fine Irish stock. Not that they had ever seen their homeland. Three struggling generations in America had wiped away the last traces of their ancestry, and aside from uproarious St. Patrick's Day celebrations, which they felt compelled to honor, their heritage was never given much thought. One of the least attractive Irish traits that had managed to filter through to the family was Timothy Freeman's love for whiskey. A flaring drunken temper and flying fists forced his son out of the household at an early age. Even the love for his mother wasn't enough to preserve the bonds of familial responsibility. Now, at fifty-one years of age, Ernest Freeman's parents were as vague as the stories his grandfather had once told about the Emerald Isle.

And so it was that Ernie came to settle—alone—in the city of Chicago. Not long after that he met and married Doris. Together, they established a relationship that had survived almost twenty-five years. Theirs was a satisfying existence that had produced a small family. Alex, Ernie's son, had now moved to a small flat near the college campus where he was attending school. And their elder, a daughter named Shawn, had taken on the duties of a new wife. Life had passed along swiftly—too swiftly. An entire generation had elapsed from the time Ernie first made his departure from the home of his parents, and now he awaited for his grown children's visits.

The thought of growing old had never occurred to him in the hectic days when he was rearing his children. He'd always known good health, thanks to his Irish blood, which had given him a sturdy body and a strong back. Even after many years of sitting behind a desk, he had never truly been out of shape. As a boy, he'd had the strength of a bull. As a man, he'd taken on the temperament. Whatever had been lost to advancing years, had been regained through sheer stubbornness. He refused to accept the fact that he might not be capable of doing all the things he'd enjoyed in his prime, and often pushed himself to the point of exhaustion just to prove he hadn't weakened.

At fifty-one, Ernie was still proud of his firm physique—handsomely contoured biceps and narrow hips. He was of fair complexion and in the summer enjoyed pararding outside in short-sleeved shirts, where he could show off the muscles of his arms as the sun beat down on them, coloring his skin to the shade of a pale lobster. In time, his hands began to freckle, and a few spots formed on his forehead and cheeks. But overall, his skin was still in excellent condition, aside from a few lines and creases. Distinction. That's what they called it. Besides, nobody ever believed it when he admitted he had a daughter of twenty-six and a son who was twenty-two. Everyone agreed that he looked much younger.

Unlike many of the people he knew, Ernie had always been fond of the city of Chicago. Oh, there were the horror stories that still lingered from the violent days when gangsters and bootlegging were the fashion, but most of them were unfounded—especially in the suburbs where Ernie and Doris had always lived. The worst part about Chicago wasn't its potential for crime. It was the winter. Blistering winds would roar down from the Arctic Circle, leaving the entire city covered in a thick blanket of snow that had to be removed before anyone could continue functioning normally. The end of November until the middle of March was a time of year that inhabitants looked upon with dread.

It came as a nuisance Tuesday morning when Ernie awoke to find that during the night as he slept, a giant winter storm had cut through. He was notified of it first as he stirred to awakening, by means of the crisp voice of a disc jockey over the clock radio. Without bothering to awaken Doris, he'd plodded out to the kitchen to take a peek through the window. It was bad. His car was almost completely buried. A good hour or more would be needed to shovel it out, and he had an appointment with a client at eight.

The neighborhood were Ernie lived was a pleasant and peaceful area. Lines of middle-class ranch-style homes lay in uniform rows along the sweeping streets. The yards were set closely together—too closely if you asked him—with only narrow driveways separating each lot. As time went on, the neighborhood had matured. Where once there had been tricycles, these were eventually replaced with ten-speed bikes, which were soon replaced by hot sports cars with loud mufflers. Then, the hot cars disappeared, and in their place were left quiet streets with stately trees that had once only been saplings.

The storm had left the neighborhood paralyzed, and a heavy shroud of shimmering snow sparkled beneath the bright morning sun, transforming the area into a frosted wonderland. Everything was coated with thick ice. Bare branches bent beneath the weight of heavy clumps, while mischievous gusts of wind danced merrily along, whipping the fine powder into sculptured peaks. Nothing moved, and the only sound that could be heard was the mournful howl of the lonely north wind as it warned intruders to stay indoors.

When he'd first opened the back door, a shower of fine ice sprayed in on his face, causing him to catch his breath and shiver. He hesitated. Then, pulling up his woolly collar and lowering his head, he plunged outside, refusing to succumb to the temptation to retreat back into the warmth of the house.

With a mitted hand, he clutched the shovel and began wading through the knee-deep drifts, searching for a place to begin. All of the usual landmarks had vanished, and it was impossible to tell where earth left off and pavement started.

Slowly, he plodded his way through until he was standing in the spot that should've marked the center of his driveway. He grasped the shovel with two hands, and bracing his legs, dug in, feeling the cold blade sink its full length before finally hitting concrete. The snow was at least a foot and a half deep. Continuing with the motion, he lifted the heavy shovel, hoisting it above his waist, and flinging it in the air over to one side. Without pause, he repeated this procedure again and again. The pavement began to peer through as he inched his way along, cutting through the drifts without stopping. With each step, he could hear the dull crunch of the shovel as it penetrated the surface, then the firm splat as he thrust the heavy load aside. Crunch —splat; crunch—splat; until he'd developed a steady rhythm. The driveway was now partially cleared, and the cotton shirt beneath his jacket was steaming with perspiration. Against the stark white background, he was a clearly defined figure attacking the snow with fury.

As Ernie continued to puff and groan, the neighborhood came alive. Others had begun to venture out as well, and the silence was replaced by roaring engines of all the residential snowblowers. He didn't bother to look up even though he knew they were there, for there was nobody he cared to greet. In all the years that he had lived in Lancaster Park, he'd never really gotten to know his neighbors. He was a busy man who didn't care whether or not the petunias were planted, or that his was the only house on the block that may have needed a new coat of paint. While he'd always tried to be cordial to the others, he felt best keeping a comfortable distance.

George Krause was an elderly gentleman who lived to Ernie's left. He was a slight man of German heritage with a pointed nose and squinty eyes who walked with a hint of a limp after having suffered a stroke many years before, just after retiring. The stroke had also left him with an irritating twitch on the right side of his face that was of great distraction when he was speaking. It was difficult to concentrate on what he was saying when your eyes couldn't help but wander over to the jerking muscle. George was extremely conscious of this, and whenever he happened to notice a listener not paying attention to his words, his face would color slightly because he knew he was helpless to stop the twitching that, by now, had intensified to the point of spasm out of sheer frustration. Most of those who knew him well had grown accustomed to this, and would deliberately fix their eyes on something else in order to avoid staring.

There were many empty hours in the day for George in which he tried to consume himself with a variety of projects. His was the house with the plushest lawn, always manicured to perfection. And the colorful awnings above his windows were always uniformly adjusted to the time of day. A neat cyclone fence encircled his backyard that was filled with dozens of different birdhouses. Religiously, he stocked them with an assortment of seeds. Every penny was invested in his home. It was all he had.

And whenver he purchased his latest piece of yard equipment, he'd step out of his garage as if he'd come across some great treasure, expecting all of the neighbors to stop and take notice. Most of them willingly obliged—like the time he'd purchased a new electric edger. All of the men of the neighborhood had clustered in his driveway, praising the new machine. George's chest had swelled with pride, and the twitching had halted temporarily. Before long, each of them had also purchased a similar device, and all the lawns on the street took on the same sharp lines George's machine had first created—all, that is, except Ernie's.

Over the years, George had tried to encourage Ernie to be more conscientious about his own home's appearance. The first year they had moved in, he'd walked over to give a few tips. The maple out front could use some pruning. Weatherbeater was the best type of paint. Once, when he was thinning his perennials, he'd loaded a bunch in his wheelbarrow and offered them as a gift. Several days later, they were sitting near the garbage cans, withered and dead. There was no time for Ernie to worry about such nonsense. So as time wore on, George tried hard to blind his eyes to the unsightly house next door, and the visits to his neighbor became less and less frequent.

In the winter, George was equally meticulous. After every snowfall, he'd haul out his monstrous snowblower—the best money could buy—and carve symmetrical paths. His sidewalks always displayed neat lines with edges so vertically straight that it looked as though they'd been carefully measured with a ruler. The affect was perfected by blowing the walk as wide as the rows of concrete themselves. It gave him a sense of accomplishment to know that passersby would feel comfortable strolling past his house if they were given enough room, and he was never stingy about it.

Ernie was still shoveling that morning, when he spotted George coming down the path towards him with the huge machine arching the snow into the air as it ground forward. But this time, he'd made a new addition. He was wearing what looked like a house —a red canvas house with a tiny plastic window that covered his body all the way down to his shins. Wearing a house? Ridiculous! Obviously, it was to serve as some form of protection, but it didn't stop Ernie from trying to hold back a sudden gush of laughter. George looked like something that belonged in a children's play, or on one of those animated commercials. The man couldn't be serious. Did it also contain some sort of heating unit? At least that would make sense. He continued shoveling, pretending not to notice even though the snowblower was less than fifteen feet away. He was not going to be one of the neighborhood admirers, and didn't want to hear one word about this latest toy. The old man had finally gone to the extreme.

"Hey, there!" George suddenly shouted over the rumble, deciding to be friendly. "See yer usin' a little elbow grease."

Ernie responded with an inaudible growl, and continued with his work.

"What?" George bellowed.

Ernie stopped what he was doing and looked up.

"What?" George repeated.

"I didn't say anything."

"I can't hear you!"

"I DIDN'T SAY ANYTHING!"

"How long you been out here?"

"About a half hour."

"You got a long way to go!"

"Yeh." Ernie studied the wrinkled face that lay hidden behind the plastic window. His cheek was twitching as usual, but he wasn't even out of breath. For a moment he felt himself toying with the idea of asking for George's help to finish the job.

The old man seemed to read his mind. "I told you to get one of these." He laughed. "You look cold."

"I'm not cold."

"Suppose not. All that heavy lifting can warm a man up."

Ernie grunted.

"Well, you have a nice day." With a vigorous thrust, he manuevered the machine around, and began making his way back down the other side of the sidewalk, away from the place where Ernie was standing. He'd stopped plowing at the exact point where his lot ended and Ernie's began.

The old goat, Ernie thought angrily! He could've gone just a little bit further. There was still five feet of snow in front of him, bridging the gap between the place where he had paused and where George had turned around. Would it have been too much? Of course he was cold—and tired. How would he feel? Did he think getting this far had been a piece of cake? The old man, with all his fancy gadgets, only enjoyed showing them off—strutting around like an arrogant rooster. But would he consider doing a small favor? No. All he wanted was to be seen in order to make everyone else green with envy.

Stupid snowblower. The old codger probably saved all of his life to get one. Now that it was his, he'd make everyone else suffer. For a moment, Ernie did feel envious. He should've made the investment. If only business had been better, perhaps he could've afforded such a luxury, throwing his money away on a seasonal item. But it would've been foolish. Spring always came, and the snow melted into great puddles that were carried away by the rain, and it never mattered that you had taken the time to clear it away at all.

It was late, and he was sure that he'd miss his appointment, and that would mean losing a sale as well as the profit that went along with it. That's the way it had always been. Something always stood in the way, and he was never able to get ahead.

He picked up the shovel and began flinging harder than ever. Crunch—splat; crunch—splat; until his face was burning and his arms ached, but he pressed on anyway with knees flexed and shoulders swinging. This time he put his back into it, plunging

19

the blade into the dense drifts and angrily tossing the load aside. It was becoming clear that the area that he had completed, in comparison to George's, was barely a footpath. He moved further to one side, deciding that he was also capable of providing a wider walkway. He could clear his portion just as well as the old man did—without the aid of a machine.

Machines! Who needed them? They took away a natural strength and caused one's muscles to turn to jelly. He glanced up, noticing that George had finished up in the front and was turning into his driveway, clutching the handles of the chugging metal monster as if it generated life itself.

Keeping up his cadence, his mind began to drift— back—back—back to the time of his father—a cruel man—a raging drunk—yet still strong. Each day of his life, from the time Ernie could remember, his father would fall to the floor every morning to complete a series of daily calisthenics. It never seemed to matter that his eyes were bleary, or that his head was pounding from a raging hangover. His exercise routine was a ritual he forced on himself each day without fail.

Ernie could still recall one morning as a child, perched above the faded rug on a chair, watching his father grunt and sweat, doing sit-ups. He'd been intrigued at the way his father's stomach muscles were rippling across his firm belly.

"Why do you do that?" he suddenly blurted out before giving the question much thought.

Timothy Freeman stopped and sat up, glaring at him fiercely. "Why?" he growled. "Ain't I taught ya nothin'?" Suddenly, his red face melted into a toothy grin. "Ta stay strong, Ernie boy. Ta stay strong." His smile faded and he frowned. "Don't ya know?

Times're changin'. Here I am, goin' out an' punishin' my body most every nighta the week. I know it ain't right. But ya know what? These muscules're hard as rock and I betcha I'm a helluva lot stronger 'n any a them other fools what never took ta the bottle. Do ya see me drivin' one of them fancy cars? No. I got two good legs an' I know how ta use 'em. Do you see me pamperin' myself? Let me tell ya somethin'." He pulled himself up from the floor and walked over to the chair where the child was cowering.

"Machines're takin' over the world. I know I'm a drunk an' a lotta times I don't make much sense, but I kin see it happenin'. They're in the factories an' in the fields. Why they're even right here in yer own home. An' it'll git worse before it gits better. Damn machines kin take over like a hoard of ugly demons. But I'll tell ya somethin', Ernie ma boy. Don't let it happen ta you. Only the weak hafta depend on machines. You remember that." His face softened and it was the only time Ernie had ever seen a flicker of love. His father reached out and placed both hands firmly on his shoulders. "Ya got good broad shoulders an' fresh pink lungs. Yer liver ain't rotted out like mine. Take care of yerself, boy. Don't ever let yer body soften. We come from good stock. Strong people. Be proud a that an' 'member what I say. Only the weak hafta depend on machines."

Only the weak. Ernie glanced over to where George's snowblower was whirling a funnel of snow onto the bank. Strange how this scene had come back to him now, to haunt him as he struggled. He'd almost forgotten about it. Somehow his father's words echoing out from the past gave him an added burst of energy, and he forgot about his growing fatigue. The path was widened, and he started back down the sidewalk feeling an overpowering sense of fulfillment.

It was strange that he'd thought of his father at all. The years had rolled by and the memory of him had faded. Most of the time he allowed himself to forget that he'd ever had a father, or that he'd ever been a son. It was unfortunate.

Ernie continue shoveling, and his mind began to wander to his own son Alex. That's when it occurred to him that if Alex were still around, he could've been helping. Even if George chose to ignore his needs, his son should've been around to assist. But Alex hadn't wanted to stay at home. It wasn't his style. He was more concerned with trying to find his own fantasies. The kid should've felt lucky he'd never had a father who was a worthless drunk. No matter how hard they'd ever had it, he'd never had to worry about having a roof over his head, or eating a warm meal. But no. That wasn't good enough. He'd needed something else—or so he said. The memory of his departure still left Ernie with a tinge of bitterness.

"I'm moving out, Dad," Alex announced one Sunday morning while Doris was still at church.

Ernie had folded his newspaper and looked up.

"I found a place near the campus. Me and a friend are going to share the apartment."

"Just like that?"

"I've been thinking about it for a long time."

"And you don't say nothing to me?"

"I didn't want to tell you until I was sure. I knew you'd get upset."

"I'm not upset. Why should I be upset? You're all grown up. You can make your own decisions. Why should I care?"

"Well." Alex coughed. "I'm glad to hear you say that."

"I just thought that after you finished school you'd be looking for work."

"That's what I thought too. But I've decided to enroll in the graduate program."

"For what?"

"I just think it would be better. I'd have more opportunities."

"Better? You've already got everything you need. A college education. It's more than I ever had. I thought that once you finished up, you'd be around to help me with the business."

"Yeh, well I wanted to talk to you about that. I know you've always planned on my taking over. I mean you've talked about it since I was a kid. But it's not for me. I'm not interested in that type of thing. I don't know how to say this, but it's just not the way I'd like to spend the rest of my life."

"Are you trying to tell me my way's not good enough? It's fine for me but not good enough for you? Is that what you're trying to say? Well, I'll tell you what. It always put food in your belly and paid for all the fancy schooling."

"I know that, and I'm grateful. But Dad, look at yourself. Look around. You never have time for anything else. I'm sorry. I just can't see myself wasting my life like that."

He'd moved out a week later. Ernie remained in the bedroom, lying on the bed as he'd listened to him pack. It was the end of an era—the end of a dream. When Alex knocked on the door to say goodbye, Ernie pretended to be asleep. It was a mistake. In the long run, his son would realize that he'd made a big mistake. But thinking back on it now, he wondered. What had he ever accomplished? Perhaps Alex had been right.

His shoveling ground to a halt, and he felt a burning lump rise in his throat that soon grew into an uncontrollable tremor of nausea. He stared down at the walk. There was no use crying over spilled milk. What was done was done, and there wasn't a thing he could do to change it.

The sidewalk was finally bare, and it was time to concentrate on clearing the driveway. His car had to be freed from the spot where it still remained deeply buried. Slowly, he trudged his way through the virgin drifts that remained, carrying the cumbersome shovel.

The blade was becoming heavier with each thrust that he made in this new location, and each time he strained to lift there was a return of the sickening wave of nausea. Nerves, he told himself. He was just frustrated at being blocked in and wasn't used to this much physical exertion so early in the day. It would pass. All he needed was a hot cup of coffee and a chance to catch his breath. The recent tension had probably created an ulcer. But at least four more feet of the frosty powder lay between him and the street. In another ten minutes he should be finished.

He was panting and perspiring profusely by the time he finally reached the place where the end of his driveway dipped out into the street. Moisture from the damp shirt beneath his insulated jacket was evaporating quickly, making his teeth chatter and his back shiver, but he refused to stop. Only a foot or two remained in one last icy ribbon that needed to be removed.

When he dug his shovel into this last mound, the blade didn't sink in as easily. He tried again. Beneath the layer of powder lay a dense bank that felt like rock. City snowplows had come through during the night, hurling their debris to the side of the road, forming an unusually compact ridge. Once more he tried to penetrate, using all the strength he possessed to try and dip beneath its surface. The roll of icy chunks was immovable.

Another machine! It wasn't bad for a person to have to cope with the natural elements like wind, rain, snow. That only seemed fair. It was nature's way—survival of the fittest, and that type of thing. Besides, weren't they all part of the same biological family—part of a life cycle that had been made by one Creator? But to have to fight against a machine, something that man himself had created to be of help and service—well, it just didn't seem right. Why should any device that served to make things easier for one man, become the penalty for someone else? Had the driver of the snowplow ever thought about that? Did it matter to him that in doing his job more easily, he'd made another's more difficult?

His muscles ached; his back was breaking, and all of his energy had been drained. Through all of this, the nausea persisted and he couldn't bring himself to lift the shovel one more time. Where was Alex? What kind of a son would desert his own father? Ingrate! The world was crawling with people like him, those who took but never gave anything in return. Wait until he needed a favor. Then the shoe would be on the other foot. And Doris. He scowled, glancing up at the bedroom window. What right did she have to sleep late when she could've been outside assisting? Females were always echoing their lament about Women's Lib—until it came time to share a little of the bull work.

He closed his eyes and leaned against the shovel, trying to gather enough strength together to go on.

There was nobody to help—except perhaps George. He strained his ears for the sound of the snow-blower. So what if he had to bend a little and ask for the old man's help? It wouldn't hurt. After all, what were neighbors for? It was a perfectly reasonable request, and George probably wouldn't refuse. But there was no more of the heavy rumbling, only silence, and a small voice inside of him warning that if he pushed himself any further, something was going to snap.

Determination overpowered the voice, smothering it with the intensity of purpose. Nothing would snap. The thought was silly. He was of strong Irish stock, and had ancestors who'd accomplished feats worse than this every day of their lives. What if he'd been born in another era, when part of the daily tasks were to bale hay each day, tossing it about with only a pitchfork and a pair of husky arms? And that was only the beginning. Had he ever had to plow a field by hand, or toil until sundown? Shoveling a little snow was nothing in comparison to the things they had done, and wasn't he made of the same tough fiber? Sure, they must've been tired, but they never gave up, and of course, never relied on a mechanically powered tool because only the weak had to depend on machines, just as his father had once said.

He picked up the shovel and shattered the surface of the mound with all his might, feeling it slice through the hardened mass; then, he sucked in his breath and hoisted the blade, carefully balancing it in the air. With arms trembling and heart pounding madly, he paused for a second to brace himself, then thrust the heavy load over to one side. Once he'd discovered this last spurt of energy, he was afraid to let go, and keeping up the momentum, dug in again.

PACEMAKER

At first, he didn't know that it was pain. It started as a tingling sensation radiating down his left arm that was startling and caused him to drop the shovel. Nothing like this had ever happened to him before. The tingling soon grew in intensity, and he tried to shake it off. After a minute or two, he was relieved to feel it subside and he bent over to retrieve the shovel. At the time, he wasn't aware that his nail-beds had turned purple beneath the thick mittens, or that his panting breaths were growing shorter. Perhaps if George had still been outside, he would've commented on the odd color that had crept along the edges of his lips—a ghastly bluish-gray. But nobody was there to point this out. If they had been, he might've been alerted to the fact that something was drastically wrong inside his body, instead of ignoring this silent warning.

By the time the real pain made its deadly appearance, it was already too late. Quite unexpectedly, two great iron hands seemed to grasp his heart and squeeze. They gripped the muscle tightly, choking out the very essence of life in a crushing steamroller sensation that left him gasping for precious air. The hands were merciless, squeezing even harder until the excess pressure began to spread up into his neck and jaws, stealing away any awareness of time and space.

Now his face took on the color of his lips—a pallid death mask with eyes opened wide in horror and a mouth gaping in an agonized grimace. Still hovering over the fallen shovel, he clutched at his chest as if trying to pull away the hands by loosening their grip. In one last moment of panic, he tried to take a step forward towards the house, but stumbled as his knees began to buckle. The last thing he remembered was a terrified feeling of impending doom.

The house, the bare trees, the shocking whiteness of the snow all blended together in a kaleidoscope of colors and he sank into unconsciousness, collapsing onto the last remaining mound of impenetrable snow.

2

When he opened his eyes, he found himself lying in a dimly-lit room. From one corner he could hear the steady drip, dripping of a faucet. Heavy blue drapes covered a wide window, blocking out the sunlight that still managed to stream through in a slender ray. It was a small room, barely long enough to contain the hospital bed. To his left was a narrow rolling table where a plastic cup and pitcher had been carefully placed. Across from him he could see a squat blonde nightstand that was covered with cards that had been thoughtfully arranged around a colorful bouquet. Next to the stand was the door, which was closed tight, locking in a heavy medicinal odor. From one of his hands protruded thin plastic tubing that snaked its way over the metal siderail up to a square blue machine from which a bag of clear solution was hanging. Just above his shoulder rested another machine that resembled a television set, with a peculiar rhythm leaving its fluorescent trail across the blackened screen. Wires dangled from the front of it, weaving their way down to his pillow and creeping over the linen where they disappeared under the sleeve of his hospital gown, attaching themselves to the walls of his chest. He stared up at the picture realizing for the first time that the pattern he saw was his own heartbeat.

Without trying to move, he was still aware of the same crushing feeling in his chest that he'd experienced just before he'd lost consciousness. He was too tired to lift his arms off the sheets, and instead, lay there listening to his own deep breaths as he watched his chest rise and fall. It was a relief to be able to fill his lungs with the rich oxygen that flowed out through the green plastic tube from two openings that entered each of his nostrils. He would never forget the fright of having that privilege taken away—the privilege of breathing. The horrible memory of the squeezing iron hands was still painfully vivid. He was better now, but afraid to move for fear of upsetting this new-found equilibrium which might set into motion that same terrible series of events that had brought him to this place.

As he rested there peacefully, he happened to notice the door open a crack. He closed his eyes, peering out curiously from behind a fringe of lashes. A woman appeared who was wearing the same type of apparel he'd seen doctors on television wear when performing surgery. He watched as she made her way over to the blue intravenous machine to check its numbers against the clipboard she was carrying. She glanced up at the monitor, studying the rhythm of his heartbeat for several seconds, giving him the opportunity to better study her. She was young. Probably close to the age of his own daughter. Her dark hair fell into a neat pageboy that framed her pert ivory face. Around her neck she wore a stethoscope, and on the front of her shirt he could see a nametag that identified her as Susan B. Werner, R.N.

"Oh, you're awake," she said, smiling down at him warmly. "How do you feel?"

"Terrible." His voice was raspy.

"Your wife just stepped out. She's been at your side ever since you came in. I'm sure she'll be glad to see that you finally woke up."

"Where am I?"

"St. Augusta's. You're in the CCU—Coronary Care Unit."

"How long have I been here?"

"Let's see . . . you came in on Tuesday and today's Thursday . . ."

"Two days?"

"Yeh, I guess that's right."

"How did I get here?"

"By ambulance. The paramedics brought you in."

He lay silent for a moment, trying to digest her words in order to fit together the pieces of the puzzle. Why wasn't she saying more? Was there something she was hiding? It was his heart. They both knew that he'd had a heart attack. Why didn't she just come out and tell him so that he no longer had to wonder?

He finally cleared his throat. "I had a heart attack, didn't I?"

"The technical name is myocardial infarction. Same thing. Yes, you had a heart attack."

"But I've never had any trouble with my heart before. I've hardly been sick a day in my life."

"That's what your wife was saying, but sometimes

31

there isn't much of a warning. Have you ever experienced any type of chest discomfort after physical exertion that tends to go away if you stop and lie down?"

"I don't know. Guess I've had a touch of indigestion every now and then. Sometimes I thought it might be my heart. But it always went away. I felt it that morning—making me sick to my stomach." He stopped and stared up at her. "You mean it was my heart all along?"

"Could've been. It's not uncommon."

He took a deep breath and sighed. "Is it bad?"

"What do you mean?"

"My heart attack. Did I have a bad one?"

She patted his hand sympathetically. "It was bad enough. Wouldn't you say?"

A vision came back to him of the strong iron hands grasping his chest in that steamroller sensation, and how he'd been helpless to pull them away. The pain had been excruciating, worse than anything he'd ever known. "Yeah," he muttered. "It was bad."

"Listen," she said. "Try not to think about it right now. The most important thing for you to do is rest. We're not going to let anything happen. Don't worry."

"Easy for you to say. My chest still feels as if it's bruised."

"It probably is, but if it starts to get worse, let me know."

"Then it could happen again?"

She shrugged. "Sure. It could always happen again."

"Well, what am I supposed to do? Live the rest of my life never knowing when I'll have another one?"

"Don't worry about it now. You're jumping way

ahead. Just rest. Would you like me to get your wife?''

She left the room, pulling the heavy door shut behind her, locking in the tomb-like quality of deafening silence, and leaving Ernie with only these new thoughts to ponder. Other people had heart attacks. Had they, too, been forced to live with the fear of one suddenly recurring, never knowing when the time would come when they wouldn't be lucky enough to survive? He'd be better off dead. Dead? The meaning of the word had taken on new impact, sending a shiver up and down his spine.

''Ernie, honey!'' The door flew open and Doris came rushing through with arms extended.

She was an average-sized middle-aged woman with mousey brown hair pulled back from her shiny forehead and tied into a tight knot. One long streak of gray, about an inch wide, ran from her left temple to the back of her head, interrupting the continuity of dull color. Her eyes were a rich chocolate and had probably once been quite beautiful, but now lay camouflaged behind dark circles beneath, and a network of fine lines that sprayed out from the corners. A long nose was nestled between cheeks that were etched with a pair of permanent creases from a lifetime of kindly smiles. The only make-up she wore was a thin splash of pink lipstick that served to enhance the sallowness of her complexion. She was as plain as the pale green dress she was wearing.

Rushing over to the bedside, Susan behind her, she reached out to smother him with a warm embrace, but at the sight of the wires, instinctively recoiled. ''Oh, Ernie,'' she whispered, dabbing at her eyes that had suddenly grown moist. ''What happened? I've been so worried.''

33

"Nothing much." He forced a smile. "The nurse here was just telling me that I had a heart attack. Can you imagine that?"

"We know that, sweetheart. But you never said anything. Why didn't you tell me you were having trouble with your heart?"

"I didn't know."

"But they said it was bad. They said you'd had them before."

Ernie's eyebrows shot up, searching Susan Werner's face for an answer.

She smiled sheepishly. "Your EKG shows that you've previously suffered other myocardial insult."

"You never said that."

"I didn't want you to worry. Dr. Spaude will talk to you about it."

Doris picked up his hand and squeezed. "And you never complained. Ernie, why? If only I would've known. You should've been taking it easy."

"I told you," Ernie mumbled. "I didn't know. I don't ever remember feeling that way."

"I've been telling you to slow down. You're always pushing yourself. That business has taken it all out of you."

Ernie's eyes darted over to her inquisitively. "How is the business? Has anyone called Jack Nelson to let him know? We had an appointment. I couldn't get the car out."

"He knows. When he called, I told him."

"Thank goodness. He's my biggest account."

"How can you think about that now? Ernie, be grateful you're still here. If it hadn't been for George . . ."

"George?"

"He was the one who saw you fall, watching from

34

his window. I was still asleep. I never would've known had it not been for him. Good thing he called the ambulance.''

''George was watching me?'' Ernie's eyes flashed in anger. The old man had been watching him struggle with the mound of ice from inside a warm house, and hadn't bothered to help? Had he enjoyed the scene? Was it a good show?

''Be grateful, honey. By the time the paramedics got there, you'd stopped breathing. If it had been a few minutes later, you wouldn't have made it. They were lucky eough to have brought you back around.''

''And what was George doing all that time? Telling them what a fool I was? That I should've bought a snowblower?''

''Now, Ernie.''

He turned his head away and closed his eyes. ''I don't wanna talk about it.''

''Shawn and Alex are outside. They've been staying here with me, taking turns the last couple of days.''

Ernie grunted.

''You want me to tell them they can come in? I know they'd like to see you.''

He shrugged.

She walked with the nurse to the door, disappearing out into the hallway. A few minutes later, a young man and woman filed reverently through.

Ernie's son did not take after him. He was taller than his father with hair as dark as Doris'. His chin was strong, and his thin lips were pursed into a straight emotionless line. He had the same long, delicately tapered nose as his mother, with wide-set eyes that were dark and soft. He reached down to pat Ernie's shoulder with his large, gentle hands.

Shawn was the female version of Ernie, having taken on the usual Freeman characteristics. Her body was small and wiry, with pale skin and golden hair with just a hint of reddish highlights. Her saucer-like eyes were set a little more closely together than her brother's, and were the color of deep lake water, cool and distant, as if all her thoughts were kept safely submerged. She had a button nose with winged nostrils that flared out slightly to the sides, a wide forehead, and a hint of a double chin, even though she was a bit underweight. She clasped her slender hands nervously, shifting her weight from side to side as she stared up at the monitor.

As different as they were in their physical characteristics, so it was with the way they chose to dress. Alex wore a pair of faded jeans and a frayed sweatshirt. Shawn was more sophisticated, in a tailored suit with matching blouse and perfectly tied bow.

"Daddy?" Shawn whispered. "Are you okay?"

"I'm fine. Guess I had a little heart attack."

"They said you'd had them before," Alex spoke up, his dark eyes boring through into his father.

"If I did, I never knew it."

"Come on. You had to know," Alex replied. "How can a person ignore a thing like that? Why didn't you say anything?"

"I told you. I didn't know anything was wrong."

"Did they tell you how long you'd be here?" Shawn's eyes scanned the room apprehensively.

"No. I haven't talked to anyone about that yet."

"Are you having any pain?"

"A little."

"Oh, Daddy," she groaned.

"Mom says you went out to shovel by yourself," Alex remarked with a hint of malice. "You could've called me. We didn't have any classes that day. I would've come over."

Ernie glared up at him. "I didn't need your help."

"So you just go out and do it yourself and wind up having a heart attack. Makes a lot of sense."

"You couldn't have gotten your car through. I had to get out. I didn't have all day."

"And what do you have now? Dad, you can be so frustrating. You act like we don't even care."

"You said it. I didn't."

Just then, the door opened slightly, and a man stuck his head through. "Excuse me, Mr. Freeman. My name is Dr. Alden Spaude. Could we have a few words?"

Alex and Shawn glanced at one another. "We'll step out," Alex explained. "If you need anything, we'll be out in the waiting room with Mom."

Shawn bent over the metal siderail, planting a quick peck on his cheek while Alex stood by waiting. Then, turning around, they walked silently out of the room.

The door opened again just as quickly as it had closed behind Ernie's children, and a distinguished-looking gentleman wearing a dark suit and tie entered. His hair was salt-and-pepper, combed neatly to the side to frame his aristocratic forehead. Thick black eyebrows were perched above steel-gray eyes that made Ernie feel uncomfortable. His expression was a buffer to their hardness, demonstrating a look of empathy and concern. He studied Ernie with his forehead knitted into a perpetual frown.

Extending a warm hand, he nodded politely. "Mr. Freeman. I'm sorry we've had to meet under these circumstances."

Ernie accepted his handshake, even though the

sudden movement caused him to wince in pain. "Call me Ernie." He grinned. "I never think of myself as a 'mister' anything."

"Ernie," the doctor said, pulling up a chair and taking a seat as he produced a pen and small tablet of paper. "I'd like to ask you a few questions if you don't mind."

"No. Go right ahead."

He cleared his throat and began. "By now, I'm sure you're aware of the fact that you've suffered a heart attack."

Ernie nodded.

"Have you ever been aware of the same sensation before? I realize that these last symptoms were the most severe, but have you felt anything that might have been remotely similar?"

"You mean did I know when I had the other heart attacks?"

"Then you know?"

"Yeh. And now everyone seems to think I'm playing the role of a martyr. Is that what you think, too? That I didn't want anyone to know? Come on doc. It was scarey. If I'd have ever gone through a thing like that before, wouldn't I have known?"

"Not always. You could've had what is commonly known as a silent MI. Then, you may not have known. Ernie do you know what a myocardial infarction is? Myocardial stands for the heart muscle, and infarction means that the tissue of that muscle has died due to some kind of blockage. Did you know that your heart was a muscle, Ernie? Did you know that like any other organ it needs a continuous supply of blood?"

"I never thought about it."

"Well, it does. This is usually supplied by two arteries that are very near the heart itself, the right and left coronary arteries. If either one of them become blocked for any reason, the blood can't get through and the dying tissue produces pain."

"I don't get it."

"How does your finger feel when it gets caught in something and the blood supply is cut off?"

"It hurts like hell."

"Well, it's the same with your coronary arteries, just on a larger scale. Your wife told me that you smoke. Well, that narrows those arteries. Your cholesterol levels are high. Cholesterol can build up plaque on the walls of the arteries, narrowing them even further. The cold has the same effect. Ernie, you were a good candidate for many heart attacks, and you're extremely fortunate you lived through this one. It was severe."

Ernie could feel his stomach twist into a tight knot. "Am I going to live?"

"Well, you've gotten this far. But you're not out of danger. Right now we're giving you a certain medicine via the intravenous drip you can see." His eyes rolled over to the blue machine. "It's helping to control your heart so that it doesn't go into arhythmia. It could easily do that, and it's important that we keep you closely monitored."

"How long before I'm outta the woods?"

"You'll never be completely safe."

"But I can't stay like this forever."

"No, and I think we'll have to consider surgery. If we can find the blockage, we might be able to make a repair. In a few days, as soon as you stabilize, I'll be arranging a few tests. After that, we'll know exactly where you stand."

"Whether I need this surgery?"

The doctor frowned. "Oh, you need it, all right. There's no doubt in my mind. What I'm wondering

39

is if it'll do any good. The blockage might be so extensive, and your heart muscle so badly scarred, that it might be more of a risk for us even to try to correct it. I don't know."

"And you wouldn't wanna take the chance."

"That's right." He shrugged. "Anyway, I did want to ask you if there were any other illnesses in your family of which I should be aware. Diabetes? Hypertension? Kidney disease?"

Ernie paused to think. "I . . . I don't know."

"Are either one of your parents still living? If not, how did they die?"

"I don't know." His face turned an embarrassed red.

Dr. Spaude raised his dark eyebrows in question. "I see." He pulled himself up. "That's okay. We'll be doing more tests. If there are any other health problems, I'm sure we'll pick them up."

Ernie watched as he tucked the pen and paper away inside his breast pocket, and strolled over to the door. "Don't you wanna know why?" he suddenly blurted.

Spaude looked up. "Why what?"

"Why I don't whether my parents are alive or dead?"

"It's probably none of my business," he replied. "See you tomorrow, Mr. Freeman."

By the next week, the pain had faded, the blue intravenous pump was removed, and Ernie was started on a series of grueling tests. He was wheeled about the hospital from department to department where they listened to his heart, watched his heart, and examined each aspect of his heart from every possible angle. Nobody mentioned a word about the results, and he found himself studying the facial expressions of the technicians and radiologists, searching for a furrowed brow or meaningful nod of the head in hopes of discovering more about his condition. But the staff was professional, never offering any telltale signs that might give away what they knew, and each night as Ernie fell into another restless sleep, all he could do was wonder.

Not long after, he was transferred out of the CCU. The nurses disconnected the wires to his chest, left one small capped catheter in his hand as an entry-way to a vein, placed him in a wheelchair, and moved him and his cards and flowers out to a bright new room on 5SW. For the first time since he'd entered the hospital he was free to come and go as he liked, taking leisurely strolls down the shiny tiled corridors to visit the dayroom, or to simply stare out the windows at the street below. Dr. Spaude made his usual daily visits, but never brought up the results of the tests, and soon he began to wonder if the physician had been wrong. With all the rest he was getting, and having finally quit smoking, he never felt better in his life.

One afternoon, while he sat dangling his legs over the side of the bed waiting for Doris to arrive, he was surprised to be greeted by a familiar voice.

"Hey, there! How ya doin'?" It was George Krause. The old man stepped into the room, carrying a brown briefcase, and pulled up a chair in order to make himself comfortable. "Thought I should stop by to pay you a visit," he explained. "Glad to see you're up and about."

At first Ernie was pleased to see a familiar face even if it was George's. Somehow it served to remind him that life had gone on outside of the institution, and that he hadn't been forgotten. But George hadn't changed, and as Ernie suspiciously eyed the briefcase, he realized his neighbor had come for a specific purpose. He could only wonder what the case contained, and wait for the old man to make his move. His mind was already made up. Anything George might come up with was undoubtedly inept.

"So . . . nice room you have here." George glanced about, nodding approvingly. "A private one, huh? That's good. Never know what kinda riffraff they can throw you in with these days."

"All of the rooms on this floor are private."

"That so? Hm-m. Hospital must be makin' a bundle." He smiled, the movement of his face starting a cluster of subtle twitches in his right cheek. "Yeh, you're lucky I was around that day. Was watching out from the window when you fell. Good thing I saw you when I did."

"I heard all about it."

"Your face was all blue an' your tongue was stickin' out. I was just tellin' Joe Morgan down the street about it the other day. Said you woulda been goner. Of course, I already knew that. When the ambulance showed up, and all of those paramedics went into a frenzy, beatin' your chest and tryin' to give you air, I knew. We ain't seen excitement like that in a long time. Guess you could say I saved your life."

Ernie's face colored slightly, and he decided that rather than make a retort, he'd get back at the old braggart by deliberately staring at the twitching.

George went on, trying to ignore Ernie's menacing stare. "Always knew something like this would happen. There you were, coming an' going, rushing around an' never stoppin' to take a rest. I don't know how you ever thought you could go out an' shovel all that snow by hand. Not like you were in good shape. Did they finally talk you into quittin' smokin'? I don't see you lightin' up. Nasty habit. A man don't look right with one of those filthy things hangin' outta his lips.''

Ernie's knuckles turned white as his stubby nails bit into the palms of his hands.

''So . . . how do ya feel?''

Ernie crossed his legs, and leaned casually back on the bed. ''Fine. Wasn't as bad as everyone seems to think.'' He looked down at the briefcase, wishing George would get to the real purpose of his visit.

''Suppose you're wonderin' why I brought this along.'' He chuckled, reaching down for the case to draw it up into his lap. ''After that heart attack, I realized just how outta shape you really were. You see, I'm a Nutrivite distributor. Never knew that, did you? Been doin' it for years. Ernie, do you know how vitamins can make the difference? Now take you for example. What you're gonna need when you get outta here is a daily regimen of B-Complex, Vitamin E, Brewer's Yeast, probably a little alfalfa . . .'' He opened the briefcase and pulled out a handful of pamphlets, handing them over to place them in Ernie's hand. ''If you don't believe me, read this.'

Ernie sucked in his breath. The old man had come to his hospital room to try and sell him vitamins? He was unbelievable! Tossing the pamphlets angrily aside, he pulled himself off the bed. ''I'm not interested in any of your home remedies,'' he snapped.

''No?'' George's facial twitching had increased. ''How old are you, Ernie? You look worse than me, an' I'll betcha I'm twenty years older'n you. I don't see how any youthful man can allow his body to go to pot.'' He shook his gray head.

Ernie's eyes flashed furiously. ''What the hell are you talking about? Just because I had a little trouble with my heart, you think I'm weak? What about you? How old were you when you had that stroke?"

Ernie's accusing question came like a cold slap in the face, and the right side of George's face went into a violent spasm. He stood up to face Ernie at eye level. "I had my trouble when I was still a fool—when I was too bullheaded to listen to good advice!"

"Are you calling me a fool?" Ernie shouted. "You old codger! I've been waiting a long time to say this. . . ." Suddenly, his face turned a ghastly shade of gray. He lurched forward, clutching his chest. Beads of perspiration sprang from his brow, and his breath came in torturous gasps.

"Ernie?" The old man stared at him in terror. "What's wrong with you?"

He staggered back towards the bed, trying to reach the call light, but crumpled onto the floor instead with an agonized groan.

The emergency buzzer blared out at the nurses station. Dropping what they were doing, two nurses rushed down the hallway. They ran into the room, immediately spotting the body of the man that was sprawled out on the floor. When they turned him over, his ashen face and vacant eyes told the story. His heart had stopped beating.

One of the nurses grabbed the telephone. "Code Blue—Room 539—Code Blue."

Together, the two dropped to the floor to begin doing CPR. One positioned herself at his head, placing her mouth over his to deliver lifesaving breaths. The other knelt above his body. With arms locked straight and palms poignantly placed on his sternum, she used all of her strength to push down in rhythmic compressions.

Within seconds, the room was alive with dozens of staff members who came flooding through the door, dragging behind them the red crash cart. Physicians shouted out orders, needles pierced his skin, and medicines and fluid poured out into the lifeless body, the room having become a place of chaotic confusion.

In the uproar, George had been shoved aside into a corner. He watched the scene unfold in horror, the right side of his face twitching violently. There had to be something he could to to help. When he noticed one of the nurses struggling with a piece of equipment, he stepped forward.

"May I?" he asked, offering to take a turn.

She looked up at him in surprise. "Who're you?"

He smiled and extended a hand. "Name's George Krause. Just happened to be visitin' when it happened. I called you on the light. It was . . . ."

"Get outta here!" she hollered. "Get outta our way! Don't you have any sense?"

He lowered his eyes and his smile faded. With shoulders slumped forward, the tired old man made his way out of the room.

When Ernie's eyes fluttered open, he found himself back in the CCU. There was the standard cardiac monitor with its green fluorescent pattern dancing across the screen. But now, several new items had been added. Instead of just one blue intravenous pump, there were four. A ventilator protected one corner, waiting to be called into use. And above his bed hung a small black box that looked like a transistor radio with its long skinny wires weaving their way down to him, going directly into his chest.

"How do you feel?" It was Dr. Spaude who bent over the metal siderail so that Ernie could see his face. "That's okay. Don't try to speak. You've had a rough time. Thank God you're awake. We almost lost you.''

Ernie's throat felt tender and dry. ''Wh . . . what happened?''

''You had another cardiac arrest, Ernie.'' Spaude frowned. ''I should've seen it coming. You're in bad shape. I knew it from the time I'd seen the results of your tests.'' He shook his head slowly. ''There's nothing I can do. Your heart's practically nonfunctional. The only thing that's keeping it going right now is an external pacemaker.''

Ernie's voice was like sandpaper. ''There's nothing you can do?''

''I'm sorry. The only hope you might possibly have is if you could be given a new heart.''

''A new heart?''

''Yeh. A transplant. But the waiting lists are long, and the odds are against it.'' He sighed. ''I don't know. I'm going to try calling a colleague of mine. We went to school together. That's his specialty. Maybe he'll be able to help.'' The physician's face fell. ''But, I can't promise you anything.''

Ernie looked up at him, trying to find enough strength to go on speaking. ''Dr. Spaude, what if he can't help me?''

Spaude tried to ignore the face of the desperate man. ''Then you're going to die.''

The room was dimly lit, and in the shadows pinpoint colored lights flashed on the faces of each of the machines. One gooseneck lamp had been turned on, and a steady stream of light flowed down upon the pillow where Ernie's head rested. A chair had been pulled up close to him, and it was Doris who had taken a loyal post, refusing to leave her husband's side.

His eyelids were heavy, and the muscles of his back ached from many long hours of lying flat.

"Dor?" he suddenly whispered hoarsely. "Where have all the years gone? I don't understand."

She reached through the siderails to take his clammy hand. "Don't talk, honey. Just rest. It's gonna be okay."

"There were so many things I wanted to do," he choked. "So much I put off, always waiting for a better day. I had big plans. Wanted to take you on a cruise." He managed a feeble smile. "You woulda been the prettiest thing on board. You know that, Dor? I woulda been so proud."

A tear trickled down her cheek, and she gave his hand a squeeze. "It's not important, Ernie. You just get better."

"Do you know that I couldn't even tell that Dr. Spaude a thing about my parents? How do you think that made me feel? Somehow, I lost track of the time." He looked up at her, his eyes swimming with hurt and pain. "I never really hated them, Dor. Guess I thought they'd always be there."

"Please Ernie," Doris pleaded. "Don't punish yourself. Just rest. There'll be time to talk about it later."

"No." Ernie closed his eyes, then opened them to stare up at the ceiling. "Dor, look at me. I'm gonna die." He began to sob softly. "I'm gonna die, honey. And I'm so afraid."

3

A few days later, Dr. Adam Sloan arrived from the Northeastern Heart Institute to pay Ernie a visit. It was the same day that the thermometer decided to venture above freezing, and the sky had darkened with the first cold spring rain. A thoughtful nurse had drawn the drapes open, and Ernie lay entranced, fixing his eyes upon the angry splats that were beating against the glass panes.

It was a middle-aged man who tapped lightly on the door before entering, gliding across the floor towards the side of Ernie's bed to peer down at him. The man was unusually tall, with sprawling limbs and gnarled hands that reached down to take one of Ernie's in a cordial greeting. His platinum hair rippled gently across his oval head, curling around his earlobes and licking the nape of his starched collar. A glowing rose complexion seemed to soften the harshness of his strong nose that swept out from the center of his face like a sturdy bough of a Christmas tree. He had high cheekbones, wry pencil lips, and moved with the graceful deliberation of dancer. But his most striking features were his globe-like eyes that protruded from behind a fringe of pale lashes like burning embers of coal.

"Mr. Freeman, I'd Dr. Sloan. Dr. Spaude called me a few days ago, and asked if I'd see you."

"Yeh, he told me he'd be getting in touch with you."

"How are you feeling? I understand you had some recent problems."

"Better. It seems as if I'm getting stronger every day, but who knows any more?"

Dr. Sloan remained standing and folded his arms across his chest. "I understand your apprehension. Tell me, what is your understanding of my being here? What are your own expectations?"

"My heart. You're here to help me with my heart."

The corners of his mouth twisted up, and he nodded. "I took the liberty of going over your chart just now. I'm afraid there's not much anyone can do about your heart."

"But Dr. Spaude had mentioned a transplant."

"So he did. Which is why he called me. How do you feel about that? Transplanting a heart can be extemely risky business. If the procedure fails, it might steal away what little time you have left. That's an expensive price to pay."

"But if it works, it could do just the opposite. . . . give me more time."

"Yes," he agreed. "It could. Let me explain something to you, Mr. Freeman. The Northeastern Heart Institute has an impeccable reputation. We've been performing successful transplants for years. To date, we have the most impressive survival rate. But this is not by accident. Each of our candidates was carefully selected. While we expect that a person's heart is damaged, it's necessary for us to evaluate their other organ systems. Do they have troubles with their lungs? Are their kidneys diseased? Are they prone to infection? What is their age and familial history? All of these questions are pertinent to weed out potential risk factors. If the pros fall short of the cons, we must refuse to go ahead. Can you understand that?"

"In other words, the only people you want are winners."

He smiled. "Winners? That's an interesting way of putting it. What we really want are those patients who, if given a new heart, could be strong enough to sustain themselves through all of the possible complications. Winners? Yes, I like that. We certainly don't like to lose."

"What about me?"

"Well, you definitely need a new heart. And in going over your chart, I was pleased to see that none of your other organs are in failure. That's something in your favor. Of course, I'm only looking at your risk potential from a very broad perspective. To be seriously considered, you'll have to undergo a few more tests. I'll talk to Spaude, and we can schedule them here."

"Then you are considering me?"

"Mr. Freeman, please don't get your hopes up too high. Many patients are considered, but few are chosen."

"When will I know?"

"We'll try to complete the tests as soon as possible, before any other complications arise. The way it stands now, another setback like your recent one, and it'll be all over. I suggest that you get your house in order before thinking about anything else. Then, if you're still around and do prove to be a likely candidate, I'll be back to give you the good news. I don't want to sound harsh, but I think it's important to be realistic. That's all I can say for now.''

With his words hanging in the air like fragile icicles that could dissolve with the first gush of warm air, he left. And when he did, he left Ernie feeling rejected, pathetically sick, and helpless to do anything in his own behalf.

Get your house in order? How did one go about putting his house in order? How could one effectively pick up the pieces of his remaining life? Make sure your insurance premiums were paid? Formulate a will? Dissolve a business that had taken years to build? Perhaps it would be wise to phone the local funeral home and order a coffin in your favorite color. Were you to call all the people you knew to say goodbye, trying to make everyone love you and feel sorry so that you would be missed? And then what? Die? Take your last breath and close your eyes forever because you're finally ready? Wouldn't it be ironic if, after all that, you didn't die at all? Get your house in order? He'd made it sound so cold and simple, the way one might plan a summer vacation. But on this trip, the person planning it would never be coming back.

By the time Doris arrived for her daily visit, he had been given enough time to brood.

"Dor, I want you to call the kids and ask them to come here. I've got a few things I want to say."

"Is anything wrong, Ernie? Is there something I should know?"

"Just tell the kids to come. I don't have the strength to bicker about it now."

There was something strangely different about Ernie's room that evening. Perhaps it was the way in which the gooseneck lamp had been twisted up instead of down, sending a wide beam of light sweeping across the ceiling that cast eerie shadows. Or, it could have been the silence—not that silence was anything new; yet, this silence was unique in that the atmosphere was filled with an aura of tension that seeped into each crevice—just like the howling March wind outside that had also managed to filter its way into the room in the form of a chilling draft, making everyone within feel helplessly exposed.

Ernie had asked the nurse to help him to a sitting position, elevating the head of his bed and propping him up with pillows. He remained physically weak, lacking enough vitality to even move his knees when they grew stiff from having remained in the same stationary position for too long. The slightest movement, caused him to become short of breath, and exchanging air had become a precious action which he found himself clinging to with fierce passion. His face was pale against the white sheets, making the sunspots and freckles stand out upon his skin like unsightly blemishes on an untouched canvas. Bluish circles encased his eyes, giving them a sunken, hollow appearance, and his lips were cracked and colorless. As he eyed his wife and children from this throne of the infirm, they noticed that one of his characteristics had been preserved. It was the firm thrust of his jaw that remained set in a grim line of determination.

Doris ushered her children through the door with an unexplained urgency, her face tense and her voice barely above a whisper as she gathered them around the bedside so that they could stand as close as possible to their father. There was only one chair, and it was offered to Shawn, who appeared to be the most unsteady of the trio. Doris hovered next to her, while Alex remained to the rear of the two women, his own face revealing an intense concern. They had all been assembled—the sum of Ernie's family.

"Dad?" It was Alex who broke the deathlike calm. "What's wrong? Mom said you wanted to see us."

Ernie smiled weakly and cleared his parched throat. "Nothing's wrong, son." His words came with great difficulty. "At least nothing any of us can do anything about."

"Then what is it?"

"I wanted you here . . . you . . . Shawn . . . your mother . . . because I've had some time to think. You see . . . I might not be around much longer. My heart . . . it's in pretty bad shape . . . the pacemaker and all."

"But Mom said they had mentioned the possibility of a transplant." His eyes were like saucers. "What happened? Did you talk to someone? Is there something we should know?"

Wearily, Ernie shook his head. "No. What good is a transplant anyway? Am I supposed to borrow someone else's heart just because mine can't cut the mustard any more?" He coughed. "A secondhand heart for a second-rate citizen?"

"What?" Alex's mouth fell open in surprise. "What are you saying? That you're giving up?"

"No . . . I'm not giving up." He sighed. "I probably never even got started."

"What're you talking about?"

"I'm talking about us. . . . our family. . . . my life. What's it all been about?"

Shawn interrupted, grasping his hand through the siderail. "But Daddy, we love you."

"Sure you do. . . . now. But no more than I've ever cared about all of you. That's just it. I've been going over in my mind, asking myself why? Why did all of this have to happen? Maybe if I wouldn't have cared so much. . . . tried so hard. . . . you know, to give all of you a decent life. I was always working. . . . pushing myself. I know that now. Oh, don't get me wrong. I'm not complaining. . . . It's just that I wonder, now, if it's all been worth it."

"Ernie!" Doris cried. "Of course it was worth it. Why in the world would you have any doubts?"

His watery eyes darted over to her. "You don't understand. It's just . . . it's just that I tried so hard to . . . to make something for us." He lowered his head. "But it all adds up to one big zero. All that slaving away . . . and I still lost."

"Slaving away?" Alex blurted. "For what? Not for us. It was your business. Is that what this is all about? Dad, forget the business. It doesn't matter."

Ernie's eyes flashed in anger. "Maybe not to you. But, it did to me. It was my life. . . . maybe it even took my life. I don't know any more. But you're right. It never mattered to you."

"So that's it," Alex muttered. "You still haven't forgiven me. Is that why you wanted us here? To get me to feel guilty about not wanting to take over your business? Listen to me, Dad." He stepped closer to stare defiantly into his father's pallid face. "You're right about that business. It did take everything from you, and never gave you anything in return. All of those long hours, and for what?"

"For you, Alex. So you'd have something. So you wouldn't have to start from the bottom like I did. So you wouldn't have to work for someone else."

"All right! All right!" Alex threw up his hands and turned away. "You want me to take over for you? Quit school? Be a good son? Okay. I'll do it. I'll take over your business. Isn't that what you wanted to hear?"

"No, Alex. It isn't. I know it's over. Why should I force you into anything? I've failed. I've never done one thing in my life that's ever amounted to anything. I understand that now."

"But Daddy," Shawn said, a tear rolling down her cheek, "how can you say that? You have us. Don't we count for anything?"

"Do a man's children count?" He managed a throaty chuckle. "I've been thinking about that, too. You, Shawn, and that husband of yours. Do you know how I felt when you told us you'd decided to never have any kids? Is that what the world's come to? That my own daughter really doesn't believe a family is important—at least not enough to start one of her own? Do you count, you ask? What about the children you'll never have? Would they have counted?"

"But Daddy." Shawn hung her head. "You know how Jack and I felt. You said that you understood, that it didn't matter. You even told us we were right."

"Guess I never thought much about it then. It's just. . . . well, now that this has happened. . . . now that I'm here. . . . I've had time to think. Everything's different. Suddenly all the things I'd never had time to really think about are important. Life's important—giving life—preserving life—making the most of your life. You never think about those things when you're in good health. But now I know how valuable life is. And my own life? What do I have? What do I leave behind?"

Alex frowned. "You're not giving yourself a chance. Why can't you be satisfied in knowing that you have us? Don't feel sorry for what might have been. It's too late for that. We do care about you, Dad. Maybe you don't think so, but we do."

"Ernie, honey," Doris spoke up, "you're tired. This is a bad time. Wait till you're feeling better."

"Wait?" Ernie hissed. "For what? Don't any of you understand? What's a man supposed to do? Of course I'm tired. . . . and I'm sick. . . . and I'm so damned disappointed. Can you understand that? I had dreams. Not just for me, but for all of you."

"I don't believe this!" Alex fumed. "So in other words, you brought us here to tell us how disappointed you are? Why? So we would feel guilty? That's not fair."

"He doesn't mean it that way, Alex," Doris tried to explain. "Of course he's not disappointed in you."

"Will you stay out of this, Dor?" Ernie groaned. "Why are you always putting them first? When will you ever learn to stand beside me?"

"But Ernie. . . ."

"Of course I'm disappointed in them. But who needs it? Who needs any of this?" He began working his jaw. "I thought that for once we could all get together and make some sense of our lives—learn to see eye to eye—put my house in order." He choked on his words. "That's all I wanted. But, we can't even do that. All of you have your own opinions. You want to read into what I'm trying to say as if you know what's going on in my head. Who needs it? Who needs any of you?" He fumbled for the call light and rang the buzzer for the nurse.

"Daddy," Shawn sobbed.

"Just leave me alone," he gasped, turning his head

away from them. "There's nothing more to say. Get out of here and leave me alone."

The door opened, and the nurse poked her head in. "Yes?"

Ernie looked up at her with eyes swimming in anguish. "Will you put my bed down? My back is killing me. A man shouldn't have to sit in one position for so long, not when he's paying good money to be taken care of."

They left the room with long faces that were unable to conceal their hurt and rejection.

"Mom, I'm sorry," Alex said, putting his arm around his mother's shoulder. "But he makes me so angry at times. Why does he have to be so stubborn?"

"He has a lot on his mind," she replied wearily. "He doesn't mean it. I don't think he knows how to act. This has all happened so suddenly."

"But did you hear him? He's wallowing in self-pity. He knows he's sick, and he's using it to get his own way. What right does he have to make us feel guilty? Doesn't he think we're also disappointed? Mom, I'm not a callous person, and I shouldn't feel the way I do; but, he was never around—not for us when we were growing up—not for you. He did this to himself. It's not our fault. Oh, I love him. I'll always love him, but I can't stand listening to him feel sorry. Maybe there's something wrong with me, but I just can't."

"And what about this thing about my not having children?" Shawn chimed in. "He never liked kids. He acted happy when he knew he'd never have to worry about crying babies and stumbling over a bunch of toys. How can it bother him now?"

"I don't know, honey." Doris sighed. "I suppose

he's beginning to question everything. We have to be patient. Don't worry. I'm sure it's just all the uncertainty. He doesn't know what's going to happen."

"Well, what about the transplant?" Alex asked. "Has he said anything to you about it?"

"No."

"Do you think it's possible? If he were able to have one, would it help?"

"I wish I knew. He's not saying much. But I'll talk to Dr. Spaude. Maybe he can explain. I wish there were more we could do. I feel so badly. You know that your father has always been independent. This is new for him. I'm sure it's really hard."

"It can't be easy on you, either," Alex replied. "You want me to stay with you for a while?"

"No, I'm fine. I just worry about your father."

The next day, tests began again. Many of the same ones Ernie had been previously subjected to were repeated, with special emphasis. Then there were additional ones that involved systems other than his heart. He didn't bother mentioning the tests to Doris, although by now Dr. Spaude had explained why they were being done. Neither Ernie nor Doris brought up the topic of transplant, fearful that it might only be a dream that could be blown away with a whisper.

It was less than a week later that Doris received a call from Dr. Sloan, requesting that she come to the hospital for a meeting regarding the results of his tests. While his voice remained cool and collected, she sensed a degree of excited anticipation in his tone. When she asked if it would be appropriate to include her children, he deliberated for a moment and then agreed, deciding that it might be beneficial for them to hear what he had to say.

Ernie was surprised to see them arrive in his room the following day. Dr. Sloan obviously hadn't thought it necessary to explain his intentions to his patient. He had requested the nurse to bring additional chairs into the tiny room that were carefully arranged around the bedside. Few words were spoken as they sat nervously awaiting his arrival.

Dr. Sloan appeared at exactly ten o'clock, wearing a white lab coat and carrying Ernie's chart. After making brief introductions, he strolled over to the window and turned to face them coolly, demonstrating the full extent of his authoritative self-control.

He cleared his throat and began. "As you are undoubtedly aware, Mr. Freeman has been undergoing a series of tests to determine whether he is a likely candidate for a heart transplant. I had spoken with him earlier and explained our position at the Institute. It has always been our policy to take certain precautions when dealing with a surgery of this nature. We try to screen out those who have systems that are weakened in order to avoid unnecessary complications. Complications are preventable if you take the proper care. After all, why take on a patient if you know that he represents an unrealistic risk? You understand?" He opened the chart and began thumbing through. "Now, the results of these tests in Mr. Freeman's case." He looked up, his pencil lips easing into a knowing grin. "I'm very pleased to inform you we believe we can be of assistance."

"You mean . . . you mean you'll do the transplant?" Ernie stammered.

"Yes, that's right." He smiled. "As a matter of fact, you turned out to be quite a surprise. All of your other organ systems are in remarkably good condition. Not only are we willing to arrange for a transplant, but we believe we are presented with a unique opportunity."

"Unique opportunity?" Doris asked.

"Yes. As you well know, the Northeastern Heart Institute has been involved in the research and transplantation of mechanical hearts. To date, we have successfully performed seventy-two artificial heart transplants. Most recently, we developed a particular mechanical heart that most closely resembled the human heart. It has now been approved and all we needed was the proper candidate. Mr. Freeman." He stepped over to the bedside. "We believe that person is you."

Ernie stared up at him in disbelief. "An artificial heart?"

"That's right. The Biotron Pump 8000, the finest mechanical heart ever created. But, allow me to continue. If you were to agree, it would be necessary for us to transfer you to our own facility. We don't have much time, and I'd like to have you there by the end of the week."

"But that's over a hundred miles from here," Alex said. "How would he get there."

"We will arrange for transportation. We have a fleet of helicopters at our disposal."

"What about the cost?" Alex continued. "How much does a thing like this cost?"

"You needn't worry about the cost. Once you agree, the Institute will be covering all expenses. It would be covered under a special research grant." His smile broadened. "Mr. Freeman, you would also be assisting us in our own research endeavors."

"I see."

"If we are able to transfer you by Friday, we could schedule your operation for the following Monday morning. By Tuesday, you would wake up to find that you had a new heart."

Ernie leaned forward in excitement. "But why wait until Monday?"

"Complications," Dr. Sloan replied, tapping his spindly fingers together. "To avoid complications. The Institute believes strongly in preventative measures. In your case, there are three areas of prevention in order to assure the success of your transplant. First, we would like to begin the prophylactic administration of antibiotics. Unwanted infections could create a serious hazard. Secondly, there's the problem of blood clotting. Even though we've worked very hard to design a heart that most similarly mimics the human heart, there are certain features we cannot provide. You see, the inner lining of the heart is composed of a resilent coating that protects blood cells from rupturing and clotting as they're thrown against the walls of each of the chambers. While the Biotron 8000 has been carefully constructed, we must still take clotting into consideration. That's why we begin each of our transplant candidates on anticoagulants—to decrease that clotting tendency. You'll be started on them before your surgery, and will probably stay on them for the rest of your life. But let's face it, Mr. Freeman. It's a small price to pay."

"And what about the third thing?" Alex asked. "You mentioned that there were three things."

"Ah yes," Sloan nodded. "The third area—nutrition. It's a crucial factor. Your father's body will have to be well nourished in order to sustain him through the operation and the convalescent period. The moment he arrives, he'll be placed on a liquid supplement in order to build him up. Every extra hour we can buy will bring him to a greater level of strength."

"Sounds like you've thought of everything," Alex said.

"Naturally." Dr. Sloan's eyebrows knitted into an intense scowl. "As I had stated previously, heart transplants are not new to the Institute. Postoperative complications could hinder our most earnest efforts, causing us to fail. They can and should be eliminated. We are not introducing the Biotron 8000 as a device that will ultimately result in failure. This transplant operation has every indication of becoming a complete success."

"But you have lost other patients," Alex reminded him. "I'm not even aware of any who remain alive today."

"That's true," Sloan nodded. "And I wouldn't be foolish enough to lead you to believe that there still aren't certain risks. In a sense, you have to think of what we do as a complicated chess game." They watched as a glimmer of excitement danced into his burning eyes. "You see, we make a move on your body in order to correct a problem. Then, your body will make a move on us in response. We then make another move to counteract your body, and it will make another move to counteract us. That's how the game of recovery goes, and it will continue until one of us wins. If we win the game, you stabilize. If your body wins, it will work us into a checkmate and you'll die. Your body will be fighting back using complications. So, it is up to us to control them. Believe it or not, we're quite good at it. After seventy-two operations, we've learned the game well. One by one they'll appear, and one by one we'll resolve them. This is where all the previous patients will work to your advantage. Since we know what happened to them, we're better prepared."

"What kind of complications can we expect?"

"The first would be rejection of the pump itself. It will be considered a foreign body to your system, and any foreign body must be destroyed. That's a built-in protective mechanism that ends up working the other way. But, we have drugs that will help, and rejection is far less of a threat when you aren't using a live organ. And then, there's the possibility of infection. The antibiotics will take care of anything that is bacterial. But we're still faced with viral attacks. The first thing we'll try to do is avoid them. But if they arise, we have a few tricks up our sleeves. Then, there's the possibility of stroke, kidney failure, sychronization of the pump. The list is endless. It's hard to say. Just because we're agreeing to take on this project, doesn't mean you're safe. Your clinical course could be long and tedious. In the end, you may lose. But even so, you will have contributed a great deal to medical research. That, in itself, is of significant value.

"Look Mr. Freeman," Dr. Sloan continued. "I don't expect your decision now. I'd like you to discuss this with your family. The battle your body will be waging is only part of the hazard. We also have to think of the press. A surgery of this nature will not go unnoticed. Privacy, as you once knew it, will no longer be. There'll be press interviews, the public peering into your personal lives, criticism, judgment, merciless exposure. You will find yourselves in the public eye. That's something that can be strenuous enough for a person in good health. You'll be forced to deal with it in a deliberated state. Your family will become even more demanding. These are some of the other problems you must consider. You may feel strong enough now, but will you be strong enough to hold up under those conditions? Think about it." He moved over to the door. "And try to think of any other questions you may have. I'll be back tomorrow. In the meantime, I urge you to weigh heavily all of these issues. Settle them in your own minds before you agree. Once you do sign the papers there'll be no turning back."

"This is insane!" Alex exploded as soon as Sloan had left. "All of the things he's asking, and for what? Nobody's ever survived more than a few years with an artificial heart. It's unrealistic to dare to believe a thing like this would ever help. You'd never be normal, and what else do you think they have planned? I don't like it."

"But Alex," Shawn replied, "even a few years is better than nothing. It might not be so bad. He said that new pump is an improvement."

"Come on," Alex growled. "Do you want hoards of reporters prying into our lives? You've heard what they've said about other people who've gone through with a thing like this. We'd never have any privacy. The whole world would know about the operation—us—what we eat for breakfast—where we were born. The thought is sickening."

Doris puckered her face into a thoughtful frown. "But we have nothing to hide."

"And what about the complications?" Alex turned to her. "How do they expect to overcome them all? He talks a good game, but think of what he's implying. The last guy I saw on T.V. who'd had this kind of a transplant was hooked up to all kinds of machinery. Is that what he means when he says they have a few other tricks up their sleeves?"

"Every case is different. Besides, it's not up to you," Doris said. "The decision should be left up to your father."

Alex pulled himself up from the chair, and walked

over to the window to stare outside. "Guess I find it hard to believe in mechanical organs. Maybe I don't believe in transplants at all. I'm not sure it's what God had ever intended. Dad, be careful. You may be wasting a lot of precious time just to be setting yourself up for failure."

"Failure?" Ernie croaked. "What do you know about failure? Didn't you hear a word I said the other night? I've never done anything important in my life. Maybe I won't come out of this okay. Maybe it'll be an inconvenience. Maybe I'll even die. But, I'm not going down without a fight. I'll have to eventually die anyway. But at least I'll be able to lie in bed and look back on it this time and know that I had been able to do something. I'll never get a chance like this again." His eyes darted over to his wife. "Dor, tell them. Am I right, or am I wrong?"

She drank in the faces of her two children, then tore her gaze over to her husband. His robust face had changed drastically as a result of his illness, but it was still the face of the man she loved. For the first time in weeks, she could see how his eyes sparkled with new hope. He was asking for her approval, maybe for the last time in his life. Slowly, she got up from where she was seated, and bent over the side-rail to plant a moist kiss on his forehead. "If you believe this is the right thing to do," she whispered, "I'm behind you all the way."

Doris Freeman left the hospital to return to a home that was empty, and, since the morning of her husband's heart attack, had only known a painful solitude. She approached the back door with key in hand and a heavy heart, taking a moment to stare up at the chipped paint that fell from the rain gutters which had grown rusted and old. The accusation he'd made several days before still lingered in her mind like a decaying piece of meat, the stench masking any feelings of relief or joy. She should've felt glad that they'd reached this decision—appreciative of this second chance. Not everyone was allowed such a privilege: to be accepted as a worthy candidate for an artificial heart transplant. Yet, any of the happiness she should've been feeling was smothered by a depressing feeling of gloom. After all their years together, Ernie had never seen her own sacrifices. Before all of life's pleasures—even before the needs of her own children—she had always put him first. But he was still too blind to see.

She glanced down at the shaggy lawn with its ugly brown patches that needed reseeding. How many times had she longed for a husband like everyone else—a man who actually liked tinkering around the house in order to build it into a place of which they could be proud? She had always wanted a garden. Silly thing. Most women fantasized over more elaborate desires like ocean cruises or fine jewels or fur coats. Not her. All she'd ever longed for was a garden—a simple garden with colorful flowers that would have lighted up her dreary existence. But a garden cost money—seeds, fertilizer, mulch, tools. Once, she'd made a list of the things she'd need. There was so much. Of course, it wouldn't have cost as much as the flyers Ernie was always having printed up for his business, or the rent on an air-conditioned office, or his intricate telephone system. When the money came in, she'd remember her list, and then listen as her husband laid out careful plans on how he could revitalize his dying business if he just had more to invest. She would bite her lower lip, tucking the slip away in a back drawer where the writing faded and the paper yellowed and her own dreams became as dim as the pictures she had

once drawn of how she had imagined her yard
would look. He was the head of the household, and
it was important that his priorities were placed first.

Over the years, she'd learned how to look the
other way whenever she pulled into the driveway,
blinding her eyes to the sight that awaited. She grew
careful not to invite people over so that they
wouldn't get the wrong impression, knowing full
well that she was only ashamed of having a home
that was so neglected. Never once had she uttered a
complaint, all the while wishing that Ernie would
finally see that she, too, needed even a small bit of
pleasure. But none of this had been enough. He'd
never bothered to acknowledge that her silence was
a demonstration of love.

He had looked up at her from his hospital bed with
hopeful eyes, wanting her approval. It was no different than any of the other times in the past. When
he'd wanted to use their extra money for a new idea,
or when he wanted to make another expensive investment when he knew that their children had
more practical needs. As always, she'd swallowed
her pride and supported him—encouraged him!
Things would work out. It was important for him to
be happy. Eventually, he'd come around. How right
Alex had been. He never had come around. He'd
never been around long enough to see how they
were only existing. And now, she had given in again.
Their lives would change as a result of this decision.
This time, would he be able to see how she had put
everything aside and placed him first? She couldn't
shake off the nagging feelings of apprehension.
Perhaps she should've stood up and told him
how she really felt. It was just that she wanted him
to finally realize he'd been wrong in his cutting
accusation when he said she put them first.

The next morning, they resumed their positions around Ernie's bed in CCU. Dr. Sloan had arrived, and Ernie cheerfully croaked out his decision. No matter what the problems, he wanted to go through with the artificial heart transplant. He was willing to take the risk.

Dr. Sloan's pink face beamed in approval. "Mr. Freeman, I'm sure you won't regret this," he crooned. "I'm sure the outcome will be positive. Now, there's the matter of signing the appropriate papers." He opened his briefcase and produced an unusually thick stack.

Ernie willingly accepted his pen, ignoring Alex's warning glare, and began to sign. Without bothering to study what was printed, he scrawled out his signature in all the places where Dr. Sloan had provided a thoughtful "X."

"Dad?" Alex finally interrupted. "Don't you think you should read those over?"

"There's no time," Ernie replied with a chuckle. "If I took the time to read all the fine print, I'd be dead and buried before I could get through."

"Did you have questions about the consent forms?" Dr. Sloan asked. "They're only standard. If you're worried about anything, I'd be happy to explain."

Alex stepped over to the side of the bed, peering down at the form his father had just finished signing. "What about this one?" he inquired. "What does this mean, 'Release of Liability Under Research Clause'?"

Dr. Sloan smiled. "It's just a way of protecting the Institute when involving patients in research procedures. As I had already explained to you, transplantation of a mechanical heart still comes under the heading of research." He shrugged. "That's why you won't by required to pay for our services."

"But what does it say?" Alex asked, reaching down to take the form from his father's hands.

"It doesn't matter," Ernie growled, refusing to release the sheet of paper. "This is none of your concern. The doctor knows what he's doing. You mind your manners."

Alex's face clouded over. "Don't be a fool. You have no idea what you're signing."

Ernie paused in his signing to stare up at him. "Look. I've been dealing with people all my life, and I'm not going to insult the doctor by questioning him. Now I've just about had it with you. Either stay out of this, or I'll have to ask you to leave." He finished signing the rest of the forms, then looked up at Dr. Sloan. "Anything else?"

"No. That's about it," the physician replied, collecting the stack and filing them away in his briefcase.

Ernie raised up both hands jokingly. "Then I guess I'm all yours."

Dr. Sloan's angular face, with those pencil lips, melted into a knowing grin, and he nodded.

4

"What time is it?"

"Twenty after eight."

"Why are they moving me now?"

"I don't know. We got a call from the flight team, and they said they wanted you ready to go by nine tonight. That's when the helicopter will be here."

"Yeh, but couldn't they have done all this earlier?"

"Maybe they were busy."

"Does my wife know?"

"She's on her way. She'll be allowed on the flight." Susan Werner started folding the get well cards that were on the table, piling them into a neat stack. "You won't be able to take these or the flowers," she explained. "But your son said that he'd be driving your wife here, so I suppose he could take them home."

"He doesn't live in our home," Ernie grumbled.

She didn't stop her packing. "Well then, he can take them to his home."

"This is a pretty crummy way of doing things."

"What? Moving you at night?"

"Not even letting me know."

"They told you it would be Friday."

"Yeh, but in the middle of the night?"

"It's not the middle of the night. Visiting hours just ended. Maybe that's why they scheduled it for now. Besides, it's not unusual. Everyone else went about this time.."

"Everyone else?" He glanced up at her curiously. "Like who?"

"The other transplant patients. You didn't think you were the first?"

"You've sent others?"

"Sure."

"How many?"

"Oh, I don't know. Who keeps count? Which reminds me." She stopped what she was doing and turned to face him. "Will you promise me you'll let us know how things are going? We never hear from any of our patients once they leave here, and it would be nice to know for a change, instead of having to read about them in the newspapers. I suppose once they become celebrities they don't think it matters. But we do care. Promise you'll keep in touch?"

"What do you mean by 'celebrities'?"

"Oh you know." She smiled. "An artificial heart is a big deal. All the press interviews and attention. It's easy to forget about the little guys you've left behind."

He shrugged. "Well, sure. Guess I'll be able to keep in touch. . . . if everything goes right."

"Thanks," she said, giving him an affectionate pat on the arm. "Now let's see." She studied the maze of different tubes and wires. "Some of this will have to go with you and some of it will stay." Systematically, she began disconnecting pieces of equipment, moving most of it to portable units that had been placed at the foot of the bed. When she'd finished, she scanned the small room. "Guess that's it." She checked her watch. "They'll be coming for you in a little while."

It wasn't more than a few minutes later when Doris and Alex came through the door. "Oh good!" Doris panted. "I thought we'd be late. Wish they would've let us know beforehand." She spotted the machines lying on the mattress. "Looks as though they have you all packed up." Her tired face melted into a worn grin. "This is it, Ernie. Aren't you glad."

"Sure," he replied blandly.

"Oh come on," she teased, playfully pinching his hollow cheek. "You look as though it's the end of the world. Honey, this is a new beginning!"

He didn't reply, fixing his eyes straight ahead on the rhythm being displayed on the new portable heart monitor that rested near his feet.

"All set?" A man wearing a blue jumpsuit strolled into the room, a bright smile plastered on his youthful face. His female counterpart trailed at his heels, pushing a narrow cart. "Good," he said, eyeing the equipment that sat waiting in readiness, then cast a look in Doris' direction. "Are you Mrs. Freeman?" he inquired.

"Yes."

"You'll be coming with us." Then, he turned to Alex.

But before he could open his mouth to speak, Ernie's son had held up both hands in a friendly fashion. "Don't worry," he explained. "I hadn't planned on going."

"Okay," the man stated as if he were relieved to have this matter settled, and anxious to move ahead with their original plan. "What we'll be doing is transferring you over to this cart. From there, you'll be taken down to the helicopter and loaded. We should be arriving at the Institute within the hour. My name is Dr. Nelson, and this is Jamie, one of our flight nurses. We'll both be taking care of you during the trip. There's no need to worry. Do you have any questions?"

Ernie shook his head.

"All right, then let's go."

The doctor and nurse positioned themselves across from each other with the bed in between, rolling up the sides of the sheet and grasping it firmly in their fists. On the count of three they pulled him onto the cart, dragging behind a cluster of tubes and wires. Once he was safely settled, they drew the blanket up around him, and wrapped it securely, using the wide belts dangling at the sides to strap him in. Doris and Alex watched them in silence.

They worked efficiently, making sure everything was in order before moving away, and when they were finished, motioned for Doris to follow as the cart was wheeled out the door. Ernie turned his head to get one last glimpse of the room he was leaving behind—a significant portion of his life.

It was a strange sensation being maneuvered down the long hospital corridor with only the ceiling in view. They traveled out of the CCU and along the hallway to an elevator with Ernie staring up at the square fluorescent lights that breezed past until he found himself growing dizzy. He closed his eyes.

From behind the barrier of his sealed lids, he could hear the steady clicking of his wife's high heels as she trotted along after them, trying to keep up with their purposeful strides.

He knew the moment they'd reached the outside. Cold air came rushing in on him as a frigid shock to his system, and his eyes popped open in astonishment. It seemed like an eternity since the time he'd last been allowed the pleasure of sniffing the aroma of the rich nighttime humidity, or to observe the shimmering moon that glowed down from the dark sky without it being tainted by a film of glass. He welcomed the picture of the stars flickering brightly in the sky like tiny diamonds spewn against black velvet, and embraced the muffled noise of distant traffic as it rushed towards some destination, completely oblivious to the scene that was unfolding in the parking lot to the rear of the hospital. And somewhere near was the sound of helicopter blades, frantically beating against a sea of calm. As they continued to move along, the chugging roar grew progressively louder, urging them onward with impatient anticipation.

His blanket was flapping madly in the wind by the time they reached the side of the monstrous machine, crawling beneath the whirling power source that appeared to be nothing more than a grayish blur. He felt the cart collapse beneath him as it was lowered to a squatting position just before he was lifted up and through a narrow door. Once inside, his world grew dim and he was acutely aware of his imprisonment, longing to have been allowed to stay outside for just a few minutes more so that he could have continued to taste the freedom that nestled snuggly outside his door. The fresh air, sweetly intoxicating, made him realize for the first time just how much his hospitalization had deprived his senses.

Within a matter of minutes, they had all taken their places inside. Doris had been given a seat to one side of him, and she glanced about the cramped compartment with both apprehension and glee. This was the first time in her life she'd ever flown, and a helicopter ride was more than she'd expected. He watched as someone handed her a pair of head-phones, and how she struggled to adjust them to her head. It didn't seem right that his own wife was being made to look like a wartime pilot, wrapped in her brown tweed coat and clutching her handbag securely in her lap, the contrast making her appear pathetically out of place.

When the rotating blades sped up, all the other sounds were drowned out, and Ernie could feel the roaring pressure mount against his ears. He could feel the machine being lifted off the ground, and because he couldn't see more than a foot around him, riveted his eyes upon Doris to read her expres-sions. She sat staring out the window with eyes open wide, not concealing the hint of a childish smile, as though she were having fun. When she noticed him watching her, she pointed to the window and mouthed a few quick words, but the roar of the thrashing blades was too loud, and he couldn't hear what she was saying, so allowed his eyes to slip shut again.

Even the stale air inside the helicopter was a re-freshing contrast to the heavy medicinal odor to which he had grown accustomed. Eagerly, he sucked it in through his nostrils, savoring its taste as a starving man might relish a delectable dish of food. The stifling bonds of the hospital had been tempor-arily broken, and although he knew he continued to remain their captive, basked in the luxury of knowing this small bit of peace—to be soaring high above the city where he was suddenly untouchable to those below. Now he knew how a bird must feel, totally uninhibited, isolated, free, and the thought of having to come down made him desperately depressed.

Life—to know the sights and sounds of all the living things on earth—to be able to feel tender slivers of satiny grass as it caressed the soles of your feet, or to take a breath of air without having to struggle—to move about without being hindered— to laugh at a joke until your sides ached, or be afforded the luxury of being thrown into a rage by a thoughtless gesture. How he missed each of these components to living. How he suddenly treasured life.

And now, he would never know its fullness again unless he were given a new heart. Why had he abused the old one? What a fool he had been. A person never thought about his heart—at least he hadn't. No more than one might consider the way food traveled through your stomach after eating a meal, or why you could wiggle a finger or a toe. Perhaps he had taken it for granted that his heart would always continue to do its job. The thought had never occurred to him that while the rest of his body continued to thrive, this one vital part could become weary.

A mechanical heart. Could it work? Could man come up with a counterfeit product of what God had first created? Now, his very life depended on the skills of mankind and whether or not this knowledge was enough to pull him through. There had once been a time when he hadn't cared, when he'd curiously review what the newspapers had to say about the latest transplant, then quickly turn the page. Dr. Sloan had mentioned that there'd been seventy-two at his hospital alone. Each of these men and women had gone before him, feeling the same way he felt. They had tried, but failed. Whereas once he'd never paid attention, now his hope rested on what they had all collectively tried to bring together and correct.

He knew the second that they halted in midair, beginning to hover. The forward sensation stopped and he sensed they were at a standstill. Then, he could feel the helicopter lowering itself and he wondered if it was only his imagination that they'd been sucked into the vacuum of a gigantic elevator that eased its way to the ground. Before he could ponder this thought further, there was a sharp jar as the machine touched down and the metal doors slid open to allow in a swarm of firm hands that tugged at his cart, dragging him outside.

The powerful lights surrounding the launch pad lit up the sky like daylight, making him feel as if he were in the center of a huge athletic field as a lone spectacle. The journey across the pavement to the rear entrance of the hospital was brief this time, and the fresh air was short-lived, coming to him only in a quick flash. Soon, the outside air had been locked behind them as they slid through the wide doors and entered a new corridor. They had arrived at the Institute.

The cart to which Ernie had been tightly buckled whipped smoothly down the spacious hallway. From where he was lying he could see the white tiled ceiling as it whisked past, different from the one in the building he had left, the more modern design given away by the fluorescent lights that cast a pinkish hue as they glowed down from massive illuminated panels. The odor was also different. The medicinal smell had been replaced by the strong scent of fresh wax and room deodorizer. From the corner of his eye he could see splashes of dark green foliage belonging to the lush tropical plants that lined the textured walls, all of these accessories apparently trying to conceal the fact that this was just another hospital.

The sounds had also changed. No audio-pages could be heard blaring out from overhead speakers as they tried to locate members of staff. The atmosphere was unusually serene, and even though there were half a dozen people who accompanied them, they could hardly be heard as they spoke to each other in hushed tones that were kept effectively subdued.

The employees of the Institute could be clearly identified, each of them wearing identical apparel—crisp electric blue uniforms with dazzling white shoes, and on the fronts of their shirts, dangling laminated plastic badges, complete with small photographs along with their embossed names and signatures. At the top of the cards rested a bold logo, symbolizing that they all belonged to the same family—the Northeastern Heart Institute.

Doris' heels clicked along beside the cart, which was the accompanying rhythm to her nervous chatter. Every so often Ernie would catch a glimpse of her face, flushed from both the excitement and physical exertion.

"Did you see how big it is, Ernie?" she chirped. "I wish you could've seen it from the air. All the lights! Stretching on and on! Can you imagine?"

He was taken to a special intensive care unit labled the CVICU—Cardiovascular Intensive Care Unit, the place specifically created for patients undergoing various types of heart surgeries. It, too, was different from one he had left. Heavy metal doors slid open when a button was pushed, opening the way to a large area that contained a long desk with monitors in the center, and a dozen or more glassed-in chambers encircling the walls. When they entered, two nurses rushed forward to assist, wheeling the cart through a glass partition to an enclosed capsule that was to be his new room. They pulled the drapes closed, locking out the obtrusive sights and sounds as he was transferred from the cart to his bed.

It was an ultramodern place where he was now being held. He lay still as the wires and tubes were reconnected. There was the usual cardiac monitor poised on the wall, a ventilator waiting for use, electronic intravenous pumps, and all the other pieces needed for the care of heart patients. Behind his bed lay an intricate electronic panel that contained oxygen inlets and electrical outlets. Suction canisters and clear plastic tubing all stood waiting, ready to be called into action should they be needed. This was a highly technical area that was meant to be utilized by those who'd been skillfully trained. For the time being, it would be Ernie's new home.

"Good evening, Mr. Freeman." A blonde nurse wearing the same electric blue uniform and laminated badge flashed a plastic smile. "My name is Holly. I'll be your nurse for the night."

"You don't have to call me Mister," Ernie objected. "Call me Ernie."

She looked down with disapproval. "I'm sorry, Mr. Freeman. The Institute does not allow patients to be addressed on a first name basis."

He glanced over at Doris and shrugged.

"Now," she continued cooly. "I will have to go

through your personal effects, making sure that all valuables are returned home. You are only allowed to keep items that are necessary. After all, you wouldn't want anything to become lost or stolen." She began rummaging through a suitcase that had been tossed in the corner.

"What about cards and flowers?" Doris squeaked. "My son will be bringing them from the other hospital."

"I'm sorry," she replied. "They will have to be returned home."

Doris stepped over to Ernie and took his hand as they watched the nurse complete her luggage check.

When she had finished, she turned around to face them. "I assume that you are Mrs. Freeman? Now that your husband has been admitted, you should be aware of the visiting policies and procedures of the Institute." They watched as she produced a small yellow pamphlet. "Please read this over. If there are any questions, feel free to ask."

"Do you think I'd be able to stay in the waiting area overnight?" she asked. "I don't have a car, and we live in Chicago. My son will be here tomorrow, but for the night. . . ."

"I'm afraid not," Nurse Holly interrupted. "Visiting hours are over at eight. Exceptions are made only in the instance of a critically ill. . . ."

"But, my husband's critically. . . ."

"As with dying patients," she said firmly.

"I see."

"However, the Institute does have contact with several local motor inns. There should be a list of them on your card. If you show it to them, they will provide you with lodging at a substantial savings."

"But how will I get there?"

"The receptionist at the front desk will be happy

to call you a cab. Let's see," she went on, checking the clipboard that had been placed on a table. "It looks as though everything else is in order. All your permits have been signed. Good. The Institute requires complete documentation of all agreements. You understand." She paused for a moment to glance up at the clock, then addressed Doris. "I see that it's already ten. I suggest you say your goodbyes for now and return in the morning. Your husband is in good hands, and we still have a lot to do. I'll need vital signs and the list of his current medications. We'll have to complete an admissions assessment that will allow for his optimal comfort and care. If you'd like, I'll see you to the door. You have our number written on the card. Don't hesitate to call at any hour of the day or night."

"Honey?" Doris looked helplessly at Ernie. "Will you be okay?"

"Sure."

"Do you need anything else?"

"I'll be fine."

"Well." She smiled meekly. "Guess I'll be going then. Holly, don't bother showing me out. I can find my way."

Ernie watched his wife pick up her handbag and leave the glassed-in room, wondering where she would sleep that night. But before he could worry about it further, Nurse Holly had popped a thermometer in his mouth, and was checking his blood pressure.

The round clock on the wall behind the nurses' desk read twelve thirty. Ernie could see it through the glass well if he craned his neck. It was late and he should've been tired, but instead, he lay in the darkened room trying to control a flood of thoughts that seemed to drown out any feelings of peacefulness. Perhaps it was the occasional cry of an alarm that kept him from sleeping, serving to nourish the flame of his anxiety as he stared out bleakly, trying to absorb all that was happening.

He was about to become the next recipient of an artificial heart. The thought was incredible! He, Ernest P. Freeman, would be known to the world within a few short days. And the heart that had been his companion all his life would be torn from its foundation, disconnected and tossed aside so that it would never be of use to him again. What would they do with it once it had been removed? Throw it in an incinerator? Bury it? Certainly it deserved more than that. It had been part of him, formed at the time of his conception. Would this mechanical replica be as efficient a servant? Could it really take on the overwhelming responsibility of keeping him alive? Had he made the right decision, or was he only taking a risky gamble? And the one thought that was the most disturbing came in the echo of Dr. Sloan's original words of warning—once he agreed, there was no turning back.

"Mr. Freeman?" It was a new nurse with auburn hair this time, wearing the same electric blue uniform.

He blinked his eyes, glancing up at the clock that now read eight in the morning, not remembering when it was that he had finally fallen asleep.

"My name is Donna." She smiled a kindly synthetic smile. "I'll be your nurse for the day."

He watched as she set a plastic basket on the over-bed table, picking out certain pieces of equipment and placing them in order.

"The doctors want me to restart all your IV's," she explained. "Everything must be kept sterile, and we can't take the chance that your exposure to the outside air may have caused them to become contaminated. It shouldn't take long. Then, you'll be started on Heparin therapy. Dr. Sloan will be in later to explain other preparations he'd intended. Do you have any questions?"

He cleared his throat. "When am I scheduled for surgery?"

Her smile broadened and he could tell from the sparkle in her eyes that this was a topic that was pleasing. "If everything goes well, it'll be Monday. That's only two days from now, so we don't have much time."

The weekend sped by rapidly, and Ernie soon found that his anxiety had been swallowed up by the contagious excitement that swept through the entire staff. It had been over a year since they'd last had a surgery of this magnitude, and they looked forward to the event with an air of enthusiastic anticipation. Even Dr. Sloan's rigidly professional attitude collapsed beneath the weight of this new exuberance. Everything was in readiness, and the Institute was confident in its ability to succeed.

The night before the operation, Ernie's family gathered around his bedside. His old heart had been faithful, pumping along long enough for the rest of his body to be physically prepared. While he still remained weak and became easily short of breath, he was content in knowing that he was rested and well nourished. The next day, he would be taking the plunge. Now that they were in the final hours, they looked upon their time together with reverence, standing quietly in the shadows as they waited for the final unfolding of a medical drama—this unique opportunity being bestowed on a person they loved.

"Do you feel okay, Dad?" Alex asked, his face

appearing unusually strained.

"I'm okay. How about you?"

Doris picked up his hand and drew it up to her lips, kissing it gently. "It's going to be okay, Ernie. I don't care what anyone else says. Dr. Sloan told me the heart they'll be using is practically foolproof. The rest of it'll be up to you, and I know you're a fighter."

He managed a faint smile. "So you think I'm strong enough?"

"If anyone can do it, you can."

"I'll be number seventy-three."

"See that? Two lucky numbers."

"Dad?" Alex asked. "Is there anything we can do? I mean, do you have any last-minute requests?"

"No." He sighed. "Guess I just wanta get this thing over with." He noticed Shawn sitting glumly. "What's wrong with you?"

"Oh, I don't know."

"These hospitals are getting the best of her," Alex kidded. "She doesn't like to face the fact that people get sick."

"Stop it, Alex." Shawn's face grew an angry shade of red. "I never said that."

"I don't mind," Ernie said. "She takes after me. The day I leave this hospital will be the happiest day of my life."

Alex frowned. "You're really counting on this, aren't you?"

"What do you mean?"

"That this mechanical heart is going to make you better." He stepped closer to the bedside and placed a firm hand on his father's shoulder. "Dad, it could work the other way, too. I don't want you going in there tomorrow floating inside a bubble of false hope. That bubble could burst.''

Ernie turned his head away and clenched his teeth. ''Don't you think I know that?'' he growled. ''You think I'm a damn fool?''

''We don't have to think of that now,'' Doris interjected. ''The most important thing is for your father to go in with a positive state of mind.''

''Well,'' Alex replied. ''If that's the case, we'd better let him get some rest. Come on.'' He nodded to his mother and sister. ''Let's go.''

Shawn looked relieved to be released from her position near the bedside, eagerly heading for the door on the heels of her brother. But Doris remained stationary, lingering at her husband's side.

''Go on,'' she said. ''I'll be right there. I just want a few minutes alone with your father.''

They nodded their understanding and made their exit, slipping through the glass door and shutting it snugly behind.

When they were gone, Doris leaned across the metal siderail and took both of Ernie's hands in hers. ''I love you,'' she whispered. ''Do you know that?''

''I love you, too.''

''I'll be waiting for you when you get out of there.''

A plump tear formed in the corner of his eye. ''And I'll be looking for you.''

''We'll pray for you.''

''Thanks.''

''Oh Ernie!'' she suddenly cried, throwing herself over the siderail and into his arms. ''I'm so afraid for you. . . . that I may never see you again! You've just got to pull through!''

The pregnant tear that had been delicately balancing, toppled off its ledge and began to descend in a slow roll down his cheek. He tried to say something—something that sounded brave, but choked on his words. In the end, all either of them could do was cling together in the still room, sobbing softly.

5

It was the morning of the transplant, and the immense
surgical team gathered together in a conference
room off to one side of the O.R. suites for a preoperative briefing. Like an army of wax manikins
they stared forward, waiting for the speaker to
begin, their expressionless faces swimming in a sea
of electric blue. The air was tense in these final
crucial moments before they were to begin, and they
waited for last-minute instructions in order to
achieve the finest coordinated effort.

"Good morning," Dr. Sloan addressed the group
without bothering to look up, his serious face turned
to stone—the captain of their surgical vessel. "I've
asked all of you here this morning in order for Ed
Granger, our Chief Biomedical Engineer, to go over
the highlights of the mechanical pump we'll be using. It's a unique artificial organ, which Ed will

explain, and one with which I would like to see you become more familiar. Mr. Granger?'' His dark eyes shifted over to a burly man with neatly clipped hair wearing a short-sleeved shirt and tennis shoes.

He hurried to the front table where Dr. Sloan stood waiting, carrying what looked like a large red footlocker. After exchanging a quick greeting, the physician gave up his place in order to slip into a front row seat. They watched as Mr. Granger set the case on the table, snapping open the latches and flipping back the cover to form a protective shield against the many pairs of curious eyes. When he had finished organizing his equipment he looked up.

''The Biotron Pump 8000,'' he began, ''is the first of its kind. You are all familiar with the standard Biotron series. This pump has all the same features of the other Biotron models and more. For instance, the 8000 has the identical CSM—Computerized Synchronization Mode. I don't have to tell you what this means, but for the sake of offering a comfortable review, allow me to explain.'' He shifted his weight, thrusting his hands into his pockets. ''Several years ago, when artificial hearts had reached the height of fashion, it was recognized that hearts, like any other mechanical devices, could grow sluggish and lose their maximum efficiency. In the same way automobiles require tune-ups after so many miles, we found that the same type of need had developed in artificial hearts. This problem was solved with the development of the Biotron. Each heart was soon supplied with a computerized mechanism for fine-tuning without ever having to reenter the chest cavity. What we had discovered was the first revolution, making any necessary adjustments through the use of an internal mechanism that was programmed to respond to electromagnetic paper.''

He reached inside the case and pulled out a roll of red and white graph paper, stretching it out for the group to see the conduction pattern already printed.

"As you can see from the rhythm on this strip, an electrocardiogram configuration has been selected to which, once the standard EKG leads are in place, the CSM will respond, changing to any new specifications by superimposing its own rhythm directly onto the tape. It was a big breakthrough." He smiled. "One that gave us an advantage. For the first time, we had within our power the ability to adjust both rate and velocity by using a simple, painless procedure.

"Another feature, the second in the Biotron revolution, was the material from which it was constructed. In the past, we had found that hearts made up chiefly of a sheer synthetic material lost their durability through normal wear. It wasn't uncommon for sudden rupturing or tears to occur, given an unusual amount of blood, as with an autonomic response. After realizing the problem, we devised a way to construct a heart using metallic fibers that had been designed to be as thin as thread. This not only made the Biotron more durable, but also created a way for it to hold a longer charge. Metal, as you know, is a uniform conductor, and putting this simple principle into use resulted in an artificial organ that most resembled our own human heart. It also served another function that was discovered quite by accident. For some reason, the metallic fibers formed a more resilient coating that has aided in the prevention of clots. Another dilemma had been solved.

"The 8000 model represents still another improvement. An advance has now been made that should prove to be as valuable as both the CSM and the metallic fibers—maybe more. You see, for the first time in the history of artificial hearts, we will be utilizing a new source of power." He scanned the group, pausing dramatically. "We have," he announced, "discovered a way to utilize nuclear energy."

Immediately, the room came alive with a hum of excited murmurs.

"Yes, that's right." He smiled broadly. "The Biotron Pump 8000 is equipped to supply its own power via a compact nuclear energy source that works at a 100 percent conversion factor. This means that we've been able to do away with cumbersome charging machines, and have provided the patient with the greatest amount of freedom. Now I'm not going to go into all the details. We'd be here all day. But I would like to assure you that it's completely safe." He reached inside the case and lifted out the perfectly constructed artificial heart that glowed under the lights like a bluish pearl. Rotating his wrist, he continued holding it high in the air for all to see the quality of technical construction that made the metallic fibers appear translucent.

"Yes," he said, lowering his voice to the level of a whisper. "An organ like this could last a good many years."

"Excuse me, Mr. Granger," one of the nurses spoke up. "In your estimation, how long could a heart like this go on?"

He looked at her solemnly and cleared his throat. "Once it's been programmed, and providing it's synchronized at least three times a week, the Biotron Pump 8000, in my estimation, could last well over a thousand years."

The room erupted into high-pitched whispers.

"People!" Dr. Sloan rose from his chair. "People, would you please subside? There are several other issues that we need to address before we can adjourn."

"But a thousand years?" a young man exclaimed. "That's utterly incredible!"

"True," Dr. Sloan agreed nonchalantly. "But before that could ever happen, one would have to consider the other physiological aspects of aging. The pump could only serve its purpose as long as the other systems of the body could hold up. It's that simple."

They came for Ernie at seven o'clock sharp. Doris and her children were standing at the bedside waiting when the cart was wheeled through the door. He'd already been given a preoperative sedative, and his thoughts had grown hazy. He remembered Doris kissing him lovingly on the lips, and Alex and Shawn giving his hand an affectionate squeeze before they were asked to leave. Then he was loaded onto the cart.

The journey down the long hospital corridors seemed like an eternity. Pink fluorescent panels flashed by overhead as he felt the cart move beneath him as it was maneuvered along a maze of sharp corners and steep inclines with only the interruption of a brief elevator ride which allowed everyone to catch their breath.

Perhaps it was the urgency in the way they moved, or the finality of their journey, or even that the generous sedative had begun to wear thin; whatever, he was suddenly aware of a nervous fluttering in the pit of his stomach, and he found himself toying with the idea of flinging himself off the cart and running. Maybe he had made a mistake. After all, it was difficult to believe what they were about to do. My God! They were going to take him into a room, and cut the heart right out of his body! Somehow, a fairy tale with a similar plot came to mind— a story he'd once read to his children when they were little. It had been terrifying, and he threw the book away. Now he was the lead character in the fairy tale. The idea was insane!

A button was pressed when they finally reached the broad glass doors that separated the operating rooms from the rest of the hospital, and he heard them slide open in response with a dull whirr.

Even in his trance-like state that left him frozen with fear, he was actually aware of all the new sights and smells. Laughing voices and running water could be heard as the team finished scrubbing up. The atmosphere reeked of the pungent aroma of disinfectant. Shiny green tiles covered the walls like a coat of ceramic armor, and the pink fluorescent panels had been replaced with stark white, making him feel small and vulnerable. The cart glided across the milky floors to another set of doors that marked the entryway to the surgical suite that had been reserved for him.

The moment those doors were opened, his palms grew moist and his entire body broke out into a cold sweat. His mouth experienced an unbearable dryness as he realized again what was about to occur. All the while he could hear Dr. Sloan's words of warning crashing in upon him like mighty waves against the sand—for him there was no turning back.

He was pulled over onto a hard, narrow table. The room was filled with a variety of machines too numerous to count—machines that even his experienced eye had never before seen. Packages wrapped in dull green cloth rested patiently on stainless steel tables, boasting a professional fore-sight. His eyes darted over to one that had already been opened, revealing dozens of glistening instruments that were waiting to be used—on him. Above the table on which he lay, hovered three broad circular lights that somehow reminded him of eerie flying saucers that were about to devour him and carry him away. They weren't turned on, yet he could still picture the intense illumination that might leave one permanently blinded. On one of the tiled walls, he noticed a round clock that was identical to the one he'd left behind in the CVICU. The time was seven thirty—time for the procedure to begin.

With this cold reality staring him in the face, his diseased heart started to pound madly, and he soon feared that it would give out. But perhaps it would be better to die now and get it all over with, rather than go through with such a ghastly surgery. At least it would be a way out—much to Dr. Sloan's dismay.

"Mr. Freeman?" A masked man wearing a drab green cap and gown leaned over long enough for him to get a glimpse of a pair of bright hazel eyes. "I'm Dr. Kelly, your anesthesiologist. I spoke with you last night."

Ernie could feel him examining the coils of intravenous tubes that clung to his right arm in an intricate nest.

"Mr. Freeman, I'm going to be giving you a medication that will help you to sleep. I'd like you to begin counting backwards from one hundred. Are you ready?"

Ernie nodded.

"Okay? . . . One hundred . . . ninety-nine . . ."

"Ninety-eight," Ernie picked up on his cadence, confident in his ability to manage such a seemingly easy task. "Ninety-seven." He fixed his eyes on the clock that now read ten to. "Ninety six . . . ninety-five." His eyelids were growing heavy, and his words began to slur. "Na-anty-fa-ave . . . na-an . . . na-anty-fa-ave . . ." No! He'd already counted that number. Try again. "Na-anty . . . fou-ou-ou-r . . . na-a-anty . . ." He was fast asleep.

As if from far away, he could hear muffled voices talking to each other, using terms that he couldn't decipher. If he was supposed to be unconscious, they'd failed miserably. He was still completely aware of what was taking place. For a while he continued to listen, intrigued at the way in which they'd been deceived. But eventually, he tired of this sport, finding it too tedious trying to concentrate on a world in which he didn't belong. Slowly. Slowly. He could feel himself succumb to a sinking sensation as if he were riding the plume of a soft feather as it floated into the depths of a rich, black void where the voices could no longer penetrate.

Now he was riding the crest of a magnificent wave with the wind pounding in his ears and the water beating against his chest. Then the pounding turned to a buzzing sound that reminded him of a saw. At first, he thought of George and his assortment of fancy power tools. What was the old geezer doing now? The sound grew in intensity, and he could feel a tugging sensation on the skin of his breast. It wasn't George's machine at all. The saw was being used on him, cutting through the very bones. It didn't matter. He didn't care. He was riding the surf and need only block the sound out so that it wouldn't interfere with his enjoyment.

At first he thought that the saucer-like lights had succeeded in sucking him up through the ceiling, sending him hurtling through space. It had to be them, for the light he could see at the end of the tunnel was absolutely brilliant—the way he had pictured the operating lights to be once they'd been turned on. He was headed in their direction.

The flight ended quickly, leaving him standing upright and walking peacefully along. It was amazing that he was able to move with such ease, never becoming short of breath. The place he was in was not familiar, and he had no idea where he was going, but it caused him no concern. All that mattered was the luxurious sensation of feeling the slender blades of plush grass caressing the soles of his feet, and to bask in the warmth of the glowing sunlight, just as he'd once longed to do.

It was strange to consider his feet, for he wasn't sure any more if he had any. They seemed to have disappeared from sight, yet he could still feel them beneath his body. And there was really no sun at all, only a majestic white light that filled him with a comforting warmth, holding him transfixed.

He was not alone. At first, he only sensed that others were nearby—until he finally saw them. From the corner of his eye he could see filmy figures in billowy white gowns who kept a safe distance. He didn't know who they were, but sensed there was nothing to fear. They were guiding him to his destination.

There was no need to talk. Somehow, he understood that he'd entered a place where words were unnecessary as a mode for sharing ideas. There was a better way to communicate—through the mind. With sweet, tinkling music dancing in the air and the warmth of the brilliant light to nourish his soul, he accepted the fact that he was in the afterworld

and was being urged onward.

He continued walking, never being aware of growing weary and absorbing the serenity like a thirsty sponge sopping up the life water that gave it substance and shape. They were on their way to the core of the white light where all the mysteries of creation would soon be revealed. It was odd how the light was far more than anything visual, permeated with a deep love that brought a lump to his throat and tears to his eyes.

Beneath his feet, the grass began to disappear, being replaced by a rocky path that made him recall the banks of a river. The billowy beings moved along beside him as they continued traveling until they came to a halt. He could go no further, for a great canyon blocked his path, and he waited for the next event for which each man is destined.

In a flash it came, the sum of his life—both the good and the bad, making him suddenly ashamed to know that the beings were also reviewing this history of his most intimate activities. One by one, each black mark appeared, and it didn't matter how many whites could be measured against them, for in order to cross over not even one black mark was acceptable. As he continued standing at the edge of the embankment, he knew that he had fallen short and was destined for condemnation, never to be allowed to cross to the other side. This was why he had been forced to stop. He couldn't be allowed to go further without first facing judgment, which filled him with a deep sadness.

Knowing now that he could not pass on, he began to look around, studying his surroundings. Gone was the luxurious grass, having been replaced by desolate clay. Gone was his feeling of contentment, leaving him with a nagging anxiety of what would come to be. But the most tragic loss of all was one which he couldn't understand. It came in the absence of the light that was leaving him behind, taking with it all its warmth. Somehow, the light had represented life and love and hope for all things, and now he was left as an empty vessel because he wasn't worthy. In an unexpected burst of panic, he began searching wildly for the billowy beings, begging them to come to his aid so that he'd be forgiven. Their reply came in a silent rejection that firmly told him there was nothing they could do. All the while, the darkness was increasing and he was gripped with unexplainable terror. Fearful to be left without the light, he ran closer to the ridge of the canyon wall, trying to follow it as it drifted off. In anguish, he fell to his knees, all the while gazing longingly at the side that was now filled with light, shuddering in the cold where he had been left.

As he continued to watch the other side, he was suddenly taken aback by a scene that was astonishing. There, lounging comfortably upon the rolling hillside, sat his neighbor George! He sat laughing and talking without a trace of the old facial twitching. His face was filled with joy, and Ernie watched in envy and bewilderment. How had he gotten there? What made him qualify? For a moment, he was consumed with rage.

George seemed to know that he was being observed. He looked up with a cheerful grin, riveting his eyes upon Ernie. As their eyes locked, a message was passed along that sent a chill up and down Ernie's spine. "You're dead, Ernie," George relayed his thoughts. "You're dead and there's no way to change." He smiled at him pathetically. "You're dead and where you'll stay was of your own choosing. Take courage, for what you now see is only the beginning. Goodbye, Ernie. Good-by-y-ye.''

No! Ernie wanted to scream out in fright. The brilliant light began to move away with George and the others in it. Darkness surrounded him, and he couldn't see anything aside from the shrinking light. He fought the feeling of being locked in a tight closet with no air to breathe. The hardened clay beneath his feet was no dryer than his own throat that was gasping in terror. He tried to run, but there was no escaping the black void that had opened its mouth to swallow him up.

Then came the sound. At first, he thought it was the heels of Doris' shoes as they clicked along the tiled floor. But that thought was silly. Doris wasn't there, and this loud clicking noise was coming much slower. The footsteps didn't belong to his wife, but to some horrible being who walked with steady deliberation as it moved in for the kill. Click-click. . . click-click. . . . Now the giant creature was skipping, creating a menacing rhythm as it made its approach. The clicking sound was growing louder, and Ernie tried in vain to get away. He couldn't move, feeling as if he'd been tied to the spot. It was a terrifying thought, knowing that he was at the mercy of the creature. He listened as the footsteps continued to come after him.

''Mr. Freeman?'' A voice was calling. ''Mr. Freeman, can you hear me?''

He didn't reply, paralyzed with fear as he felt the clicking sound take possession of his body.

''Mr. Freeman,'' the voice called again. ''Your surgery is over. You're in the recovery room and doing fine. Open your eyes, Mr. Freeman.''

The consuming clicking began to harmonize with a pounding in his head. His mouth felt like gravel, and his tongue seemed to be stuck to the roof of his mouth, coated with sticky plaster. It took a moment to digest her message. He was not dead after all, nor was George. It had all been a bad dream, and he was safe inside the hospital with the dreaded operation in the past. He struggled to open his eyes, straining against the weight that kept them tightly sealed. For a fraction of a second, they flickered open and he tried to focus, noticing at once the all-too-familiar cardiac monitor. The usual fluorescent trail was now different. Click-click. . . . click-click. The configuration on the screen was a perfect match for the mighty clicking within his chest. The sound he had heard was no giant being. Instead, it was the synthetic beat of the artificial heart, synchronizing perfectly to pulsation in his temples. He tried to reach up to hold back the mounting pressure, but discovered that his hands were firmly tied. In a panic, he fought against his bondage, trying to call out for help. But to speak was useless, for a thick plastic tube blocked the passageway to his throat. He continued struggling for a short while, but eventually tired and allowed his eyes to slip shut again as he sank back into the world of darkness.

"Ernie, honey?" It was Doris. "Ernie, can you hear me? This is Dor. Come on, hon. Squeeze my hand if you can hear me."

He tried, but was too weak to move.

"It's no use, Mom." Alex was near. "He's been like this ever since they brought him back to his room. Maybe tomorrow. You've got to give him a chance to rest."

Doris pulled her hand away, and the absence of its warmth left Ernie in helpless desperation. If only his body didn't ache so, perhaps he would've been able to respond.

"Suppose you're right," she replied with resignation. "We'll come back tomorrow. Maybe he'll be better."

"Yeh. Besides, we should check up on Shawn. I knew she wasn't looking right. I was going to call Jack, but she wouldn't let me."

Ernie strained to listen, wondering what had happened to his daughter.

"She'll be all right," Doris said. "It was the strain. She never was a strong child."

"Do they know what it is?"

"Dr. Sloan thinks it's probably physical exhaustion, but they're running some tests to be sure."

"Too bad. I know how badly she wanted to be here once it was over. When Dad wakes up, we'd better not mention it. No need to cause him to worry."

Ernie's stomach tightened. With all his strength, he tried to show some indication of life—that he had heard them and already knew something was wrong. But it was impossible to pry open his eyes, and before he could concentrate on it further, he'd drifted back into darkness with only the dull click-clicking lulling him to sleep.

Doris and Alex made their way out of the glass cubicle, stopping at the desk in the center of the unit to talk to the nurse. They were a somber pair who faced the youthful woman in electric blue as she sat calmly charting.

"Excuse me," Doris said. "How long do you think he'll be this way?"

The nurse stopped what she was doing and looked up. "Nobody knows for sure. It's not uncommon for a patient undergoing this type of surgery to slip into a coma."

"Coma?"

"A very light coma," she said reassuringly. "There was a bit of trouble during the operation. We almost lost your husband. The neurological disturbances you're seeing are due to a temporary loss of blood flow to his brain. But it only lasted less than two minutes, and I'm sure he'll recover without any permanent damage. Hasn't Dr. Sloan explained all of this to you?"

"Yes." Doris nodded wearily, casting her eyes downward at the shiny tiled floor. "So we just have to wait. Is that it?"

"That's right." The nurse smiled. "Please don't worry. Everything's under control. The Institute is very good at handling these types of problems."

They left the CVICU in silence, plodding down the corridor to return to the waiting room. It was still too early to go back to the hotel. Perhaps if they waited, there would be a change.

"Mrs. Freeman?" A perky, middle-aged man strolled into the room before they could get comfortable. He planted his feet in front of the chairs in which they were seated. "My name is Warren Beacher. I'm with public relations." He extended a hand.

Alex leaned forward in his chair, eyeing him suspiciously.

"What can I do for you?" Doris asked, trying her hardest to sound pleasant.

"I'm glad you asked that," he replied, motioning to an empty chair across from them. "Do you mind?"

"No, please."

With a sigh, he sank into the chair and crossed his legs. "I wanted to give you a little time before I contacted you," he explained. "We gave out a press release earlier this afternoon about your husband's surgery, and now we have reporters all over the place. They'll be interviewing Dr. Sloan, but I thought it would be a good idea to include you. You know, give it more human interest." He glanced down at his watch. "We'll be holding a press conference in about an hour. I'd like you to be present."

"I don't think my mother's up to it," Alex said with a hint of disgust over the man's apparent lack of consideration. "It's been a long day, and my Dad's not doing well."

"Not doing well?" Beacher's eyebrows shot up. "I wouldn't go so far as to say that. No. I think it's better to think positively at a time like this. All we want out of you is a simple comment from the heart. You know, tell them how relieved you are that it's finally over—that he's made it this far. You could probably mention your gratitude."

"Gratitude?" Alex asked in disbelief. "We don't even know where my father stands—whether he'll ever wake up or not, and you want us to talk about gratitude?"

"I never mentioned you," Warren Beacher commented dryly. "I was referring to your mother."

"But my husband isn't doing well," Doris objected. "You see, there was a problem during surgery and . . . ."

"Problem?" Warren snapped. "I'm not aware of any problem at least not any problem due to the Institute. Now, there may have been a problem with your husband. We try our hardest to screen all candidates. But nothing we can't resolve. Problem?" He scowled. "Perhaps you're right. This probably isn't the right time for you to be talking to the press. We'll talk about it further down the road."

Later that evening, Doris and Alex sat watching the ten o'clock news. The Northeastern Heart Institute's seventy-third artificial heart transplant had become official, and Dr. Sloan stood before a podium with microphones poised.

"The surgery went well," he was saying with confidence. "Of course, I'm not going to deny the fact that we encountered a bit of trouble—nothing that we weren't able to get immediately under control. Mr. Freeman's now back in intensive care. His vital signs are stable. His family has been in to visit. The heart is functioning well."

"You said that you'd had trouble," a reporter spoke up. "Exactly what kind of trouble?"

"Synchronization of the pump," Dr. Sloan replied aloofly. "We were meeting with unexpected vascular resistance, and couldn't get the heart to properly synchronize."

"Did this endanger Mr. Freeman's life?"

"Yes it did. It was necessary for us to act within a matter of seconds. Fortunately, our transplant team is one of the finest in the world. They were able to move in swiftly, making all the proper alterations before it could have any serious effects."

"And Mr. Freeman is no worse for the wear?"

"That's right. As I said before, his vital signs are stable and the heart is functioning perfectly."

"Dr. Sloan." Another reporter stood up. "We understand that the heart you used today is the first artificial organ to be powered by a nuclear energy source. Is that true?"

"Yes."

"Could you tell us a little more about it? This seems to be a big breakthrough."

"You're quite right," he agreed. "The Biotron Pump 8000 is the first of its kind. We expect to see results that are most beneficial to the patient. With this type of continual power being supplied, there will be no need for the usual charging devices that you had previously seen. It's a mechanism of convenience; that is, convenience for the patient so that he won't be burdened with lugging around heavy machinery. We believe it's the thing of the future."

"But nuclear energy? Is it safe?"

"Completely safe. As you well know, we would never attempt using any device that hasn't already been approved by the FDA. It's been in the working for several years. It's a giant step forward in the area of heart transplants."

"And this heart will never have to be recharged?"

"Correct."

"Just how long do you expect that it will be able to function? For an average lifespan?"

Dr. Sloan stared down at the reporter. "That's one of the issues we'll be examining most closely," he replied. "But just how long is a lifespan once a disease has been resolved? We may be moving into a new era of medicine."

"Could you . . ."

"Excuse me," Sloan interrupted, calling on another reporter who'd held up his hand.

"What about the family?" he asked. "How do they feel about all of this?"

"Mr. Freeman has a very supportive family. I spoke with his wife and son earlier. They're delighted with the results so far, and are relieved that it's over. This has been a wearing experience as I'm sure you can imagine. They were in to see him and were amazed at how well he looked."

Alex pulled himself up from his chair, and walked over to snap off the set. "Can you believe that guy?" he growled. "Making everything sound all sweet and dandy. Why didn't he tell them Dad's in a coma, and that we're worried sick? And did anyone ever mention to you that the heart they'd be using would be powered with nuclear energy?''

''They may have said something,'' Doris said softly. ''I can't remember. It all happened so fast. And your father was the one signing all the permits. He probably knew and didn't want to tell us. You know how he hates for us to worry. Alex, it's okay.'' She stepped next to her son and patted his arm. While she tried to maintain her composure, she couldn't help but wonder why it had been so important for Dr. Sloan to present such a glossy picture. She couldn't quite put her finger on it, but there was something about the Institute that she was beginning to find unnerving.

6

The first impulse Ernie had was to rip everything from his body in order to set himself free; but instead he lay still, afraid to move for fear of upsetting the tangled network of tubes and wires that encircled him. It wasn't that they were merely external pieces of artifact, for his lengthy stay in two hospitals had already taught him to feel at ease with those types of harmless accessories. No, these were more complex internal perforators that sprouted from every orifice, and from some places where there were no natural openings, as if he'd somehow grown a host of new appendages. So he chose to lay quietly, listening to the steady tick-ticking of his new mechanical heart.

A few minutes later, the glass door opened and a tall, lanky woman clothed in a yellow gown with blue surgical cap and mask appeared. Ernie watched her closely, wondering why she was wearing that type of apparel. Did she plan another operation? He observed her movments, watching as she walked over to a corner to drag to the bedside a large, box-like machine that resembled the ones used to perform standard EKG's. On the top of the machine sat rows of knobs and dials, and on the side he could see the usual wires loosely hanging, with colorful plastic clips at each end. Without saying a word, she reached over the siderail with a gloved hand to open his gown and expose his naked chest, and began attaching four of the colorful clips to sticky white pads that had already been pasted to his flesh in a lopsided rectangle—two near each of his armpits bordering his gaping chest incision, and two just above his belly. After making certain all was in order, she stepped back to the machine to turn it on.

He didn't feel anything, just watched as the red and white graph paper on the top of the machine began to roll. From all indications, it appeared to be the same as any other regular EKG, with only one difference. Instead of the paper being free from any pattern until the tracing of his own heart could be transposed, this paper already portrayed a perfectly printed rhythm. As the paper continued to roll along he could see how his heartbeat differed, falling erratically around the other pattern. She reached over to adjust one of the knobs, and gradually the patterns began to merge into one. The picture of the spindly woman hovering over the machine, her thin shoulders and neck arched in concentration, somehow reminded him of a movie he'd once seen where a miserly tycoon stood licking his lips as he waited for the next stock market report to roll off his ticker tape machine. She watched the configurations with the same type of intensity—waiting for the reaction of his mechanical heart as if it were her own financial investment.

When she was satisfied that the two rhythms would remain unified, she turned one of the dials to cut off the power, and began disconnecting the colorful clips. As an afterthought, she flipped the gown back up to cover his bare shoulders. When her arm happened to brush against his, he reached out to grab her, and she looked down at him, eyes open wide with surprise.

He couldn't speak. A thick tube in his throat blocked the movement of air, and he noticed that it was connected to a ventilator. Not wanting to lose her attention, he tried mouthing a few words.

"Oh, you're awake," she said. "Well, that's good. Let go of my arm and I'll go tell your nurse."

He moved his lips again, forming words that could be read more easily, but she showed no interest in what he was trying to say. Finally, he let go of her, deciding that it might be better if she were allowed to leave in order to relay her message and bring back someone who could help.

It was a relief to see Rita Lawry come through the door a few minutes later. Hers was a familiar face that he'd grown accustomed to over the past several days. Slipping in and out of consciousness, he'd caught glimpses of her as she'd gone about her work. Once, she'd gotten close enough for him to read her picture I.D., just before he'd sunk into his world of darkness, which is how he'd come to know her name.

He'd liked her the moment they'd first met. Towering over his bed that first morning like a mighty mountain of flesh, her large bosom heaving from just the physical exertion of having to move her weight and her pudgy hands perched daintily in the place where there should've been hips, she reminded him of a plump mother hen. Fuzzy reddish hair floated about her animated face with its smooth forehead and invisible brows, and she had wide-set eyes that were honest and filled with expression, a comical pug nose, and an elastic mouth that could easily twist itself into a puckered grin whenever she felt the inclination. Working diligently in his room while she thought he remained asleep, she'd hum softly to herself, filling the air with the sound of a rich alto melody that he always found comforting. In spite of her plumpness, she carried herself with unusual grace, her flowing motions demonstrating a certain gentleness of spirit, and with each passing day it became more apparent that she was one person who didn't fit the usual plastic mold of people who made up the staff of employees at the Institute. Perhaps it was through her flaws that she came across as being genuinely human, and he sensed that she was a friend.

She came through the door, strolling purposefully to his side, and looked down at him to study the eyes that now remained open. "So you really are awake," she commented. "Can you wiggle your fingers? If you can hear me, wiggle your fingers."

She watched his hands as they attempted a weak flutter.

"Good!" she sang out in delight. "Dr. Sloan will be happy to hear about this."

He mouthed a few words and she concentrated on his lips, trying to decipher the message.

"What day is it? Is that what you want to know?"

He nodded eagerly, glad that someone had finally understood.

"It's Tuesday the sixteenth, over a week since your surgery."

His eyes rolled upward in amazement.

"Yes," she replied with a note of compassion. "It has been a while. I'm going out now to call the doctor. He wanted us to notify him the moment you awakened. Just relax." She started for the doorway, then turned around. "And try to stay with us."

It wasn't long afterwards that Dr. Sloan came marching into the room wearing the identical yellow gown with cap and mask that both Rita and the ticker tape lady had worn. The skinny white ties to the mask formed a bow in the back of his head, and against his silver hair, making him look like a loosely wrapped Christmas package. He sauntered about eyeing the equipment, then turned around to face him. "Mr. Freeman?" he asked with authority. "Can you hear me?"

Ernie nodded.

"Good." A smile formed behind the covering on his face. "That's very good indeed. The reason you aren't able to talk is because we have you on a ventilator. That tube in your mouth passes beneath your vocal chords. Once it's out you'll be able to speak again, so don't let it concern you."

Ernie motioned to the mask the doctor was wearing.

"This?" Sloan pointed to his face. "Are you wondering why I'm dressed this way? It's because I've placed you in a type of isolation. Just a precaution. I don't want you catching any bugs—an ounce of prevention, you know. Anyway, every person coming into this room must wear the same getup so they don't carry in any germs. Do you understand?"

Ernie nodded.

"How do you feel?" the doctor asked. "We adjusted your heart today. I thought it might have been turned up too high. Maybe that was part of your problem. Do you feel any better? Any ringing in your ears?"

Ernie shook his head, noticing for the first time that the pulsating pressure in his temples had been relieved.

"Good," he said, reaching down to take a peek at the chest incision. "Looks like you're healing nicely. Everything appears to be going well. Try to rest now, and don't worry. We're not going to let anything happen to you."

Later that morning, about the time Rita had started to give him a bedbath, Doris popped into the room. From the glow of excitement on her face, it was apparent she'd been given the news about his return to consciousness.

"Oh Ernie!" she cried, rushing through the glass door and over to his side. "It's so good to see you with your eyes open! You had us worried!"

Ernie reached up to give her hand a squeeze.

"You're going to be okay." She looked over at Rita hopefully. "Isn't that right?"

The hefty nurse, who was standing with a soapy washcloth in her hand, winked. "We sure hope so." Then, glancing down at Ernie, she noticed that he was beginning to shiver beneath the skimpy towel, his naked body partially exposed and forming goose bumps. "Look," she explained. "I've got to finish this bath before he catches cold. Why don't you step out, and I'll call you when I'm finished?"

Doris nodded politely and began to step away, but Ernie clutched at her hand, refusing to let go. She found herself remaining anchored to the spot, throwing the nurse a look of helplessness.

"She'll be back," Rita tried to console him. "It's okay."

But he refused to let go of his wife's hand.

"Oh what the heck," she finally said good-naturedly, tossing Doris a warm washcloth. "You wanta help? Maybe between the two of us, we can get this job finished a little faster."

Doris beamed with joy, dropping her purse on the table and rolling up her sleeves.

Together, the two women went to work on him, scrubbing each of his limbs. When they were finished, Rita drew back the towel to begin washing his torso, and at the unexpected sight of her husband's mutilated body, Doris' face suddenly paled. It was the first time she'd actually seen the results of his surgery, and the raw incision and deeply inbedded tubes came as a shock. She took a deep breath, pretending she hadn't noticed the change, and set about the task of helping to finish bathing him. All the while he studied her face, trying to understand her strained expression. There was so much he wanted to say, so much he wanted to tell her—the apprehension, the pain, the surgical experience, and most of all he wanted to confess to her his discovery during the brief encounter with death. He wondered if she could possibly understand, and he watched her carefully in order to read her alteration in behavior, realizing that she was treating him a little differently and hoping that whatever it was that had caused this change would eventually resolve itself.

Being awake and aware in the tiny glassed-in room was not without its consequences. Time seemed to drag along in an endless stream of having blood samples taken, being poked with needles, and every third day undergoing another encounter with the ticker tape girl. The round clock on the wall outside of his door moved slowly as the big black hands pointed to whatever time it was, and there was no way to tell whether six o'clock meant day or evening, since the moon and the sun had become forgotten entities that now only existed as memories in the room without windows.

But progress was made, and it wasn't long before the tubes in his chest were removed, which made each breath on the ventilator come more easily. Shortly thereafter, they began the stages of weaning, and before long he was breathing on his own with only the thick tube in his throat to act as an airway. It came as a surprise one morning when Dr. Sloan announced that this tube could also be removed. In a hurried procedure, the tube was suctioned clear and then yanked free, leaving him gasping for air and croaking words in a voice that was raspy from lack of use.

When Doris arrived for her daily visit, she was thrilled that he could finally talk. Leaning over the metal siderail, she threw her arms around him to give him an encouraging hug.

"What do you have to say about all of this, honey?" she asked through joyful tears. "I know there's been so much you've wanted to tell us."

"How . . . how's . . . Shawn?" he managed to ask.

Doris looked down at him in surprise. "You know? You heard that something happened?" She pulled away from him, and turned to stare out the glass door where she could pretend to be concentrating on the view outside. "It's nothing much. Some kind of an influenza. She'll be fine."

"Has she been in to see me?"

"No. You see, we all have to be careful. Don't I look silly wearing this mask? I feel like a surgeon." She giggled nervously. "Good thing I'm not."

"Where is Shawn?"

"She's here, at the hospital. But she should be going home soon." Doris turned around, brushing aside a tear that had rolled from her eye. "Honey, I don't think they'll let her see you. At least not until she's better."

"How about Alex?"

"He'll be back. He had to go back to finish his classes, but he'll be here for the weekend."

Ernie stared down at the sheet, then looked up at her with eyes filled with anguish. "Dor . . . it was terrible."

She rushed over to him, taking his hand in her own. "I know, sweetheart, but it's all over now."

"No. You don't understand. I've . . . I've been to hell and back."

"Of course you have. You had a rough time."

"No," he croaked impatiently. "I mean it. I've seen the other side. I've seen what's waiting. It was a . . . a nightmare. Horrible!"

She patted his hand. "And that's how you have to look at it. It all has been like a bad dream."

"Dor, when I die I'm going to hell. Do you . . . do you understand? That's what I saw."

"I understand," she cooed sympathetically. "But I don't think you've been that bad a person. Whatever you saw was probably only a bad dream. Don't worry about it."

"Just a bad dream?" he asked. "You think so?"

"Of course," she replied. "Lots of people have strange reactions during surgery. Don't worry about it. We'll talk about it later."

"A bad dream," he repeated to himself. "That's probably all it was." He tried to sound convincing, pushing the memory aside so he wouldn't have to deal with the frightful thought any longer.

His recovery continued, and IPPB treatments were started in order to insure proper expansion of his lungs. As he stabilized, the tube going into his stomach was removed and he was allowed to eat. At first it was only a few sips of water and several chunks of ice chips, but gradually his diet was increased until he was tolerating at least half a tray of food at each mealtime. Hunger was a desire that had never plagued him, but his thirst could never be quenched. Once he was allowed to drink, he consumed glass after glass of any kind of liquid beverage available until Dr. Sloan found it necessary to set limitations. All the while, complications were gracefully skirted as he continued to grow stronger each day.

By the time one month had passed since his transplant, he was looking especially well, considering he had survived the short bout with cerebral anoxia that had occurred during the procedure. He remained in the CVICU under close observation, but gradually expanded his activity tolerance to not only being assisted to a chair, but to also take brief walks out of the glass cubicle and about the unit with a nurse poised on each arm. Since he was still required to remain in reverse isolation for the prevention of infections, everyone continued wearing their gowns and masks during their walks, including him. Together, they made up a crawling parade each day when he ambulated, boldly exhibiting their bright uniforms to all the other patients who curiously watched them travel to the front door and back—the same wide doors that had once slid open to admit his cart from the helicopter. It was exhilarating, knowing that he could now walk past them on his own strength, and each time he accomplished this feat, it represented another victory that was more nourishing than any of their medicines.

It was about this time that Warren Beacher decided to pay another visit. He called upon Ernie one afternoon, overflowing with exuberance at his splendid progress. Doris and Alex were both in the room at the time, but it didn't seem to bother the man from public relations since he liked the idea of classifying any type of transplant as a family affair. In fact, he seemed delighted that they were there to hear what he had to say.

"One month," he said to Ernie, smiling approvingly. "You're a real champ. This is the first time I'm actually getting the chance to meet you, and I want you to know that it's a real honor. Let me shake your hand, Mr. Freeman." He reached down and pumped Ernie's arm enthusiastically. "The reason I'm here is because I think it's time for you to consider making your first public appearance. The press has been calling every day to check up on your progress, and we've been telling them you've been doing well, but I think it's time for them to see for themselves. I've already spoken with Dr. Sloan and he gave his permission for me to drop by. You see, I'd like to set up a time for them to film you."

"Film me?" Ernie asked, suddenly aware of how he must look. It had never occurred to him, during the days following his surgery, to check on his appearance. Now vanity overruled, and he tucked away a mental reminder that the first chance he had, he'd ask to see a mirror.

"I'm sure they'll have lots of questions. Their viewers are undoubtedly curious," Beacher continued.

Alex crossed his arms. "What kinds of questions?"

"Oh, the usual. How are you feeling? What was it like? You know, things like . . ." He paused the chuckled. "Say, haven't you ever seen any of these transplant interviews before? They're all basically the same. No reason why this one would be any different. They'll bring in their cameras to show everyone how the place looks, take a few shots of the different machines, maybe catch you walking. You are walking, right?''

"Yeh," Ernie muttered.

"It would probably be best for you to stick to the positives. Don't use your time on the air to complain about anything or feel sorry for yourself. People don't wanta hear that kinduv stuff. Right now, you're a national hero. You have to talk like a man who only knows success. That's what they want. Know what I mean?''

"Are you trying to tell me what I should say?'' Ernie asked, growing angry at the man's flippant attitude.

"Not at all. I'm just trying to give you a few tips so that you'll present the best possible picture.''

Alex scowled. "I don't see how it matters. What business is it of yours how my father presents himself?''

"You're quite right. After all, I don't work for your father. But I do work for the Institute, and it's my job to care. I suggest you think about that. The Northeastern Heart Institute. . . . well it has done its best for you.''

Later that week, Ernie made his television debut. Deciding to take Warren Beacher's advice, he said all the right things at the right times, and was congratulated later. Alex disagreed, grumbling that his father was being exploited until Ernie grew confused. He found himself torn between the desire for public recognition and not wanting to think that he had been manipulated. His son was right about one thing. The people at the Institute had a way of taking charge, and he began to wonder how he fit in with their own achievements. What motives could they have for wanting his meager verbal endorsement? After several days of brooding, he decided there was only one person there who might be truthful. He'd ask Rita Lawry in hopes that she'd be able to shed some light.

"The Institute's a funny place," she explained frankly after he asked. "I've worked in lots of different hospitals, but never one like this. Don't get me wrong. The research they've done is phenomenal. It's like they have a special insight, but I've always thought it a little weird."

"Weird?"

"Yeh." She wrinkled her pug nose. "I suppose it's their attitude. They want everything to be perfect, or at least to look that way. It's very important for them not to tarnish their public image. And there's something else. It's always been a sore spot with me." She stopped to think. "I don't even know if it's worth mentioning."

"What is it?"

"Well, it's like they have a certain arrogance. Take all these transplants for instance. Everyone here seems to pride themselves in the fact that they've mastered the human body. I don't know. It shouldn't get to me, but it does. I mean, there are just some things I don't think we have the right to tamper with—things that we shouldn't know. But they would never agree. They think they've got all the answers. They believe they've discovered all the secrets that make our bodies work. Sure, they talk about complications, but they'd never let it happen, and if you developed a problem, they'd have a way to solve anything your own body might come up with. You're lucky because you haven't had anything go wrong, but if you did, they'd come at you

121

with everything they've got. And believe me, they've got methods and equipment you've never dreamed of. Suppose that's not so bad in itself, but after a while, it begins to develop into a type of sport. They lose sight of the patient and worry more about winning this ridiculous physiological game they classify as science. I don't think it's right that the patient should become secondary just because they're bent on success. Maybe I'm wrong but. . . ."

She didn't notice Dr. Sloan standing at the doorway, listening to her speak. When he finally managed a subdued cough, she spun around, her face turning pink with embarrassment.

"Miss Lawry," he said coldly. "Could I have a few words with you?"

Rita had spoken too soon. A few days later, Ernie suffered a major setback. The doctors became alarmed when they noticed him growing weaker, and immediately began a new series of tests. Like bloodhounds on the scent of a trail, they pursued the threat of complications, determined to discover what it was that was causing the problem in order to eradicate it. In the end, they came up with a diagnosis—viral pneumonia. Within a matter of hours, the thick plastic tube was back in his throat, and he was breathing with the aid of the ventilator again. And that wasn't all. He learned of a new method they had been successfully researching—plasmaphoresis. While he struggled to fight off the infection, they offered their own scientific assistance. Each morning he was taken to a laboratory where two veins, one in his left arm and one in the opposite leg, were utilized to drain the blood from his body, spin it clean, and then replace it using a new supply of plasma. He watched in astonishment, realizing that in addition to giving him a new heart, they could also supply him with a fresh source of blood. Along with the viruses that were wiped away, also went his natural immunities to even the most basic of childhood illnesses. The reverse isolation would continue until there was no longer a threat of picking up the simple germs of measles or chicken pox. After several weeks of undergoing the same procedure, he began to show a marked improvement. Thanks to the Institute's advanced technology, a complication that could've proved fatal had now disappeared. Once again, the tubes were removed and he began another uphill climb of eating and regaining his strength.

The last tube to be removed was the slender rubber catheter that ran from his bladder to a bag below the bed. It was a major landmark in the journey toward recovery for him to take on the responsibility for this most basic function—urinating. The act symbolized his newly-gained independence, and he was determined to prove to them that the transition could be made with ease.

Not long afterwards, Dr. Sloan made another surprise announcement. "Mr. Freeman, you've doing extremely well." His eyebrows were knitted into a thoughtful frown. "How would you like to be moved out of the CVICU and transferred to a regular room on the floor?"

At first, all Ernie could think of was the last time he'd been allowed to make another such change. Everything had gone fine for a while. He could still vividly picture the look of shock on George's face when his body had drained of color the moment his heart had stopped beating, and his stubby nails bit into the palms of his hands.

"Are . . . are you sure I. . . . I'm ready?" he

stammered.

Dr. Sloan stepped closer to give him an encouraging pat on the shoulder. "Of course you are. You're doing fine. We know what we're doing."

The next day, two nurses came in to pack up his belongings. Stacks of gift cards wishing him well that had been tucked away in a drawer because the rules had stated they couldn't be displayed, were now nestled in a large plastic bag to go along.

"At least I'll be able to set them out where I can look at them," Ernie remarked half-jokingly.

"Mr. Freeman," one of the nurses replied coolly. "There're enough cards here to cover all the walls in your new room, and maybe even another room besides."

Ernie glanced over at Doris and smiled. It was a comforting thought to know that so many people had cared.

"Is Rita off today?" he asked as they continued packing. "I hate to move out on her without saying goodbye."

The taller nurse stopped what she was doing and stared at him through eyes that had suddenly narrowed. "Rita?" she asked. "Rita Lawry?"

"Yeh, you know, the chunky one."

"I'm sorry. Rita Lawry is no longer an employee. She was asked to resign."

"Resign? Why?"

"I'm not at liberty to say."

Ernie's stomach twisted into a tight knot as he recalled the tone of Dr. Sloan's voice when he'd stood listening to her divulging information about the Institute. "Was it because of me?" he finally asked.

"Of course not. There were several reasons. She wasn't the type of person who had learned to follow hospital policy. I know she hadn't kept up her CPR certification, and she'd lost her plastic I.D. card and never tried to get it replaced. Things like that can go against an employee. I'm certain that it all added up. It's not like she hadn't been warned. No. It had nothing to do with you. Losing her job here was by her own negligence."

"I see," Ernie replied glumly, refusing to believe this story and feeling badly that the one person he had come to trust was now gone.

He was transferred to his room in a parade of yellow gowns and masks, with television cameras lining the halls and efficient nurses clustering around him. It was the first time since he'd arrived at the Institute that he could travel upright. Perched snugly on the seat of a wheelchair, he was whisked along to an entirely new setting. A spacious private room waited near the nurses' station, complete with carpet and T.V.

At first, Ernie was delighted with his surroundings. It wasn't merely the freedom of not having to be connected to a host of machines, nor the exhilarating thought that he no longer required the suffocating monitoring. No longer was there the nagging cardiac monitor that he had grown accustomed to being connected to his chest, always reminding him that the mechanical heart was still clicking along. No longer was there the maze of tubes and wires that prevented him from even rolling onto his side without assistance. The blue intravenous pumps had been taken away, and blood pressure checks dwindled from once every hour to once every four, which offered him more time alone in order to reflect. All of these changes were an indication of his progress, still none of them could compare to the one thing he found in his room that was the most meaningful—the windows. At long last, he was able to gaze through the glass and see the sun and moon and stars. Dusk would tiptoe in at the end of each day in a splash of warm colors, and the glow of dawn as it peeked over the horizon welcomed him as a member of the earth—a participant in living, and the vision of such an awesome sight oftentimes left him breathless. Once again, he was part of the scheme of things, and each day gave cause for a new celebration. The hours on the face of the round clock that had once been important, now seemed insignificant. The window was his timekeeper, and whenever he looked in its direction, he was reminded that outside the walls of the hospital there awaited a world from which he'd been abruptly taken—a vibrant, active, purposeful place to which he longed to return.

As his strength increased, so did his awareness, and he began to notice all the little things that made up his environment. Perhaps it was the need to keep up with the ever expanding mind that had been deprived of stimulation for too long, and now hungrily devoured any new input. He began to notice the steady drip of the faucet that needed repair, and a smear on the edge of the glass pane that was never wiped clean. The telephone at his bedside sat idly, and he began to notice that he'd never heard it ring. The room seemed bare and it took a while to decide what it was that was missing, the quality that made it different from the other hospital room he'd known. There were no flowers. The last time he'd lived in a room outside of intensive care, the tables had been covered with attractive floral arrangements. Now there were none. Colorful petals that could've offered a refreshing contrast to the hospital's monotones were not there, and as the weeks passed by, he began to resent the fact that he was not being allowed this simple pleasure. He also noticed that the number of people permitted to see him was kept limited. Aside from Doris and Alex, he rarely saw anyone other than hospital staff, and even their visits were marred by the masks they were still required to wear. It had been a long time since he'd last seen a pair of lips that weren't covered, or enjoyed the color of his wife's dress. Yellow isolation gowns always covered their clothing, and this became a new source of irritation. All the while, in spite of his strong desire to return to a state of normalcy, he was constantly reminded that he was the one who was different. And when the lights were turned out at the end of another long day, he lay silently in the darkened room, staring out into space and listening to the one ever-present companion that he couldn't forget. He would drift off to sleep listening to the rhythmic click-clicking of his mechanical heart. It was this haunting sound that was a constant reminder that he could never be the same, and he knew that the continuation of his life depended on the artificial pump and the ticker tape machine.

It came as a surprise one day when Dr. Sloan appeared in Ernie's room not wearing the usual gown and mask. His dark eyes twinkled merrily and his pencil lips were twisted into a wry grin. Ernie sat in his chair, watching the physician curiously and wondering what had brought about this change.

"You're not covered up," Ernie commented, trying to sound casual even though his piercing eyes gave away the fact that he was intensely interested.

"That's right," Sloan replied in a soothing voice that attempted to instill confidence in his patient. "I've decided it's time to discontinue your reverse isolation. I think you're out of danger."

Ernie's fingers clutched at the arms of his chair, and he leaned forward in disbelief. "You mean no more masks and gowns?"

"That's right."

He gulped, trying to contain a sudden burst of uncontrolled laughter. "Does this mean I'll be able to get out of this room? Take walks?"

The stately physician slowly shook his silver head, clasping his chin between his fingers. "No, not just yet. Perhaps in the future. We'll see. Discontinuing the isolation only means that your body can begin to build up a tolerance for a select group of people."

"But can't I have other visitors? I get tired of talking to the same people every day. My wife was telling me that some of the nurses from the old hospital had come to visit. They were turned away. I had promised to keep in touch, but I haven't even been able to call. Something's wrong with the phone."

"There's nothing wrong with your telephone. We took the liberty of having it disconnected to avoid the strain of calls. You still aren't completely recovered, and you didn't need that as an additional pressure." He drew his slender hands behind his back and shifted his weight. "As far as other visitors, I'm afraid that's something I can't allow. Gaining an immunity to a specific group of people is going to be difficult enough. I can't take the risk. I know the nurses who cared for you at the other hospital have your best interests at heart, but they don't understand that your condition remains guarded. I can't imagine how they expected to help you by coming here. Excessive stimulation through idle chatter interferes with the healing process and could be detrimental. Obviously, our publication on this finding hadn't been passed along. That's unfortunate."

Ernie listened with pursed lips, and after Dr. Sloan had finished, sat sulking. After a few moments deliberation, he looked up. "What about my daughter? Will I be able to see her?"

"I'm afraid not. I hadn't wanted to tell you this, but I can see there's no sense in avoiding it any longer." He sighed. "We've found that your daughter is the carrier of a virus. This particular virus could be extremely dangerous to you."

"What do you mean by a carrier?"

"She carries the virus on her person—in her nose, her hair, her mouth, her hands, all over. It doesn't have much of an effect on her, unless of course her resistance is down. That's probably what made her grow ill the day of your surgery. She hadn't been taking care of herself. But what's most important is that she could easily spread this virus to you—if we allowed it to happen, which we will not."

"So what does that mean?"

"Mr. Freeman." Sloan stared at him without emotion. "I doubt whether you'll ever be able to see your daughter again."

"What?" Ernie shouted.

"Now there's no sense in allowing yourself to get worked up. It's just one of those things that can't be avoided. Of course, you'll still have other forms of communication with her. It's just that you won't be allowed any physical contact. It's not as bad as it seems."

"But . . . but not to be able to see my own daughter," he choked.

"Precautions," the physician stated emphatically. "It's vital that we maintain certain precautions. You've got to learn to trust us."

At first Ernie was angry. How dare they tell him who he could and could not see? What right did they have to control his life? His life. It was then that he realized how much control they did have over his life—the new life they'd given him as a result of the mechanical heart. It wasn't as if he could sign himself out of the hospital, or even change doctors. They were in control of him—completely. The only thing left was to grudgingly submit to their authority and follow their set of rules. The lab work continued being done each day, and he began to anticipate the arrival of the girl with her ticker tape. This was his new life that would never be the same, and the rhythmic tick-ticking in his chest was the constant reminder.

"Good morning, Mr. Freeman," his nurse chirped through the doorway. "My name is Ann. I'll be your nurse today."

He glared angrily at her, disgusted with this daily ritual of having to listen to the staff make their regular synthetic introductions. "I know who you are!" he shouted. "Damn it! After all this time don't you think I know who's taking care of me? Of course you're Ann, and there's Denice and Gloria and all the rest of you! I know all of you—every last one of you, and I wish to hell you'd start acting like it instead of treating me like an idiot!"

She didn't react to his outburst, remaining at the door like a stone figure. "The Institute requires that we identify ourselves at the beginning of each shift," she recited.

"But I know who you are!"

"It's a policy of the Institute."

"Well to hell with the Institute! To hell with you and to hell with this place!"

"Mr. Beacher, from public relations, is here to

speak with you," she went on, ignoring his mounting rage.

"For what? To tell me what I'm supposed to say? Like I don't have a mind of my own? Another press interview? Is that it?" His eyes were reddened with fury.

"I suggest you discuss it with him. Shall I tell him to come in? Are you ready?"

Ernie allowed his head to drop forward in defeat. There was no use in fighting. "Sure," he mumbled. "Tell him I'm ready. What the hell else do I have to do?"

He was grateful for Doris' afternoon visit.

"Dor, I've got to get out of here. It's getting to me."

"Honey, you've got to be patient."

"Patient? I have been patient!" She jumped, startled at how his voice had risen, and he tried to calm down, rubbing his forehead to soothe a rapidly developing headache. "I can't take it anymore," he continued with restrained composure. "This room, the hospital, all of it is beginning to wear. It's been such a long time since I've been home. I want to see my house, pull into my own driveway, sleep in my own bed. I want to watch my own television set and sit at my own kitchen table to eat a meal that my own wife cooked. I wouldn't even mind seeing George again." He smiled wistfully. "It was strange that he was in that dream. Wonder what he's really doing now. Him and all those fancy gadgets." Ernie's eyes lit up. "Hey, you know what?"

"What?" Doris asked softly.

"I'd like to see him match this machine with any of the ones he owns." He laughed, playfully thumping his chest.

Dr. Sloan stood with his back to Ernie as he gazed through the window to the street below. "So you want to go home," he muttered. "Of course you have been doing well, and I had considered writing for your discharge."

"Then I can go home?"

The physician turned around. "Not home. There would be too many problems. You'll still require the CSM three times a week."

"You mean the ticker tape?"

He smiled grimly. "Yes, the 'ticker tape.' You see, you'll always need the CSM. It keeps your heart functional. But let's face it, it's a small price to pay."

"Why can't someone do it in Chicago? There's plenty of big hospitals—not like I'd be stuck out in the boonies. It can't be that hard for someone else to operate it. Doris or Alex could drive me, and Shawn. . . ."

"I thought we'd already settled the matter about your daughter."

"All right, I understand that she's a . . . a carrier. God! I hate the sound of that word. It's like she's diseased . . . a leper or something."

"There are other problems to consider. You can't be exposed to dust or pollen. Our latest research shows that all green plants are out, including grass. That leaves you somewhat limited. Even the air you breathe must be filtered."

"For what?"

"To avoid complications."

"But I can't avoid them forever."

"Perhaps not, but we must try."

"Why?"

"To keep your heart functional."

"I don't see what any of this has to do with my heart."

"Then to keep you functional," Dr. Sloan said

with exasperation. "To keep your other organ systems in balance."

"When will I be able to go home?"

"Mr. Freeman," Sloan said patiently. "Didn't you read any of the forms you signed? One of the conditions to performing your transplant was that you remained under our care. Now that doesn't mean you can't be discharged. You will leave this room and this hospital. But you can't go home. The distance is just too great."

"Then where will I go?" Ernie tried to contain a rising degree of panic.

"We have a lovely apartment complex on the grounds only a few minutes away. It's called Winnow Cove. The rooms were designed especially for people like you. I'm sure you will find it most pleasant."

"What about Doris?"

"She'll live there with you. Of course, a nurse will be checking in on you regularly, and I'll be paying visits. We'll have a special hotline set up, but basically it'll be just like it was before your transplant."

"Just like it was?"

"Okay, not exactly." He cleared his throat. "But as close as we can come. Mr. Freeman, we don't want you to be unhappy. We're trying to work with you. Everything can't possibly be the same. Not with. . . ."

"With an artificial heart," Ernie completed his sentence bitterly.

Later that week Dr. Sloan met with both Doris and Alex to discuss the plan. Ernie would be discharged in two weeks, providing there were no problems, and arrangements would be made for them to settle themselves at Winnow Cove. Alex notified a realtor, and he and his mother returned to the house to pack.

They took along a letter that Ernie had written to Shawn, promising to return as soon as possible. During the journey home, they told themselves that many people were forced to move to new locations, and their situation was really no different. While it might take time to adjust, it was still another step forward. Ernie waited anxiously for their return so that he, too, could prepare for his departure.

Doris was gone for over a week. Each day passed more tediously than the next, and when she finally did return, Ernie was excited to hear about the old neighborhood.

"They were all thrilled," Doris reported, smiling from her chair as she sat at his hospital room. "I don't think any of them ever thought you'd become famous. They saw you on the news, and everyone had so many questions. Here." She reached into her handbag for an envelope. "They all signed this card. Wasn't that sweet?"

"What about George?" Ernie asked. "What did the old geezer have to say?"

Doris' eyes clouded over. "Honey, George is dead. He had another stroke. As a matter of fact, it happened the same day as your surgery. Isn't that odd? Anyway, it was fast and at least he hadn't suffered. Mr. Kearney was there and. . . ."

Ernie was no longer paying any attention, lost in a sea of thoughts. The experience he still vividly recalled during his operation seemed more real than ever. All this time he'd led himself to believe that it had only been a bad dream—the light moving away from him, George sitting contentedly on the other side of the great canyon, his fright over his own judgment—death and hell; these were the things that awaited. His brief glimpse of eternity had only been a sample of what was ahead. George had warned him that it would get worse. The footsteps had been coming to claim his soul, but he'd been foolish enough to convince himself that it was only the sound of his mechanical heart because George couldn't have been there since he was still alive. But he wasn't alive. George was dead. He'd died the very same day! And it all wasn't a bad dream. What had happened was real, and he'd been shown what was waiting for him on the other side.

Well, he wouldn't die. He wouldn't allow it to happen, at least not yet. Thank goodness for people like Dr. Sloan who insisted upon taking safety precautions, and he was fortunate for having the ticker tape girl. So what if he couldn't return home, and might spend the rest of his life inside Winnow Cove? And it wasn't his fault that Shawn was a carrier. Now, the only thing he cared about was his sudden passion for life, which like the primitive craving it was, began seeping through his veins with each pulsating click-click that he could feel being generated by the artificial heart.

7

Winnow Cove was the picture of gracious living.
Nestled snugly in the midst of a park-like setting, it
was a sprawling network of condominiums that
were designed in rich cedar and flowed together to
form a rustic sanctuary. Sweeping streets wound
their way through, forming attractive boulevards
that were lined with elegant streetlamps. There was
hardly a hint of traffic on these roads since this was
an area that was kept deliberately secluded.

The atmosphere was peaceful, and the outside air
was so quiet that even the sound of chirping birds
came as a startling intrusion. Nobody was ever seen
outdoors. There were no loud engines or squealing
children at play, no neighbors tending to their yards.
Any more obtrusive sound, like the slamming of a car
door when there happened to be a visitor, was like
an explosion, echoing through the empty courtyards

and causing dozens of anonymous heads to curiously bob up behind the windows. However, this was a rare occurrence, for those allowed on the inside of Winnow Cove were carefully selected, and all visits were kept to a minimum.

The apartments boasted a futuristic design with immense windows that were made of treated glass, allowing the residents to look out, but blocking the view from outsiders peering in. There were spacious rooms with plush carpeting and contemporary furnishings that gave the illusion of space. When one first entered these quarters, it was difficult not to notice the remarkable odor of freshness that had been achieved through the use of filtered air. In fact, some might've considered it an unnatural environment that harbored the strong scent of plastic and wax. The climate inside was always kept temperate with just the right mixture of mist to provide the proper humidity, and a temperature that was always kept at a constant seventy-two degrees.

Doris and Ernie lived on the corner of Vassal and Lyceum in Apartment 314D. It was a building that sat at the end of the road where the two streets came together in the form of a T, and offered the widest view of their surroundings. From their kitchen window they could see the broad, concrete steps leading up to the house next door, and from the living room it was possible to spot whomever might be coming down the road.

Ever since they'd moved in, Alex had tried to be faithful in his visits, but gradually the time between them lengthened. He tried to explain that he had other responsibilities, and that it wasn't that he didn't care. Life must go on, and he would come whenever he could. They assured him that they understood and told him not to worry. At least they had each other and there was enough to keep them occupied. But he was still missed. In addition, where once they could easily identify his red convertible as it inched its way down the street, this eventually became impossible as his vehicles began to change in models and colors.

Time had a way of slipping by unnoticed at Winnow Cove. Perhaps it was because there were no trees to indicate the seasons. The years were neatly divided into summer and winter, with only a telltale sign of snow that periodically covered the earth to give away the time of year. They weren't completely isolated. There were newspapers and the television set. Still, from the inside of their apartment there was little change—nothing to look forward to—nothing to plan—and it became an impossible feat to remember whether it was Monday or Friday or any other day of the week. Oftentimes, as Doris sat writing letters, she'd find herself searching for the correct date, and it was at these times that she found it hard to believe they'd managed to sustain themselves for so long at Winnow Cove.

Neither of them were ever allowed to leave. Doris could never respond to the ads she saw in the Sunday paper by attending any of the local sales. New clothing and household items were supplied by the Institute and delivered to them whenever they made a request. Groceries arrived on a weekly basis, so they never had to worry about these kind of trips. It was explained that even the simple exposure to crowds in the outside world could result in unwanted diseases, and it wasn't worth the risk. Every so often a dietician would stop by to explain Ernie's daily menu with suggestions on how his food should be prepared. Certain nutrients and the amounts he ingested of sugars and salts were vital to his good health. Telephone calls were monitored. Their numbers were kept limited, and anyone trying to reach them was first carefully screened. The Institute was wise in its ways; the press could take on different disguises. It was because of concern for their protection that all these measures had been taken. The Institute always had good reasons for any of the rules they made, and after a while the couple adjusted to this lifestyle and learned not to ask for explanations.

When they'd first moved into the apartment it was exciting, almost like learning how to live together again. Hours were spent reliving the past, and they shared thoughts that had been suppressed over the last several months. In one sense, it was like a second honeymoon. In awe, they ventured about their luxurious surroundings, feeling like guests in a hotel suite; all of their furnishings being far better than anything they could have ever afforded. Towels in the bathroom were neatly stacked and waiting for use. Sparkling dishes graced the cupboards, and there were fresh linens on the bed. The bed. How long it had been since they'd last shared a room in private? The flame of passion that had once brought them together intimately was rekindled behind drawn drapes, as they shared in spontaneous lovemaking. This act put such a physical demand on Ernie's body that by the time the ticker tape girl showed up, it was necessary for her to make substantial adjustments. Later, Dr. Sloan spoke with them and advised that they learn to set certain limitations.

There was much to keep them occupied at first, but soon Doris had read every book in the small library, and from there she and her husband took up playing cards. As they sat together at the cozy kitchen table, old times were once more recalled. Sometimes they simply sat quietly, staring out the window at the house next door and tried to imagine whom their neighbors might be. But eventually, they grew tired of this, too, and the time came when they began to get on each other's nerves. Television took on a more important role, soon becoming their main source of entertainment, and before long, they requested a second set since they found that their tastes were beginning to differ greatly.

As time passed, there were subtle changes in Ernie. He began to walk with a bit of a stoop and the skin on his upper arms turned flabby. Doris noticed how his hair had thinned, and from the way he squinted, she knew that his eyesight was beginning to dim. The incision on his chest had long ago healed, and there was only a wide grayish scar to act as a reminder of why they were there, except when he held her close enough so that she could feel the pulsating click-click of his artificial heart.

He never complained about being locked inside. She thought it odd, since all of his life he'd been so active. Ordinarily, he wouldn't have accepted being caged in, but to her surprise he was usually quite chipper, and whenever she happened to make a negative remark, he was quick to put her in her place. After all, these measures had been taken for his own good, and they mustn't forget their importance. His heart was the greatest priority. As a matter of fact, his heart was the excuse for almost everything. It was the reason why he could never help with the dishes or get up to pour himself a glass of milk as he watched T.V. If they were in the midst of a heated discussion, he could always bring an impending argument to a screeching halt by tapping on his chest and reminding her of what it contained.

No matter what the situation, he soon learned how to control his wife for the sake of his life-giving heart.

Doris had also changed. The streak of gray she'd had in her hair at the time of his transplant widened until there were only a few thin patches of brown left. The kindly lines around her eyes and mouth had grown so deep that the skin around them began to sag. Age had steadily crept up on her, and instead of being the middle-aged woman she once was, she'd taken on all the characteristics of an old lady.

The sparkle that had, at one time, danced in her dark eyes had now faded, undoubtedly because there was no reason to laugh. While she tried her hardest to accept their situation, she often struggled with feelings of bitterness. All her married life she'd made sacrifices; still, none of them had ever been appreciated. She grew weary of hearing about her husband's heart, and was tired of having to wait on him. In all their years together, she had lived with the faint hope that her situation would improve, but now she knew it would never come to be. There was no hope inside the apartment at Winnow Cove—no quality of life to cling to. The worst part of all was that she couldn't share these thoughts with Ernie, for he was the one who was responsible for causing her anguish. Rejecting this lifestyle would mean rejecting him, and she loved him enough to remain silent. Her duty was to stay with her husband, her responsibilities of motherhood having come to an end. So she learned to bite her lower lip and face each day as cheerfully as possible, all the while unaware of how far into herself she was withdrawing.

Life was predictable at Winnow Cove. They could

always depend on the nurse showing up every Thursday to bring news from the outside world. Dr. Sloan continued to make regular monthly appearances, complimenting him on his splendid health. And three times a week they welcomed the ticker tape girl who was there to keep the Biotron 8000 in check. Each of these visits was like a light in an otherwise dreary existence, and the couple dreaded the moment anyone had to leave. When any of the medical staff was there, they were bombarded with questions that ranged from the temperature outside to what was happening in the world politically. The conversation was usually kept coolly professional, for the arm of the Institute had a long reach, and even in this informal setting, only a scant bit of information could be safely shared.

It must've been sometime in September or October when there was an unexpected knock at the door. It wasn't the day for the nurse's visit, nor was it time for the ticker tape girl or Dr. Sloan. Doris rushed to the front window to take a peak, noticing a shiny blue sedan, and then tried to crane her neck to the left to see who it was standing on the doorstep. The effort was futile, and she finally gave up, walking over to open the door and allow the stranger in.

"Mom?" a man said, hovering out in the cold with his collar turned up against the wind. At first she didn't recognize Alex. Perhaps it was the gray near his temples, or the permanent crease that had etched its way in between his brows. He looked down at her, smiling uneasily. "May I come in?"

Flustered, she nervously smoothed the wrinkles in her dress and opened the door wider so that he could enter. "Why, Alex," she chirped. "It's so good to see you. I wish we'd known. Come in. Please. Let me tell your father."

They sat together on the white living room furniture. This area was rarely used, kept spotless for the entertainment of guests. Now, they sat across from each other, Alex perched on a plush chair with his back errect and his parents glued together on the couch.

"Mom, you look pale. Are you okay?"

"I'm fine. Don't be silly. How's Shawn? She never answered my last letter. Did she and Jack go to Florida?"

He nodded. "Yeh, they went. As a matter of fact, they both found work and will be moving down there next month." He reached into the breast pocket of his suit. "Here. Shawn wanted me to give you the new address."

Doris accepted the piece of paper, staring down at it gloomily.

"You look a little peaked yourself," Ernie remarked, leaning back and crossing his arms against his chest. "How's the job going?"

"Great. I'm up for a promotion next month. It's been a long haul. Work has a way of getting the best out of you."

"Yeh, work." Ernie cleared his throat. "Sure can take its toll. Say, did I tell you they interviewed me a few weeks ago? They wanta do a cover story. Did you know that I'm the longest living survivor of an artificial heart transplant?" He smiled. "Can you imagine that? Never thought your old man would ever do anything right, did you?"

"You always did right by Mom and Shawn and me. Guess now that I'm a little older, it's easier for me to appreciate everything you did. Dad, I want you to know I'm sorry about your business. I still think about it every now and then. After being out in the business world myself, I can better relate to what you went through. I hope you understand why I made my decision."

"Don't worry about it," Ernie scoffed. "My business was going under anyway. I realize that now. Don't give it a second thought. Now this heart thing, well that's another story. There's not another human being alive who's hung in there as long as me."

"Yeh, that's great. How long has it been? Ten years?"

"That's right. Eleven next spring. I don't think anyone expected me to last this long. But I found that the secret is learning how to pace yourself. That's the only way. That, and having a good woman behind you." He reached over and patted Doris on the knee. "Say, how about you? Are you finally getting serious about anyone?"

Alex grinned. "No, haven't found the right one."

Ernie shook his head. "How old are you now? Thirty-two? Thirty-three. Hell, I had both you and your sister in braces by this time. Come on there. You'd better get on the stick."

"Well, a man's gotta find the right woman to share the rest of his life."

"Suppose you're right. Me and your mother . . . well . . . guess we were just lucky. But I'll tell you one thing. I've never regretted the day we met."

Alex glanced over at his aging mother and drew his eyebrows together in a frown. "You're a lucky man to have a woman like Mom. I hope you know that."

"Of course! You think I'm blind? But we're happy. All we need is each other. She gives me a reason to live."

"Are you living, Dad?"

"Why sure I'm living. Don't you see me sitting here? Think you're talking to a ghost?"

"When was the last time you were out?"

Ernie chuckled self-consciously. "I can't go outside. What do ya mean? You know I need special air."

"But what about Mom? I mean, do you really think it's healthy?"

"Healthy? Didn't I just tell you I'm the longest survivor? Do I look like I'm in bad health? We've got to be doing something right."

"I just don't like the way she looks." he studied his mother's face. "Mom? Are you sure you're feeling okay?"

She nodded. "Of course. Please don't worry."

Alex pulled himself up and walked over to where she was seated, offering his hand. "Mom? Do you think Dad and I could be alone for a few minutes? I'd like to talk to him about something. We won't be long."

She accepted his hand and drew herself up off the couch. "Take all the time you need. I've got to start supper anyway."

The two men watched in silence as she made her exit, and when Alex was sure she was out of hearing range, he sank onto the couch next to his father.

"Do you see her?" Alex asked nervously. "Do you see the way she looks? There's got to be something wrong with her. She doesn't look right."

"There's nothing wrong with her. If there were, don't you think she'd tell me?"

"No," Alex taunted. "I don't think she would. I think she'd hold it inside, just as she always has done. My God, Dad. There's no reason for her to be caged in here with you like an animal. She only stays because of you."

"I don't think you understand. Your mother and I love each other. It would kill her if we were apart."

"Dad, we're worried, both Shawn and me. Her letters have strange undertones, like she's giving up. That's why I came, and now that I've seen her, I know she's lost a certain spark."

"I don't see anything different in her."

"Of course not. You see her every day. But take a good long look at her for once, and compare her to the way she used to be. And while you're at it, look at yourself. Look at both of you. How can you live in this fishbowl? Neither one of you is living. You're only existing like specimens in a bottle. Dad, let go of her. If you have to live this way, fine. But don't make her feel as if she's obligated. Any fool could tell that she's not happy. Who knows how much time she has left. Have you ever thought about that? At least let her make her own decision."

Ernie's eyes turned to ice. "She did make her decision," he hissed. "You've gotta lot to learn about marriage. A man and woman become obligated the minute they take those vows. They make a promise, a promise that they'll stay together 'til death . That's serious business. You think your mother didn't know what she was gettin' herself into? Of course she's obligated. But you'd never understand that. You and your wishy-washy generation think the rules have changed. You look the wrong way at a woman nowadays, and right away she's asking for a divorce. Maybe that's why you're afraid to get married. I don't blame you. It's not worth the gamble. Maybe you don't have what it takes. But your mother and me, we know what marriage means. And that's something you'll probably never understand."

Alex cradled his head in his hands. "Dad, you're

not hearing what I'm saying." He sighed. "When two people love each other, they look out for each other and make sacrifices. They want their partner to be happy. All I can see is that Mom has made a big sacrifice for you. What about a sacrifice on your part? You've had her this long. If she wants to leave, at least be willing to let go of her, but let her be the one to tell me she wants to stay in this place. I want to hear it for myself. You owe it to her to find out."

"Are you crazy?" Ernie shouted. "She wouldn't go with you!"

"She always wanted a garden, Dad. Did you know that? I can remember her talking about it when we were little. I found old pictures in the house right before I sold it. She had dreams—dreams that were never fulfilled. Look around at this place. Where's her garden? Where is that one lousy dream?"

"We've got plants here."

Alex stood up and walked over to one of the large potted plants. He tore off a leaf and held it up for Ernie to see. "Artificial!" he cried. "Artificial plants! Artificial air! Artificial grass outside! Your whole damn world is artificial—as artificial as your heart!"

"Shut your mouth," Ernie lowered his voice threateningly. "Shut your mouth before she hears you."

Alex walked back over to the couch and sat down. "I want to talk with her. I want to convince her to leave with me. I've given it a lot of thought. I have a nice home and a big back yard with plenty of room for a garden. Let go of her. Tell her it's okay, that you want her to leave. For once, Dad, think of her."

Ernie clenched his fists and began working his jaw. "Get outta here! Get outta here and never come back. You're not welcome here any more. I'll notify Dr. Sloan in the morning. You're not good for my health, and I don't want you allowed in this place."

"Dad, stop it! Stop talking so foolish and think about what I'm saying! My God, where's your conscience?"

"My conscience?" he snarled. "You're asking me about my conscience?" His face twisted into an ugly sneer. "When was the last time you came to visit? Five years ago? Six? Who the hell do you think you are, coming here after all this time and thinking that you've got all the answers? Well, I'll tell you something. This has always been a two-way street. You think you're too good to come and visit? Who needs you? When I get through with you, a court order wouldn't get you into this place. Not get the hell out!" He sprang from the couch and pointed to the door.

"Dad, please. At least think about it. Don't do anything you'll regret later."

"Get outta my house."

"At least let me say goodbye."

"I'll tell her goodbye. She doesn't have to talk to you. Now get outta here or I'll forget that I'm an invalid."

"Honey?" Doris called out after Alex had gone, wandering back in from the kitchen. She glanced about the room in surprise. "Where's Alex?"

"I told him to leave."

"What?"

"I told him to leave and never come back."

Her eyes opened wide in disbelief. "Why?"

"Because you don't need a son like him."

"But, Ernie!"

"He's no good. He never has been. Do you know why he came here tonight? He came because he wanted to take you away. Can you imagine? He actually thought you'd leave me and go with him."

"And because of that you told him never to come back?"

"That's right. I'm calling Sloan in the morning. I'm having his name taken off the visitors' list."

"But he's all we have. You can't do that to him."

"We don't need him."

"But who else do we have? There is nobody else!" In a sudden wave of panic and frustration, she began to cry. "Ernie, we never see anyone else. We don't even know who we have for neighbors. The only thing you seem to live for is the time you'll next be interviewed. And everything you or I say to the press is completely controlled. They control the food we eat—the clothes we wear. They pick who we can talk to. Everything we do is under their control. Don't let them control him, not our son. They've already taken our daughter away. Please, Ernie. Don't let them tell Alex he can't visit." She buried her face in her hands, quietly weeping.

Ernie stared at her as if she were a traitor. "Is that how you feel? Maybe Alex was right. Maybe you don't like being locked up here with me. Maybe I was wrong and you really did want to go with him. Well, you're free to leave. I'm not holding you. You think I'm gonna be the one to stand in your way?" He pointed to the door. "Go on. Go after him if you want. But I'm not going back on my word. I never want to see him again. And if you leave, I never want to see you."

Doris sank onto the couch, rocking back and forth as she continued to sob deeply.

A week later, they sat silently at the kitchen table. Doris' face was more ashen and her eyes were unusually dull.

"What's wrong with you?" Ernie asked. "You're not eating."

"I'm not hungry."

He looked at her with concern. "You're losing too much weight, Dor. It's got me worried. You're gonna get sick."

"You don't have to worry about me."

"Why do you say that? You know how I hate that kinda talk. Maybe I should give Dr. Sloan a call." He reached for her hand. "I just don't want anything to happen to you."

The moment Ernie notified Dr. Sloan of the change in his wife, they took action. Not less than an hour later, they had come to take her away. Two nurses dressed in electric blue and wearing plastic laminated I.D.'s stood at the door inquiring as to her whereabouts. They explained that it was necessary for her to be transferred to the hospital in order to undergo a series of tests. Her husband had been the one to alert them, and any impending illness could be a threat—to him. Surely she agreed that it wouldn't be right if she spread any diseases; after all, it was their duty to prevent such a thing from occurring. As they helped her out the door she looked back at Ernie sadly, not bothering to conceal the hurt look in her eyes, as if she'd been the one who'd ultimately been betrayed.

With Doris gone, the apartment at Winnow Cove became nothing more than an empty shell that was as hollow as the pit of his stomach. Somehow it had been her presence that had filled these same rooms with life and joy and love. Now through her absence the silence mocked him, and each day represented another painful, bitter journey through time. She was no longer there to play cards with him, so he sat alone at the kitchen table thinking to himself and toying with games of solitaire. Each time a car passed, he'd watch until it was close enough for him to see the faces behind the windows, hoping it might be her returning. He consoled himself with the assurance that he wouldn't have allowed her to be taken away had Dr. Sloan not first convinced him that it was his only logical choice. It was imperative to act swiftly in order to achieve the earliest possible recovery. He had done what was necessary even if she didn't understand. Besides, it might not be anything serious. The tests would be conclusive, and Sloan promised that he'd be immediately notified of the results. Then both of their minds would be put to ease. So several times a day he found himself unconsciously pacing in front of the phone as he waited for the call. It wasn't as if she were a person who was easy to forget. Doris was his wife, and everything around him was a reminder that she'd been dissected away, like a useful limb being amputated from a body. Once, in the bathroom, he came upon a loose bobby pin that had fallen into a corner. He picked it up, rolling it gently between his fingers and swallowing the lump that had risen in his throat before lovingly tucking it away with the rest of her belongings. Another time, he'd gone to get something out of the closet, and found himself standing transfixed at the door, gazing at her favorite green dress and trying to imagine how she'd looked wearing it. He longed for her return with the same intensity of a loyal animal brooding over the return of its master. And in his lonely bed at night, the rhythmic ticking of his mechanical heart was no substitute for the warmth of her companionship.

During his most solemn moments, he struggled with the memory of the conversation with Alex, trying in vain to fight off any feelings of guilt. Perhaps his son had known that she didn't have much time, and for that reason had put forth such a valiant effort. Had he been wrong? Should he have been more willing to treat her to the happiness she deserved during her last dying days? What disease had sunk its teeth into her? Cancer? Of course! Fool! That was why she'd been losing weight, and he had been too blind to see. Would they allow her to come back to end her life with him? Oh, the tragedy of it all! What were his meager choices? He could either watch her endure a painful death inside their apartment, or request that she be kept away and only hear from Dr. Sloan about her end. Which was worse? How could it be? All this time he'd thought it would be him who'd be the first to go. Never had it occurred to him that it would be he left grieving. Being the one who'd been debilitated had always placed him in a position of safety that prevented him from coming to terms with any great loss. Who would have thought that fate would step in, blinding his eyes as careful measures were taken for his sake, while all along a monstrous illness had been creeping up on her unexpectedly?

The days turned into weeks and he continued to wait for word. When Thursday came, and the nurse paid her regular visit, he'd inquire about his wife. But her answer was always the same. She'd put him off with the claim that this wasn't her department. The ticker tape girl divulged even less information, and he soon found it useless to bring up the topic. All he could do was wait for the call that would finally deliver the fateful message, and he forced upon himself the virtue of patience, even though his anticipation was gnawing away at a mind that was rapidly growing bewildered and confused.

The call came unexpectedly. Office hours had long since ended, and he had retired for the evening, lounging comfortably in his bed. The shrill ring of the telephone was startling. At first, he was paralyzed—fearful of hearing the caller's message. Four rings. . . . five. . . . six. Perhaps something had happened. Why else would they be calling now? Seven rings. . . . eight. But he had to find out sooner or later. There was no point in skirting the inevitable. Slowly, slowly, he inched his hand over to the receiver to pick it up, all the while unaware of the fact that he was holding his breath. "Hello?" he finally whispered.

"Mr. Freeman?"

"Yeh?"

"This is Dr. Cramer from the Institute. Dr. Sloan had asked me to consult on your wife. I apologize for calling this late, but I wanted to notify you as soon as possible on the results of her tests." He paused.

Ernie's knuckles turned white as he gripped the receiver in his moist hand, waiting motionless.

"Everything looks fine. We didn't find anything unusual."

In sudden relief, he let out the breath he'd been holding. "You mean. . . . you mean she's okay?"

"As far as we can tell."

"But what about her weight loss?"

"We don't know. It's possible that she experienced a bout of clinical depression. In her situation I could understand. But we're positive that she shows no signs of any type of infectious process, so I believe it's safe to release her back to you."

"But is she better? Is she eating?"

"Not exactly, but I doubt if there's much more we can do. I've spoken with Dr. Sloan, and we both agree that returning home to you might be the only thing that will work to her advantage.''

"When? When will she be discharged?''

"Well, if you're up to it, it could be as soon as tomorrow.''

Ernie couldn't control a gush of laughter that burst forth in hearty cries, representing all of the pent-up frustration that, at long last, was being released. "If I'm up to it?'' he roared between throaty chuckles. "Of course I'm up to it! Just bring her home to me." He reached up to brush away a happy tear. "You don't know how worried I've been.''

"Yes, I understand. You can be expecting her at around one.''

"Dr. Cramer?''

"Yes?''

"Thanks.''

Perhaps he expected to see more of an improvement. In his mind's eye, he'd never lost sight of the picture of a vibrant, enduring woman. He wasn't prepared for the teetering old lady with dull gray hair who came hobbling through the doorway on the arm of a nurse. It took a moment for him to realize that this pathetically frail grandmother was his own wife, but he still welcomed her with open arms, and when she smiled up at him with her dark eyes speaking silent words of love, he knew that it was Doris and was glad that she had finally made it home.

"Dor, you had me worried. You know what I thought?'' He giggled foolishly to himself. "I thought you had cancer.''

"Cancer?'' she asked. "How did you come up with that?''

"I don't know, the weight loss I guess. I'd always heard that's the way it happens.''

"I tried to tell you I was okay, but you wouldn't

believe me."

"I'm sorry. I just didn't wanta take any chances. Dor, if I lost you . . . well, I don't know what I'd do. The time you were gone was like a . . . a living hell."

"We can't stay together forever, Ernie. We're both getting older. Eventually, there'll have to be an end."

His smile faded. "You know, I haven't thought about this for a long time, but I'll never forget that experience I had. Dor, I know it was real. George was there as plain as day, and I couldn't have made it up because I didn't even know he had died. I saw him. I saw the whole thing. I know what's waiting for me. Maybe the same is waiting for you. We have to hang in there for as long as we can."

Doris took his hand and gently squeezed. "Ernie, you can't run forever. There comes a time when we all must die."

He tore his hand away, and turned his head. "Don't talk like that, Dor. I don't wanta hear it. We aren't gonna accept defeat just yet. Neither one of us is ready."

"Ernie?" she whispered softly. "When will we be ready?"

Doris did not get any stronger. Every day Ernie watched helplessly as his wife continued to wither away. Soon, she was too weak to get out of bed, and he would carry trays of food to her room, encouraging her to eat. Her eyes became two sunken pits that rested above jutting cheekbones with skin that fell in loose flaps to frame her colorless mouth. Her expression was frightening because it was quietly accepting, glowing with an inner peace.

Most of her day was consumed with reading the Bible, and that was an equally threatening gesture.

The Bible was for people who were preparing to meet their Maker, and he shuddered each time he found her poring over the tissue-like pages. On Sundays she'd watch every church service, and this nudged him with feelings of anger. It was almost as if she were deliberately flirting with death in order to torture him, and he resented the fact that she spent more time on this game than sharing their moments together.

One morning during the middle of what sounded like another boisterous sermon, he marched in and snapped off the set. She didn't get angry, simply watched him serenely, her face having taken on the peaceful expression he'd come to loathe.

"Well?" he bellowed. "Aren't you gonna say anything? Aren't you gonna get mad at me that I turned off your precious program?"

"Why should I get angry with you?" she asked in a voice that was sickenly sweet.

"Because I'm not allowing you to eat up that crap. All I had to do was walk in here and turn the dial and poof! Your favorite program was gone!"

"And you think it's that easy?" she asked. "You think the message that man was giving is limited to a television set?"

"Cut it out, Dor!" he shouted. "You know how that stuff gets on my nerves."

"You don't have to listen."

"Oh no? Well what the hell am I supposed to do? You never talk to me, and I can hear that crap from every room of the house. I'm tired of it. You lock yourself in this room reading the Bible all hours of the day and night. It's not like I can get away from it. I can't escape and go down to the local tavern. Don't you see? We're in this together. Talk to me for once. Give me a break."

She reached over to the nightstand for her Bible. "Ernie, I want to show you something. You see, it was you who was most instrumental in bringing me to the truth."

"What're you talking about?"

She began thumbing through the pages. "Ernie, you know how you've tried to explain to me the experience you had during your transplant? That one where you were left in a terrible place, and your throat was dry, and you couldn't cross over to the other side—the side where George was seated?"

"Yeh?"

"You know how you keep claiming the whole thing was real?"

"Yeh, I know it was real."

"Well, you're right. It was an authentic experience. I found it one day right here in the Book of Luke. Look, it's in Chapter Sixteen, verse nineteen. It's a story Jesus told of the rich man and Lazarus. Here Ernie, read it for yourself. It's the same thing that happened to you. The rich man couldn't cross over to the other side either. He was so thirsty he begged to have Lazarus come over to bring him a droplet of water on his finger. The rich man felt exactly the way you did. He couldn't believe he'd been condemned to such an awful place."

"Big deal," Ernie scoffed. "So it proves I didn't make the whole thing up. There is such a place and I was there."

"But Ernie. In the story, the rich man asked if he could come back and tell everyone about it. But he wasn't allowed. You have been allowed to come back. Don't you see? God was giving you a warning."

"I don't see nothin'. All I see is that you're reading into Bible stories you can't understand. You're filling your head with a lotta nonsense because you think there's nothin' better to do."

"No, Ernie. You told me yourself that because of your black marks, you couldn't be allowed on the other side. But George was there, and we both knew him. We know he wasn't perfect. How do you think he got there? Why were his black marks erased?"

Ernie rubbed his forehead. "I don't know, but since you seem to have all the answers, why don't you tell me."

"Because that's the beauty of Christ. He came to this earth to take away all the black marks. All a person has to do is believe. George believed, and he was allowed to cross over. Now, I believe and I know there's nothing to fear. Ernie, all you have to do is believe, too. Then we'll all be there together."

"Will you stop with that crap? Have you lost your mind? You sound like one of those religious fanatics! Dor, I'm talking about reality. What you're trying to tell me is a fairy tale. I need you here with me!"

"But Ernie, death is a reality. We all have to die. Nobody gets away with living forever. Think about it. Do you think I could talk this way if I were afraid of judgment? Of course not. You see, I know that there is a beautiful place waiting for me." Her eyes filled with joyous tears. "There's fresh air to breathe and brilliant sunlight and freedom and happiness. And Ernie, there are beautiful gardens with the most wonderful flowers. I'm going to ask the Lord if I can care for them when I get there. Ernie, I want you there with me. All you have to do is believe."

He watched as her eyes took on a distant look, almost as thought she could actually see the place she was describing. The lines on her face seemed to dissolve magically, but he knew that she was old. All the endless days of being locked inside had finally taken their toll. At that moment he knew why she had been losing weight. It wasn't just that she'd become dangerously depressed. She had given up. Dreaming these dreams, thinking these thoughts was her only way of escaping. She was giving up on the dreary existence with him, and was willing herself to die!

Well, he wouldn't give up without a battle. He needed her, and she wouldn't be allowed to get away this easily. Now at each mealtime he arrived with a trayful of food and sat cramming each biteful into her mouth. Dr. Cramer ordered potent vitamins upon Ernie's request, and he forced them on her every day. He talked to her—tried to reason with her that what she was doing was having a negative affect on him, but his words fell upon deaf ears.

"Dor," he pleaded one day, sitting on the side of the bed. "Why are you doing this to me?"

"Doing what?" she asked innocently.

"You're not even trying."

"Trying to what? To stay in a world that doesn't need me?"

"But I need you! Can't you see? You're everything to me. You are my only happiness."

"You're not happy, Ernie. Living this way isn't happiness."

"Oh Dor!" he cried, gathering her frail body into his arms and burying his head against her shoulder. "I love you. Don't do this to me."

She pulled away and looked at him. "What am I doing to you? Don't you see? I've had it. I'm all worn out. Right now, I have the promise of a bright, new life. I'm not doing anything to you. It's out of my hands. God will take me when it's time."

"But what about me?"

"God will take you when it's your time."

"No!"

"Ernie, I've tried my hardest all our married life. At least give me that much credit."

"Dor, you're playing games. You know you shouldn't get me all worked up. Think of my heart."

"I have thought about your heart. Now you think of mine."

He called Dr. Cramer later in a state of panic. "You've got to do something to help her," he groaned.

"Mr. Freeman, there's nothing we can do. We have found nothing clinically wrong with your wife."

"You mean with all your fancy research there's nothing you can do? I don't believe it! You can give a man a heart that your scientists designed and built, but you expect me so sit by idly as my wife wastes away, believing that you're not capable of helping?"

"I don't know. I suppose we could bring her back to the hospital and feed her through a tube, but is that really you want?"

"You don't know? Hell, I don't know. Right now, I'm willing to try anything. Maybe if we give her a little more time she'll snap out of this."

"If that's what you want. Tell you what. We'll be there tomorrow morning. Please don't worry. You know how Dr. Sloan feels about allowing yourself to get worked up."

That night, Ernie crept into the bed and snuggled close to Doris, taking her hand in his. He couldn't tell her they were coming. She'd never agree. But even if she were gone for several months, at least the could rest assured that she'd eventually be back. It was better than allowing her to commit slow suicide. There was no way he could force her to eat, but they could. They had tubes and intravenous drips. The Institute had many different ways to help a body to sustain itself. She would get stronger, just as he had. Life would appear brighter once she returned. For once, she would be able to see how much she truly was needed. She was too young to die. There were so many days ahead of them in which to live.

He awoke at the crack of dawn. She was still sleeping, and he was grateful that he wouldn't have to face her long before they took her away. He noticed that he was still holding her hand, and gave it a loving squeeze. The moment he pressed against it, he instinctively recoiled. Something was wrong! It was cold! He jumped up, staring at her in horror. She lay with her head resting on the pillow, strangely still. Her eyes had taken on a hollow appearance, and her forehead and cheeks were grotesquely mottled. He continued staring at her in disbelief, stunned. She was dead! Without even saying goodbye, she had slipped away during the night. The Institute had never been given a chance. She was dead. She was gone, and on her pallid lips was left the hint of a smile.

"Dor!" he screamed, gathering her limp figure in his arms. "Dor! My God! What have you done?" He clutched at her cold body hysterically.

Unknown to him at the time were the physiological effects of the shock of her death on his body, setting into motion a deadly chain reaction. Immediately, his autonomic nervous system was activated, releasing adrenalin into his bloodstream. Had his heart still been normal, it would've been madly pounding. But it was not a normal heart, and the Biotron 8000 could only respond to the ticker tape. The excess adrenalin continued being secreted, and his blood vessels began to constrict. Unaware of this alteration, the artificial heart continued at the same rhythm and rate for which it had been synchronized, all the while his arteries narrowing until his blood pressure began to rise uncontrollably.

He sat on the bed rocking her corpse and moaning. "I'm so sorry, Dor. Please forgive me. God forgive me. I believe, Dor. Do you hear me? I do believe and I want to be with you."

The last thing he remembered was a knife-like pain in his temples. He was still holding his wife's body, but it was the last thing he recalled. Alone in the bedroom inside their apartment at Winnow Cove with nobody to see, he suddenly slumped forward, covering her chilled body with his. The rising pressure within the vessels of his head was more than his brain could tolerate. He lay there motionless, having suffered a massive stroke.

8

Winnow Cove was ageless. As the seasons passed little changed, for time seemed to hold no authority over the sprawling network of rich cedar buildings. The same desolate streets that had wound their way through years before, continued to form attractive boulevards that were still lined with elegant street-lamps. Windows with treated glass stared out vacantly to the courtyards below. And Apartment 314D still sat, as it always had, at the intersection of Lyceum and Vassal. Winnow Cove was a stable environment, identical to how it had once been and the way it would undoubtedly remain.

On the inside of Ernie's apartment, there was no great noticeable difference. Filtered air was still being supplied, filling the spacious rooms with the distinct odors of plastic and wax. The furnishings boasted the same contemporary style, with each item looking just as fresh and untouched as it had in the very beginning. Tall potted plants continued to stand in their containers, never needing watering and never having grown, for they were nothing but artificial decorations. And the cozy kitchen table rested in the same spot, facing the window that viewed the broad concrete steps that led to an anonymous neighbor. It was at the table that there had been one change. A lone figure, who had not been included among the original inhabitants, sat posted in this location—a nurse wearing electric blue.

Now there was always a nurse assigned to the apartment. She'd remain seated at the table reading a book or chomping her gum, the only interruptions coming at the time her shift was over, when she was being relieved, or if Ernie happened to need assistance. Several times a day, she expected him to call for help in order to walk to the bathroom, or to join her at the table for a meal. But these interactions were kept brief, and lengthy conversations were never shared.

After the stroke, he'd been left with a slight unilateral weakness that made it necessary for him to have continual supervision, but he had worked hard to improve this minor disability. On Tuesdays and Thursdays a physical therapist would come to help him with exercises so he could continue to make progress. At first, he was started with simple tasks, like combing his hair using his affected arm and squeezing a hollow rubber ball. From there he'd advanced to riding an exercise bicycle in order to strengthen his legs. The therapy had been a tremendous help, and he had reached a point where he knew the nurse was only needed to insure his stability as he moved about. He didn't like the idea of being dependent on anyone, but only went along with it because he'd been warned of the dangers of falling. Besides, she was always there and why allow her skills to go to waste?

Three times a week, he also received regular visits from the ticker tape girl. Synchronization of his heart had become a way of life, and he never paid much attention to the rhythm being displayed any more. There was no need for her to remind him to unbutton his shirt so that she could attach the brightly colored plastic clips. He'd notice her standing at the doorway and without a word, begin preparing himself. When he saw that she was finished, he'd sit up and help her to remove the white pads. Then she was gone, the entire procedure having lasted only a few minutes where no words were ever exchanged. It had become as common to him as taking a daily bath or brushing his teeth, and he accepted the ritual without question or complaint.

Most of the day was spent planted in front of the television set, not that he could enjoy any of the programs, for it was difficult following story lines while under the effects of sedation. Ever since he'd been a patient in the hospital after Doris' death, he'd been drugged. Twice a day after that, he was given a small blue capsule that helped to dull his senses and turn his surroundings into a hazy blur. He didn't mind. The sedated world was quite enjoyable, offering him a chance to have all his thoughts and fantasies drift together into an endless sea of warm scenes that kept him from growing depressed. With the help of the medication, he could imagine conversations with Doris, and if the trance were deep enough, could even picture her standing beside him with a smile on her face, appearing to be as young as she was the first time they'd met. He came to fear the moment when the drug would wear thin, casting him back into the world of pain that he'd first experienced the day of her death.

Dr. Sloan had thought it fortunate that he'd been found in time that fateful day. Two nurses had arrived to take Doris, and became concerned when there was no answer at the door. They'd forced their way in, only to find the couple lying in bed, Ernie's body crumpled over his wife's corpse. It was a frightening scene, and at first they weren't sure of what had happened. Rushing forward, they'd worked together to pull the pair apart, and when they separated, quickly examined them both to see if anything could be done. It was obvious that Doris had been dead for several hours, so they left her where she was and went to work on Ernie. His breathing was labored and he had lapsed into coma, but at least he still had a palpable pulse. An ambulance was called and he was rushed to the Emergency Room and back into intensive care.

His recovery had not come easily. He was forced to start out from the same condition where he had once begun. No sooner had he been rolled through the door when the all-too-familiar machinery was brought into play. Within minutes he was back on the ventilator and connected to the cardiac monitor. Plastic tubes were snaked around his body, leading to the various bags and containers, and near his bedside stood an army of blue intravenous pumps. For weeks he remained unconscious, never responding to the staff's painful pinches and rubs that were administered for the purpose of trying to awaken him. The medical staff hovered over his limp figure and shook their heads sadly, agreeing that it was still too early to measure the full extent of cerebral damage. A Cat Scan had been done at the time of his admission, which reinforced the clinical diagnosis—intracerebral hemorrhage. Each week the scan was repeated, showing how the excess blood was being absorbed, and each week they watched for any sign of improvement. Nobody knew, at that time, whether or not he'd survive, so all they could do was wait and try to keep him as stable as possible. All the while, adjustments continued being made on the Biotron Pump 8000, until his soaring blood pressure gradually began to decline.

The day finally came when his eyes fluttered open, and the medical staff rushed to his bedside rejoicing in the knowledge that the most crucial stage had ended. They watched him glancing about the room as if he might be searching for his wife, and when he could not find her, noticed how his face fell in sorrow. It was as if he had recalled all that happened before they had arrived, and all they could do was nod their heads sympathetically when his eyes filled with tears. It was at that time they became sure of what had caused the complication, and left the room mumbling words about the autonomic effect. The next day he was started on tranquilizers, and they closely monitored his sedative blood levels once every twenty-four hours. When they felt he had reached his therapeutic peak, he was continued on a maintenance dose. That was when the real world first began to fade out, and while he continued to respond to them from behind the stuporous wall they had created, they marched about the hospital with gloating expressions. After all, they had succeeded in their attempt to rescue him from this danger, regardless of his subsequent quality of life.

All the while, his body continued to heal and since

he was finally stable, the day came when he was transferred out. He was on the road to a promising recovery, and the press was alerted to this fact. As he was rolled down the halls to his new room, pictures were taken that proved to the world he had survived, left with minimum deficits—thanks to the Institute.

He was aware of the moment he was back in the apartment. The medication wasn't strong enough to wipe away the heavy sensation of loss as he roamed about the rooms. His wife's portion of the closet seemed hauntingly bare, and the bed felt a bit too large as he lay on his usual side alone—reaching out to her unconsciously that first night for a hand that he would never again touch. The next morning he took the medicine graciously because he knew that it was the only way he could possibly endure this new existence, and when he accepted the glass of water, looked up at the nurse hoping that she would somehow be an adequate substitute as a replacement for his wife.

Although he existed in a dazed state, he still tried to make the most of a meaningful relationship with his newly appointed companion. During his first few days home, he made it a point to come to the table to eat his meals, encouraging an air of friendship. Even as slow as his mind had become, he'd continue attempts at light conversations.

"What's yer name?" he slurred one morning, managing a sloppy grin as he sat facing the nurse over breakfast.

"Alice," she replied. "Alice Sweeney. But Mr. Freeman, I thought I'd introduced myself when I first came in."

He winked. "So you did. Don't worry. I was jest testin' you."

She shrugged, going back to her reading.

"Say, Alice. Do ya ever play cards?"

"Sometimes. When I'm off duty."

"What ya say you an' I have a game? Would help ta pass the time."

Her eyes narrowed and her face turned to stone. "Mr. Freeman, it is a strict policy of the Institute not to become involved with our patients in any extra-curricular activities. Playing cards with you is not allowed."

"Yeh." He hung his head. "Well, ya can't blame me for trying."

The nurses were always coolly professional, making it clear who it was they had as an employer. It wasn't their duty to formulate personal relation-ships, and the Institute's policies clearly outlined their duties of having only to see to his physical safety and care. So even though he longed for any form of human interaction, there was none, and more so than ever he welcomed the tiny blue capsules twice every day.

The months blended together into years, but Ernie never paid attention, for he seemed to have become part of Winnow Cove, just as permanent, just as ageless. He would take his medication, then sink back into a tranquil state where only those he chose were allowed to appear. It came as an unexpected surprise when one day the nurse stood at his bedroom door, announcing that he had a visitor.

"Dad?" a man with steel-gray hair inquired, towering over the bedside.

Ernie looked up, trying to break through the chemical haze in an attempt to focus.

"Dad? This is Alex."

"Alex?" Ernie muttered to himself as if trying to

171

recall the name. Then his eyes turned misty and reached out, clutching for his son's hand. "Alex?"

"Dad," Alex echoed, crumpling onto the mattress and encircling the old man with his arms. "I thought you'd still be angry."

"Angry?" Ernie asked through a flood of warm tears. "No. I thought I'd never see ya again."

"I had to come. I know the last time I was here, we exchanged some pretty hot words. It took a lot for me to have the visitation restriction lifted. But I thought you may've changed your mind—especially after Mom died."

Ernie squeezed his eyes shut and twisted his face into a wretched grimace. "You'll never know how I've missed yer mother."

"I do know, Dad."

"So, how about you?" He brightened, studying his son's lined face. "Looks like yer gettin' on in years."

"Same as you. What happened to your hair?"

Ernie reached up to run his palm against the skin of his bald head. "Guess I lost it." He chuckled. "Must run in the family." He nodded in the direction of his son's receding hairline.

"Yeh, guess we're both a little older."

"Ya look tired. Been pushin' yerself? How's the job?"

"It's always hectic, but there's not much I can do."

"Can't ya quit? There's always somethin' else. Yer bright an' talented. Pressure's no good. Nobody knows that better'n me."

He grinned. "There's no point to that. I'll be retiring next year. Already have almost twenty years under my belt."

For a moment Ernie was stunned. Twenty years? What had happened to the time?

"Mr. Freeman," the nurse said, walking over to the bed. "I hate to interrupt you, but it's time for your dialysis. If you'd like, you son can go along with us so that you can continue with your visit."

"Dialysis?" Alex asked in surprise. "When did you start that?"

"Oh, I had a little trouble with my kidneys a while back. It's no big deal. They do it right here. Afterwards, I'm as good as new."

Alex furrowed his brows, watching as the nurse helped him out of the bed and across the floor to a small room that was connected to his bathroom. He followed behind, taking a seat across from the vinyl recliner where his father had been placed. She inserted a needle into his wrist that was connected to wide plastic tubing, and when the machine began to whir, bright red blood came rushing through. Ernie closed his eyes and leaned back.

"How long have they been doing this?" Alex finally asked.

"I don't know. A while. When my kidneys went into failure. Had something to do with my blood pressure after I'd had the stroke."

"Stroke? Nobody told me."

"Yeh, well, I guess I went off the deep end the day yer mother died. I ended up back in the hospital."

"So that's why you never answered our letters. Shawn and I thought you hadn't cared."

"How is Shawn?"

Alex cocked his head to the side as if he hadn't heard the question correctly. "Well, Dad." He cleared his throat. "Didn't they tell you?"

"Tell me what?"

"That . . . that Shawn died."

Ernie's jaw dropped open, and he gripped the arms of the dialysis chair so tightly that his knuckles turned white.

"I thought . . . I thought you knew."

"How? How did it happen?"

"She had a lump. They said it was cancer. The whole thing went so fast. There was hardly any time."

"When?"

"Well, by now it's almost three years."

"Three years?" He pressed his eyes shut.

"I'm sorry. I thought you knew. There was nothing that could've been done. It had progressed to a point where it was inoperable."

"But she was so young."

Alex slowly nodded. "Yes she was. She was only forty-four."

The hazy fog around Ernie suddenly lifted. Alex close to retirement? Shawn dying at forty-four? If that was three years ago, she'd be forty-seven years of age, almost as old as he'd been at the time of his transplant. He stared at his son, then allowed his eyes to fall upon his own gnarled hands. How old did that make him? For how many years had they kept him alive inside Winnow Cove?

"So, I haven't heard much about you in the papers lately," Alex went on. "Of course, it's been a while and they've done dozens of other transplants."

Ernie managed an audible grunt.

"Well." Alex pulled himself up. "Looks as though you're getting tired. Tell you what. I'll be back." He turned to leave, then as an afterthought, pivoted around with a smile. "I almost forgot. One of the reasons I came was to tell you that I finally did find the right one."

"Right one?"

"Yes!" he announced happily. "The right woman. I know I've been a bachelor all of my life, but I plan on getting married in the near future. I haven't told her about you yet. I think this is something I'll have to break gently. It might come as a shock to her to find out I'm the son of the famous Ernest P. Freeman, longest surviving artificial heart recipient. Maybe I'll bring her here to meet you—if I can get her on the visitor list.''

"Yeh, you do that.''

Alex reached down to shake his father's hand. "I'll see you, Dad.''

"Alex?" Ernie grasped his son's fingers tightly. "Promise me you'll be back?''

"Sure. Just as soon as I can.''

Once Alex had gone, Ernie stared blankly at the walls of the room, milling over this unexpected bombardment of information. The news of Shawn's untimely death had come as a shock, and his eyes still stung from the blow of the message. He struggled to contain the scream of panic that had risen in his throat, for the first time understanding the severity of his situation. Now each click of the mechanical heart came as a menacing trill that set into motion a cursed effect that started in the base of his chest and radiated into every other part of his body until it had accumulated in his head, making his ears pound unmercifully and his skull feel as if it were about to burst. Each rhythmic beat seemed to ridicule him for having been foolish enough to have exchanged all that was of value just for the opportunity to live. To live? He glanced about the room. In exchange for all of this he had sold everyone else out. Years that should've been shared with his family had been traded off for this type of existence, and now as he huddled in the dialysis chair, he realized how little his life was really worth.

He spotted a pencil and paper next to him

on the table, and reached out for them with trembling hands. How long had he actually been there? He began to think. Shawn had been twenty-six at the time of his transplant, and now would've been forty-seven. He scrawled out the numbers and subtracted. Twenty-one. That's how long it had been, an entire decade from the time of Doris' death. His own age? He added the numbers together. Seventy-two!

The pencil slipped from his fingers and rolled to the floor. For a moment he watched it lie there motionless, then his eyes wandered over to his hands. There, bluish veins stood out upon the pale tissue skin like tortuous ropes, and where once there had been a few dark discolorations, these had now been swallowed up by unsightly blemishes that covered their backs. He reached up, running his palm over the skin of his head, then allowed it to explore the contours of his face. The flesh of his cheeks and neck hung in loose folds, with no sign of its former youthful elasticity, and he found himself pulling it, twisting it, and pinching it together as he felt how freely it moved over its boney base. Then he let go, and it fell back into place like an ill-fitted suit with no more consistency than a glob of dead chicken skin.

Originally, they had talked about only a few years of any life extension, but the few years had expanded to over twenty, leaving him nothing more than a lonely old man. Not that there weren't others who shared this same age category, but their situation was different. They had a quality of life, never having been locked inside an isolated apartment where it was easy to be forgotten, nor ever having known the feeling of being limited to a world within an artificial bubble. What had it all been for?

He shuddered. Why had he ever been willing to make such a sacrifice? For life? What life? He closed his eyes, trying to block out the hum of the dialysis machine. What else had happened over the years of which he was unaware? How much more had the Institute actually stolen?

Slowly, he opened his eyes, studying his surroundings as if he were seeing them for the first time, and trying to fill in all the empty gaps that were once kept hidden. What were the clues that should've tipped him off to the nightmare that was taking place—the nightmare that he had invited?

It wasn't as if he'd been completely in the dark. Each day he'd received the newspaper. Still, he'd never paid much attention to the small dates that were printed on the tops, as if it had never occurred to him that they'd ever been significant. Then there had been the television, but changes in programs had always been made gradually enough so that time had been able to slip by unnoticed.

How could you effectively gauge time when you weren't even aware of your own age? By people. It was continual contact with others on a regular basis that provided a type of mirror to help form images of where you stood in time and space. And how could you hope to measure yourself if there was nobody to serve as a comparison? Perhaps if Doris had still been alive, he could've seen the way she was aging, or if Alex hadn't been banned for so many years. Still, there should've been others. He thought back. The ticker tape girls were forever changing, and besides, they all looked the same. Dr. Sloan. He suddenly pictured the silver-haired physician. Sloan had always appeared much older than himself. Where had he gone? He tried to remember the last time he'd visited, and then found himself cringing in terror. He couldn't recall when it had been. What had happened to his transplant surgeon? Nobody had ever said, and he had never bothered asking. He'd simply accepted the fact that he'd always be there, just as he once thought of his own parents, never suspecting that time would eventually play its own hand.

The nurse, who had stepped out for several minutes, came rushing back in to check the equipment. Without saying a word, she took a stool near the dialysis machine until the procedure was finished. Every so often Ernie found her glancing over at him curiously, trying to see what he was writing, but he was careful to shield the slip of paper from view. When his dialysis had ended, she stood up and began detaching the tubes.

"How long have you been working with me?" he asked as he searched her face.

She smiled. "About four years."

"What happened to Alice Sweeney?"

Her manicured eyebrows shot up in question. "Alice Sweeney? Why she's no longer with the Institute."

"But what happened to her?"

"She was getting older, Mr. Freeman."

"So?"

"So, it was time for her to retire."

"And what happened to her after that?"

She lowered her eyes without responding.

Her silence was conclusive. Alice Sweeney had grown older and retired, and then she'd probably died, just like everyone else. It had happened to Doris, happened to Shawn, and probably had happened to everyone else he hadn't seen over the last several years. Everyone was being allowed to die—everyone but him.

That evening he made it a point to go to the table for supper. Seated across from the nurse, he watched her with an intensity she found peculiar.

"So how did the visit go with your son?" she finally asked in an attempt to conceal her own feelings of nervousness that had been triggered by his piercing stare.

"Fine. It was nice seeing him."

"Well, that's just wonderful, and I'm glad for your sake that he came."

Ernie did not take his eyes off of her as he set down his fork. "How am I doing?" he suddenly blurted.

"What?"

"How am I doing? You know, my health."

"Why, you're doing just fine."

"What about my heart? Are there any problems?"

"Of course not. The Biotron 8000 is running just as perfectly as it was the first day."

He sighed, then leaned forward to push his plate away. "Tell me something," he said as if it were a challenge. "Why have I lived this long?"

She glanced over at him with a scowl. "I don't think I understand your question."

"Why haven't I died?"

"Mr. Freeman, you have an amazing stamina. For some reason your body's able to adapt."

"But if I have so much stamina, why don't my kidneys work, and why did I have that stroke?"

"Those were merely complications. It was already explained to you that there might be complications with the heart."

"And what would've happened to me if nobody had been able to step in and correct those complications?"

"Why . . . why you would've died."

"Then it's not my amazing stamina at all."

"I don't see what you're driving at. We're only here to keep you on the right track."

"So that I'd continue living?" he asked dryly.

"You're extremely fortunate."

"And my heart, this Biotron 8000 that's packed away in my chest, how long will it last if everyone keeps helping me back to the right track?"

"I have no idea. Nobody does."

"What if it never stops?"

"Don't be ridiculous."

"I mean it. What if this contraption can never stop? What if it just keeps going on and on and on? Is someone going to eventually decide to turn it off? Who's gonna make that decision?"

"Mr. Freeman, is something bothering you?"

"Of course not," he replied bitterly. "Why should anything be bothering me?"

Later that evening, she came to his room carrying the usual medicine cup. He accepted it, studying its contents. Nestled among all the other pills was the tiny blue capsule. This had been part of his problem, the chemical thief that had robbed him of any awareness of time. When she turned around to pour a glass of water, he removed the capsule and stuffed it into his pocket, planning to flush it down the toilet at the first opportunity. He had to be in control of his faculties if he wanted to work out this problem. Then he could find a solution and bring the nightmare to an end.

Alex would help. When he returned they would put their heads together and figure out a way to resolve his dilemma. He would tell him that enough was enough—that he was ready to call it quits. Perhaps his son could use his influence to put pressure on the Institute, even if it meant appointing an attorney. In the end, they would be forced to release him from this bondage and he would at last be free. Even if it meant returning to an unprotected world where he would soon become its victim, it was still far better than this, being held as an unwilling captive.

Without the sedation, he began to change. For over a week he experienced symptoms of withdrawal that left him trembling severely enough that he dared not show the nurse his hands. Several times a day it was necessary for him to crawl alone to the bathroom to wipe the beads of sweat from his brow so that she wouldn't grow suspicious. The thought occurred to him that he might die, but by the time he'd reached the second week, his system showed signs of stabilizing and he knew he was out of danger.

Now that his head had cleared, each day dragged on more endlessly than the last. All of the details within his environment had surfaced and he found their monotony unbearable. He began to notice the similarity in meals, and that he was served chicken at least three times a week. Where once it had not mattered, he now found himself forcing himself to eat so that it wouldn't become obvious that his senses had sharpened. The walls began to represent barriers locking him inside, and each day he seemed to spend more time at the windows until the nurse would catch him looking out, and then he'd tear himself away pretending it had only been a coincidence that he had been standing there. When he found himself relating to familiar faces on the television set as if they were old friends, he began to wonder if he might be going insane. The sedation may have been more significant than he had originally thought.

At times he found himself controlling a temper that dangled on the end of a shorter fuse, and he tried hard to keep it from reaching a level of explosion. Like the day the nurse came in to explain that the newspaper hadn't been delivered. It was the only thing he had looked forward to in the evening hours, and he fought the rage that festered inside. But if he were to lose control, his secret would be known, and he couldn't afford the luxury of making such a costly mistake. Biting his tongue to keep from showing his anger, he'd turned away passively to look for something else to read. That was when he'd discovered Doris' old Bible.

It was only a book. He thumbed through the pages looking at the small print. How could these words have given her peace during her last days? Did they hold some mystical enchantment? He read a few verses then turned to another section, noticing specific sentences that she had underlined. He placed his hand over her markings. These had been the pages her own hand had once touched, and as he ran his finger over her penciled tracing, he suddenly felt closer to her. Alex would come, and then his loneliness would be brought to an end. He needed something a little more solid, and knew that the solutions to his problems couldn't be resolved just through the words of a book. If only she had known what had been in store.

Depression was a physiological threat that stalked him unrelentlessly and finally succeeded in taking hold. It started with a feeling of exhaustion, where he found himself requiring more and more sleep. Breakfasts were missed, and oftentimes his desire to sleep stretched out to almost include lunch and supper. It wasn't unusual for him to be found taking a nap at any time during the day. Gradually, he began to lose weight, which caused the nurse to observe him more keenly and question whether or not he was having any other symptoms—like pain. He knew what she was driving at, but managed to shrug it off by explaining that he was just bored. This reply seemed to satisfy her temporarily, but he would still catch her watching him from a distance. Throughout this period, he was enshrouded with an overwhelming sadness that he couldn't seem to shake; nor did he have any desire to do so, for he was caught up in a web of apathy where he no longer cared. It had been five months since Alex's visit, and he was beginning to wonder if his son would ever return—in spite of his promise.

Ernie didn't know why he decided to start the project. The depression had lifted long enough for him to realize that he had to use some protective mechanism to keep himself from going mad. One day, he announced to the nurse that he'd like to begin packing away his wife's collection of china curios. They'd been seated on the shelf ever since the day they'd moved in and had only been collecting dust. Since his son would soon be getting married, he thought Doris would've wanted them in their home. Besides, if he were to pack up this treasure, it might give him an excuse to inquire about his son's current address. Then he could send out the package with a letter tucked safely inside, explaining the urgency of his plight.

The nurse smiled approvingly when she brought in the stack of old newspapers and a large cardboard box. He took a seat in one of the living room chairs, carefully wrapping each piece and packing it away.

Why he happened to turn to that particular page, or why he was drawn to the article he'd never know.

As he scanned the headlines he noticed that it was a newspaper he hadn't read, and was probably the one that hadn't been delivered that day. The nurse must've brought her own newspaper from home. His eyes fell upon the bold print at the bottom of the page, leaping out at him with an immediacy he couldn't ignore. *Marketing Executive Found Dead In Auto.* He began to read, and suddenly found his hands trembling at the sight of the name. "Alexander E. Freeman, a forty-three year old marketing executive of the Kuepfer Corp. was found dead in his automobile in the parking lot of Hillview Mall." The cause of his death was unknown, but they suspected a heart attack. A complete autopsy was scheduled. Alex! The newspaper slipped out of his hands and crumpled in his lap.

He rested his elbows on his knees, rubbing his forehead and groaning. When he'd sufficiently recovered from the initial blow, he picked up the paper again and checked the date. It had occurred over two months ago!

Poor Alex. The strain on his face was apparent the day of his visit. Heart problems ran in their family. He should've known. But instead, he pushed himself to the limit, dying the same kind of death that had originally been intended for him. Poor Alex. Ernie thought back to the squeezing pain he'd experienced in his chest. Had his son known? Had it caught him off guard? Had he also been afraid in those last isolated moments? Couldn't he have called for help? Oh God! He began to sob. Now all of his loved ones were gone, leaving him nobody to turn to; his whole family had been taken, leaving him in the world alone.

When the nurse returned, he looked up at her with tear-stained cheeks and reddened eyes. "You knew," he hissed accusingly. "You knew all along that my son was dead and you never even told me."

She glanced down at the newspaper and her face colored slightly. Then she folded her arms across her chest and eyed him coolly. "I couldn't tell you."

"But I talked about him. I told you he was getting married. And you stood there and lied right to my face."

"I didn't lie to you. I just didn't say anything. There's a difference."

"But you led me to believe this package would be going to him, but how could it?" Angrily, he kicked the bottom of the box and the contents went flying across the floor.

"The activity was good for you. You weren't eating properly, and you needed something to keep you busy."

Giant tears welled in his eyes. "He was all I had left—the last of my family. Did you know that? Did you care?"

She nodded. "Yes, we knew. But you reacted quite severely to your wife's death, and we had to protect you from another autonomic response." She reached out to place a firm hand on his quivering shoulder. "Mr. Freeman, calm down. You wouldn't want anything to happen."

He stared up at her in anguish. "Why not? Why the hell not? What else do I have to live for? Why?" he cried. "Why do you people want to keep me alive?"

She became alarmed. "Mr. Freeman, please keep calm. If you don't, I'm afraid I'll be forced into taking action."

"What? And help me to get back on the right track again?" His face had turned purple with rage.

Without saying another word, the nurse dashed

out of the room and returned with a loaded syringe. Thrashing and screaming, he fought against her, but she still managed to roll up the sleeve of his shirt, and in a flash had plunged the tip of the needle deep within his flesh.

The room was deathly quiet when he awakened, and the drapes were drawn, locking him in a shroud of darkness. As his eyes fluttered open, he strained to hear any sound that might warn him if he were being observed. He was in his bed, and could see all the familiar objects of his room. The scene with the nurse still remained as vivid as if it had just happened, and he could feel the sting of the wound that had been inflicted through her deceit. Alex would never be returning. He was gone, just like the others. Everyone he had ever loved had been taken, leaving him alone in the world to fend for himself.

He tried to sit up, but his head was too heavy and he let it fall back upon the pillow. There was no way out—no hope of being rescued, and his artificial heart would continue beating forever inside a body that had become decrepit and frail. There would never be any visitors—no comforting words from the outside world. He would go on forever and ever at the mercy of the Institute. Something had to be done. Now, the problem rested solely on his shoulders.

Mustering up all the strength he possessed, he eased his way over to the side of the bed and swung his feet to the floor. He pulled himself up to a sitting position and took a few deep breaths, trying to decide upon his next action. When he was sure of his own stability, he drew himself off the mattress and staggered his way across the room to the door.

The apartment was still, and as he slipped past the kitchen noticed the nurse at the table, her head nodding as she dozed. Good! She didn't see him, and he rushed across the plush carpet of the living room to the front door.

It had been over twenty years since he'd last set foot outside, and the afternoon sunshine exploded in his eyes, forcing him to falter in his tracks. He collapsed against the porch railing, filling his lungs with the fresh outside air, and welcoming the warm breeze against his face as he tried to focus. In the distance, he could hear the wail of an ambulance racing to some destination with a persistent urgency that was no different than his own, for now he understood that he was being driven by a state of emergency, too. The only solution to his imprisonment within Winnow Cove was escape.

At first, his movements came with great difficulty, and he found himself weaving down the front walk as if he were drunk. The stroke had left him unbalanced, and his body swaggered over to the right as he tried to maintain his footing. Gradually, he began to pick up speed, and even though his affected foot trailed behind the other, he rejoiced in the fact that he could almost run. He was racing away from the apartment, freeing himself from the bondage of the dialysis machine, the ticker tape, and the entire Institute staff. In that moment he longed to scream out in pleasure, the way a child might do at the end of a school semester when he was beginning his summer vacation. Even though there was no destination in mind, it didn't seem to matter because for the first time in years there was nobody watching him. He was moving on his own merit. He was free!

It happened before he had time to react. He'd leaped off the curb, when his knee suddenly buckled beneath the weight. Excruciating pain knifed its way up into his hip, and he was hurled into the gutter in a writhing heap. The sun was too bright, and he tried to blink away the stars that flashed before his eyes like a display of burning fireworks. There was no way to control the whirling of his head, or the tidal wave of panic as he struggled to maintain consciousness. The last thing he remembered was the grate of the pavement, like sandpaper against his cheek.

When he awoke, he was back in the apartment, lying on his bed where he could see all the familiar objects in his room. His hip was throbbing, the pulsating pain having moved up into the small of his back and when he tried to turn over, the motion of his limbs sent him into an acute spasm. He decided it was best to lay still.

"Mr. Freeman?" a man's authoritative voice cut through the haze.

Ernie looked up at him helplessly. The man wore a stethoscope around his neck, but appeared too young to be a doctor.

"What you did today was very foolish," he scolded. "Now, you've broken your hip. An ambulance is coming, and you'll be taken to the hospital where it'll have to be set. I don't know how long it'll take for that bone to heal, if it ever does." He shook his head. "I doubt whether you'll ever be able to walk again."

The nurse marched in and began to prepare him for transport. As a last minute gesture, she brought in the usual medicine cup. He glanced down at its contents and noticed the tiny blue capsule. This time he swallowed it willingly. At least it would help him to forget.

9

"Where's . . . my . . . pill?"

"These are your pills."

"But . . . where's . . . the . . . blue . . . one?"

"The doctor discontinued that one. You won't be getting it any more."

"Wh . . . hy?"

"I don't know. He probably thinks you don't need it."

"But . . . I . . . do . . . need . . . it!"

"Well, why don't you talk to him about that. He'll be coming to see you this afternoon."

Ernie's eyes slipped shut and he drifted back into a world of sleep. He could see Doris walking towards him carrying a bouquet of flowers and wearing her favorite green dress, and he was anxious to meet her.

"You've got to get up," she said with a smile. "It's

almost time.''

"Time for what?''

"The party. Everyone'll be there, so the grass has got to be mowed. I want everything to look especially nice. We don't have much time. Come on.'' She reached out to him, and he took her hand.

Together, they moved down a long, narrow corridor and its pink fluorescent lights glowing from the tiled ceiling. He could hear the click of her high heels along the shiny floor as he tried to keep up with her, but she was moving too swiftly and he found himself becoming short of breath.

"Slow down!'' he finally cried out in exasperation. "You know I can't move very quickly!''

She turned around to toss him a look of disapproval. "But you have to. Everyone'll be here and we're not ready.''

Without further complaint, he tried his best to pick up speed, but his legs felt weighted and he seemed to be moving in slow motion. Each step came as a struggle when he found himself using all of his strength just to pull his feet off the floor, as if the soles of his shoes were glued.

"Hurry, Ernie.''

"I'm trying.''

"Can't you go any faster?''

"No, I can't. Are we almost there? I've got to sit down and rest.''

"But you can't. The yard isn't ready, and it's going to be a garden party.''

A door opened at the end of the hallway, and a burst of sunlight flooded through, almost blinding him. Against the brilliant background he could see two silhouettes. He squinted.

"Daddy? Daddy are you ready?''

"Shawn? Is that you?''

"Yes, Daddy. We've been waiting."

"Are you coming to take me away?"

"Come on, Dad." It was Alex's voice that interrupted. "We've got to hurry. There's a lot to be done. We've got to get our house in order."

Ernie could see his children now, their faces looking just as young as he'd remembered. Doris stood beside them, and they wrapped their arms around each other, smiling.

"What do I have to do?" Ernie asked.

"The yard. The guests will be arriving any minute."

They turned around to open the door, and Ernie followed them through.

The scene that awaited was not what he expected. High mounds of muddy clay formed mountainous ranges for as far as the eye could see. There was no foliage, only the reddish slime that clung to his shoes when he tried to take a step forward. Off to one side was a patio table with a colorful umbrella opened wide. It teetered in the wind, looking as if it were about to fall over. On the opposite side rested a large glass vase that was partially covered with mud. Doris seemed to glide across the wet surface in order to place the flowers inside, the small splash of color appearing strangely out of place. A lawn mower was there, and Alex bent over to pull the chord and start the engine.

"I can't do anything with this!" Ernie cried out to them. "You can't have a party here!"

"But you have to. They're all invited."

Ernie stared down at the lawn mower, then gazed out across the mounds of desolate clay. "There's no grass. I don't see any grass that has to be moved."

"But the seeds have been planted," Alex replied accusingly.

"You don't understand," Ernie went on. "I just want to be with you."

"Dad." Shawn grasped his hand. "You've got to help. Everything must be put in order before you can leave."

"And the guests will be coming," Doris reminded him. "What will they think?"

"They can't come here."

"Why not?" A man approached them. It was George carrying an electric edger. "Here, use this. Maybe it'll help."

"Nothing will help!" Ernie cried.

They formed a small group, staring at him in disbelief. "Why not?" they asked in unison.

"Because . . . because I'm not ready."

"When will you be ready?" Doris asked with a scowl.

"I don't know. It'll take forever. I'm just not ready, yet." He looked at them pathetically, and his eyes filled with tears. "Can't you understand?"

"Then you can't cross over," they said.

"No! I want to go with you!"

They didn't reply, simply stood there staring at him with eyes that were cold and unforgiving. When he tried to reach out, they turned around and began to fade away.

"Please!" he entreated. "I'm sorry. I'm sorry. Give me another chance!"

"Mr. Freeman?" a man's voice boomed.

"I'm sorry," Ernie sobbed.

"Mr. Freeman." The man shook his shoulder. "Wake up. You're having a bad dream."

"Huh?" Ernie stopped crying, and slowly opened his eyes.

"Mr. Freeman, I'm Dr. Roberts. Can you hear me?"

"A-huh."

"The nurse said you were asking about your sedative."

"My . . . blue . . . pill."

"Yes, that's right. You see, Mr. Freeman, I think it's about time that we begin weaning you from that drug. It's been severely affecting your level of consciousness. I wouldn't want you to appear stuporous during the program."

"Program?" He squinted, trying to see the doctor's face, but everything was a blur.

"They're going to be doing a television special. They'll be interviewing you, along with thirty-eight other artificial heart recipients."

"Thirty-eight?"

"Yes, you didn't know there were that many, did you? Science has certainly come a long way. Thirty-eight people have survived; twenty-three men and fifteen women who have been just as fortunate as you. It'll be a two-hour special, so I hope they'll be able to get everyone in. Naturally, you'll be the highlight. We agreed that your spot should be done live. I think it's important for the world to see you just the way you are. After all, you are the longest survivor, and your birthday is coming up. It's absolutely amazing! There are very few people who've managed to reach your age without the use of an artificial heart. So you've really set a record. It should be an inspiration to others. You'll even be receiving recognition from the President himself. It's a real miracle that you've been able to make it to one hundred."

"One . . . one hundred?" He tried to lift his head off the pillow so he could better see the man who was speaking.

"I'm sorry," Dr. Roberts apologized. "You don't

have your glasses. Here, allow me." He reached over to the nightstand and pulled out a pair of bifocals. "Good thing we removed those cataracts when we did. You were practically blind. But you've got to remember to ask for these. Otherwise, you won't be able to see."

"A . . . a hundred?" Ernie repeated.

"I know you're still a little foggy, but don't worry about it. In a week or two you should be as sharp as ever. We had to keep you a little snowed for your own protection, but you'll be fine as soon as the drug wears off."

With the glasses on, Ernie was at least able to see the physician. He was a young man with rich black hair that framed his face like a neatly clipped hedge. His skin was smooth and shiny, and the dark stubble of his beard, in spite of the fact that he was cleanly shaven, smothered his upper lip and jaw with a perpetual shadow. He was of slight build, with narrow shoulders and delicate hands that appeared almost feminine, except for the tell-tale sign of matted hair on their backs, lending proof of his masculinity. He smiled down at Ernie, revealing a set of pearl teeth that dazzled with a brilliancy that could have only been attained through meticulous grooming. Most striking were his eyes, and as Ernie studied them, he found his own curious stare being matched by two bottomless pools of icy blue.

"What . . . happened . . . to . . . Sloan?" Ernie asked in confusion.

"Sloan?"

"My . . . my doctor."

Dr. Roberts scratched his chin, then his crystal eyes lit up like a pair of iridescent candles. "Oh! That Sloan. Say, you do go back a long way. He hasn't been around for over thirty years.'"

"Is . . . he . . . still . . . alive?"

"No. As a matter of fact, we were just talking about him the other day. Seems he died of congestive heart failure. The Institute offered him an artificial heart, but he refused. Can you imagine? Why would one of the best transplant surgeons we ever had, refuse the one thing he had worked so hard to build? You got me. I'll never know. But that was before my time, and it's really none of my concern. The important thing was that Sloan was good while he lasted. He did manage to get you this far."

"Doctor?" Ernie looked up at the smooth face, suddenly recalling all that had happened.

"Yes?" The physician smiled down warmly.

"You . . . said . . . I . . . was . . . having . . . a . . . bad . . . dream."

"That's right. It was bad enough that I found you crying."

"No." Ernie shook his head slowly from side to side. "This . . . is . . . my . . . only . . . bad . . . dream."

Once Ernie had awakened, he was forced into a rude introduction to the body he now possessed. It was worse than anything imaginable, and he looked upon it with horror and dread. Time had taken its toll, and along with a continual lack of mobility while he'd remained in a semiconscious state, he had been left a mere shell of a man who barely resembled a functional human being.

He soon discovered that his own teeth had become decayed over the years, and that after they'd been extracted, it was necessary for him to wear a full set of dentures. A tube hung from his nose that originated from the depths of his stomach, and it was through this plastic vehicle that he had been fed purely liquid meals. It came as a shock the first time he tried to use his hands, only to find that they had shriveled up into contracted claws. His arms and legs had not been spared either, permanently molded into a spindly fetal position, and even though a physical therapist had been assigned to work with them, trying to pry them apart was an impossibility as they creaked with each painful attempt. The most humiliating experience was to find that the nurses had been donning him with adult-sized diapers, and more often than not, he chose not to wear his glasses, rather than look upon the creature into which he had evolved.

Oftentimes, in the silence of his room, he would concentrate on the mechanical heart. He'd close his eyes and strain to listen for each metallic click, for it was this merciless instrument that had become a demon, urging his worn body onward when it only longed for rest. By now, he knew he was reaching levels that his cells had never anticipated at the time of his conception, and what he was left with was a biproduct of its effects. With every beat he could almost feel the blood surging its way through his aged vessels like gelatinous sludge, and at times he toyed with the idea that if he concentrated hard enough, it could somehow be willed to stop.

The ticker tape girl was ever faithful, never failing to show up for her scheduled appointments, and three times a week he watched as the colorful plastic clips were snapped into place for the synchronization process that would adjust the Biotron 8000 to a level that was always as good as new.

"Did you have to go to school to learn how to work that ticker tape?" he asked her one day, trying to be cordial as she adjusted the dials.

"Ticker tape?" She looked over at him inquisitively. "What's a ticker tape?"

"That." He nodded in the direction of the red and white graph paper. "You're probably new, but the other girls knew that's what I always called it."

"I never thought of it as a ticker tape, but I guess it kinda fits." She smiled. "You certainly have quite an imagination. I could come up with a lot of other names to describe it."

"Have you been doing it for a long time?"

"Long enough. We only have four other girls in our department."

"It must keep you busy—now that there are thirty-eight."

"Thirty-eight? Where'd you get that number?"

"From Dr. Roberts. You see, they're going to be doing a television special, and we'll all be on." He paused for a moment, glad that he'd broken through the usual barrier of silence, but afraid to say anything that might cause her to clam up. "I suppose you've met the other ones," he finally went on. "People like me."

"Oh, yeh. I've met them."

"What're they like?"

"I don't know. We never really talk."

"Are they all in places like this?"'

"Not all of them."

"What do you mean? I thought we were all sent to this kind of special apartment."

"Some of them are." She tapped her finger nervously. "Some are right here in Winnow Cove. Some are still in the hospital. You know, because of complications. And some of them . . . ." She stopped, her face coloring slightly. "Look, I really shouldn't be talking about it."

"What?" Ernie replied, deciding that her response was worth another long bout of being ignored. "It's okay. What were you going to say?"

She lowered her eyes, refusing to answer.

"Do any of them get to go home? Is that it?"

"No," she stated emphatically. "None of them ever get to go home. . . . at least not yet." She sighed. "I mean, I wish they could, but the researchers are still trying to find the right drugs. They feel that it isn't right to allow complications. Still, they're always looking." Her face softened, and she smiled. "Have you seen Mr. Presta on T.V.? He's the first Biotron 9000 recipient. He was done last week."

"The Biotron 9000? What does that one do?"

"It's pretty much the same. All they did was add a new computer chip so that it doesn't have to be synchronized quite as often. It'll be a big help to me."

"And how does this Mr. Presta feel about it—being the first one to try it out?"

"I don't know. How did you feel?"

After their discussion, Ernie began to pay more attention to the television news. Each day he looked forward to the latest update on this new transplant patient, somehow feeling a common bond between them since they'd both been first. Pictures flashed on the screen during the different phases of his recovery, showing him surrounded by his family, and somehow he felt responsible to them for he knew that if this man were to survive, he would be in for a rude awakening. If only they could talk, perhaps he could warn Mr. Presta of the mistakes he'd made along the way.

It was the late night news that alerted him to the fact that one of the thirty-eight had died. Her name had been LaVern Cook, and as he listened to the account, he couldn't help but feel a twinge of envy. Her procedure had been done several years after his, and, like himself, she had no surviving relatives.

What else had she known during that time—the same feelings of agonizing loneliness? But she had finally succeeded in an escape, and he began to wonder how this had been managed. The real surprise came when they showed where she had lived. At last, he'd been able to meet his neighbor. The camera moved in, showing an ambulance stretcher that was carrying her remains away, rolling down the broad concrete steps that led to the apartment next door.

It wasn't the last of his surprises. Early one afternoon, the Institute's latest public relations man came to pay Ernie a visit. He wanted to meet with him to discuss the scheduled television special.

"Mr. Freeman, we're just delighted to see how well you're doing. Too bad they can't do something about this tube." He waved his hand in front of Ernie's nose. "I'll talk to Roberts. Maybe he can take it out just for the interview. I was thinking." The man scratched his chin. "Since this will be live, I can't help but wonder if it wouldn't be nice to include a close relative."

Ernie smiled wryly. "Don't think I can help you there. I'm the only one in my family left."

His eyebrows shot up in question. "Why, that's not true."

"What do you mean?"

"I mean that you're not the only survivor in your family. You have a granddaughter."

"A granddaughter? That's impossible. You see, I only had two children. My daughter, well . . . well she was fixed, if you know what I mean. And my son, he never got married."

"But you do have a granddaughter. We've been able to trace it back." He reached into the breast pocket of his suit, and emerged with a tiny brown notepad. "Yes, that's right." He glanced down at it. "Her name is Katherine. Has your last name. She's living in Colorado, and is about twenty-seven years old."

"Katherine," Ernie muttered. "That was my mother's name."

"So it is." The man checked what was written, then added his own brief note. "I like that. Has a nice touch. Maybe we can use it."

Warm tears began to form in Ernie's eyes. "But if I do have a granddaughter, why she hasn't ever come to visit?"

"Mr. Freeman," the man stated, "from what we understand, she didn't know."

"Know what?"

"That she even had a grandfather, or that he was living in this place."

It was later that Ernie found out that the public relations man's name was Sid Chandler. He wanted to know more about him. The wiry fellow with his bushy brown hair and electrifying personality had made quite an impact, and Ernie wanted to know who he was and how he had managed to sift through the details of his life. More important, he wanted to know whether or not he'd been telling the truth; so after he left, Ernie bombarded the nurse with an onslaught of questions. But she had been meticulously trained by the Institute, and he received little satisfaction from her replies. It shouldn't have been of much concern, for he'd waited this long and it was only a matter of time before he'd see for himself if this Katherine Freeman were really a member of his family.

The weeks before the interview dragged on, but the surprise announcement Sid Chandler had made added a promising spark, and during quiet moments he'd find himself wondering about his grandchild, trying to picture her face, and making feeble attempts at trying to piece together bits of information that were never enough to solve the riddle. Whose daughter had she been? If she was twenty-seven years old, he would've been seventy-three at the time of her birth. But his son had never said anything. Perhaps she wasn't a blood relative at all. She could've been an offspring of one of his children's spouses. Still, she'd taken the name Freeman, and he couldn't understand how this had come about. It could've been a lie. The Institute was good at deception. In the end, he rested in the knowledge that he would know for sure when they were finally allowed to meet.

By the day of the television special, Ernie gave little thought to how he looked or what he would say. Instead, he continued focusing upon Katherine. If she really were his granddaughter, perhaps she would care enough to help. At long last, there might exist a relative who could move against the Institute and set him free.

He expected her to arrive at six o'clock that evening, but at five thirty there came a light tapping at his door. He turned around in his wheelchair just enough to catch a glimpse of a figure hovering in the shadows.

"Who's there?" he called out.

A delicate voice tinkled its way across the room, filling his ears with sweet music. "Grandfather?" she replied, and then stepped forward so he could see her face.

She was young, with a dewy complexion and lithe limbs, and wore a flowing frock that was painted with picturesque roses, making her stand out in the dreary room like a bright bouquet of flowers against dull clay, just as he'd seen in his dream. Her lovely

201

chestnut hair fell to her shoulders in gentle ripples, and he watched as a fragile hand reached up to brush a strand away. She gazed at him with eyes that were warm and sensitive, soft grayish-blue lagoons that swam with serene passion. Her pert nose rested above a pair of perfectly sculptured lips, and when she smiled at him he knew that she shared more than just the name of a woman he'd once loved. As she stood there waiting for him to speak, he realized that she was the image of his own mother.

"Katherine?" he whispered.

She took another step forward.

"Who were your parents?"

"My father was Alex Freeman, but I never knew him. He died before I was born."

"Yes." Ernie nodded. "I thought that might be it."

Before they'd had a chance to go on, Sid Chandler burst into the room. Excitedly, he groped for their hands, trying to bring them together. "Just look at the two of you!" he exclaimed. "Such a stunning couple! I wish you could see the expressions on your faces!"

Ernie glared at him. "Do you think we could have a few minutes alone? I'd like to get acquainted with my grandchild."

"You can take care of that later. You'll have all the time in the world, but right now we've got to get everything straight. I spoke with the program director, and we agreed not to mention the fact that the two of you have never met. It's better that way. After all, we don't want to create any viewer confusion. Now, as far as the questions go . . ."

"Excuse me," Katherine's velvet tone melted through the air like butter. "Am I to understand that this will be a staged interview with prompting?"

"Prompting? Why no! It's just that there won't be

much time, and your words will have to be weighed very carefully. You're expected to portray a certain image."

"I'm not concerned with images."

"Perhaps not. Up until now, it probably hasn't been very important. However, when you appear on this program you'll be representing the North-eastern Heart Institute, and what you might say becomes our concern."

"I didn't agree to come here for the purpose of tarnishing your public image, if that's what you think. You have no need to worry. And I would appreciate your recognition of that fact, and choose not to dwell on it further." She folded her arms across her chest, indicating that the discussion was closed.

Ernie watched her respectfully, deciding that she had definitely been endowed with her father's fighting spirit.

"Anyway." Sid shifted his weight nervously and turned to Ernie. "You've been through all of this before, so you know what we expect."

It wasn't long before the apartment was swarming with a host of strange faces. The first to appear was an overweight man wearing a loud cotton shirt with a cigarette hanging from his lips. He planted himself in the center of the living room floor, and began directing traffic.

Sid Chandler's face turned purple when he saw the cloud of smoke. "Put that out!" he yelled, rushing forward. "You can't smoke in here!"

The obese man shrugged his rotund shoulders, and sauntered over to one of the large potted plants, stomping his cigarette out at its base. Then, he turned back to face one of the cameramen. "Okay, I think we should set up here. The heart guy can sit on the couch and Dawn can take a place across from him on this chair." He framed his fingers in the air as if to visualize the effect. "Yeh, that's good. Why don't we move one of those plants over there to give it added dimension?"

"Are you going to be the one conducting the interview?" Katherine asked, stepping up beside him.

"Naw. That's Dawn McDonald's department. We're just here to set up. By the way, my name's Stewart Ness." He extended a pudgy hand. "And you must be Katherine."

"Right."

"We'll have you sitting beside your grandfather over here." He pointed to the location, then turned around to call out to a member of the staff. "Hey, is he ready? Why don't you bring him in?"

Ernie was moved into the living room and carried from his wheelchair to be placed in the spot Stewart Ness had indicated. Katherine took her position at his side, and together they watched as the lights and tiny microphones were snapped into place.

Dawn McDonald arrived in a whirlwind of confusion, her makeup and hair flawless. The moment she drifted through the door, Stewart descended on her with last-minute instructions, with Sid Chandler close at his heels.

"You think they can keep the camera off his hands?" Sid asked. "They make him look like some kinduva freak. Maybe if you just used head shots."

Dawn puckered her lips. "Please, Mr. Chandler, we know what we're going."

"Okay," Stewart announced, donning a pair of headphones. "We're almost on the air." He grabbed Dawn by the air and led her over to the chair while everyone watched and waited in silence. The cameraman stood poised at his tripod, waiting for the cue. When Stewart waved his hand, they sprang into action.

"Good evening." Dawn's face was plastered with a dignified grin. "This is Dawn McDonald coming to you live from the house of Ernest Freeman, the world's longest survivor of an artificial heart transplant. Up until now, you've heard about the Northeastern Heart Institute's scientific advancements. You've seen other recipients and met their families, but Mr. Freeman is very special, for he was the first pioneer of a unique mechanical heart that was different from any of the others used previously. The Biotron Pump 8000 that has been serving Mr. Freeman for an incredible forty-eight years was the first heart to have been powered by a nuclear energy source. With the aid of this heart, it has enabled him to reach a miraculous one hundred years of age. This has given us new insight into heart research, and certainly offers us hope and inspiration. Seated across from me are both Ernest Freeman and his lovely granddaughter, Katherine." She turned to them. "Katherine, I can imagine that you're quite proud of your grandfather's outstanding achievement."

"Yes I am. And I'd like to add that not only am I proud of his physical condition, but for a man of his age, he's amazingly bright and alert."

"How does it feel to be the granddaughter of a man who's been in the public eye for so many years?"

"It's an honor."

"Had you ever thought a thing like this could ever happen—that an artificial heart recipient could survive this long?"

"Well, you have to understand. When I was born, artificial hearts were already well established. I guess I had taken the process for granted. Some of the transplant patients were already surviving for more years than I had lived."

"That's an interesting point. I do suppose that after a certain period of time, we tend to take a thing like this for granted." She paused. "Seeing your grandfather, and being able to talk with him . . . does it put any of your own fears about artificial hearts to rest?"

Katherine turned to him adoringly. "Just knowing that I still have a grandfather is enough."

Dawn McDonald smiled warmly, then looked at Ernie. "What about you, Mr. Freeman? You have been the first person to prove that complications could be mastered, and have been able to go on with your life. I'm sure you have many stories. Forty-eight years is a long time, and it's true that you've succeeded in living longer with your heart than some of us are old. Tell me, when it all began, did you ever think you'd survive for this long?"

"No."

"Was it difficult making all the necessary alterations in your lifestyle?"

"Yes."

"You are truly a man who's been fortunate to have been blessed with life extension due to scientific technology. You've gone through what had to be a frightening surgical procedure, made dramatic adjustments, and are now able to sit with us this evening as a vital human being. Through all of this, is there something you've gained that you would like to share?"

At first he couldn't speak. She'd referred to the endless years as if they'd never happened. How could any normal person know the hell of his isolated existence, the desperate feeling of being locked inside with no hope of escape? He pictured Doris, and how their life inside Winnow Cove had destroyed her will to live. He thought of Shawn, and how they'd forced her to stay away. Alex, his loyal son, had warned him, but he'd been too stubborn to listen, and by the time he understood, it was too late.

He glanced over at Katherine, a beautiful young woman who was tragically deceived. How much she resembled his own mother. Had his mother also been deceived—by him? How long had she gone on living, believing that he might return? Were those days just as endless and lonely as his? Then she was gone, disappearing forever like everyone else. Would he have to live long enough to see this new Katherine vanish? Would she be the next victim who would never come back?

Millions of people were watching him, anxious to hear what he had to say. Mr. Presta with his Biotron 9000 might be listening to those words from his own bed, along with all the other recipients who were too blinded by the Institute's brilliance to see what was really in store—if it were allowed to continue. Everyone was waiting to hear him speak. All the many people who were at that moment contemplating a similar surgery, being lured into taking the plunge into a rancid pool where they would eventually drown. He owed it to them to be truthful, no matter what the consequences. Besides, what more could they do to him that hadn't already been attempted? What penalty could be terrible enough to compare with what they'd already done?

"Mr. Freeman?" Dawn McDonald cut through his thoughts.

"Yes," he finally replied. "I do have something to say. He leaned towards the camera so that his anguished face was clear. "I never wanted any of this. Nobody would. People have got to know what they're doing here. They're just keeping me alive—against my will!"

"Mr. Freeman," Dawn gasped, the color of her face having faded. She began to wave her hand indiscretely so that the camera could be turned away.

"No, please!" he cried out pathetically. "Please help me. I'm nothing but a prisoner." He drew his contracted hands up to his face and began to weep.

Sid Chandler came rushing into the room, and Dawn's eyes darted over to him helplessly, her face ashen.

"Did any of that come through?" he asked in panic.

"Yeh, all of it came through." Stewart Ness stepped forward, removing the headphones. "By now the whole world has heard him."

They turned to Ernie angrily, but he had collapsed into his granddaughter's arms.

"I didn't know," Katherine sobbed softly. "I wish I would've known."

10

"Perhaps we did go a bit far," Dr. Roberts said, pacing back and forth in the huge, mahogany-paneled office. "But we just wanted to prove to the public that it could be done."

"Damn right you went too far!" Otto Armstrong, the hospital administrator, thundered. "Over three million people heard that old man last night. He went nuts right on national television. How could you have allowed it to happen?"

"We . . . we didn't expect it," Roberts stammered. "It was an accident."

"Accident?" The burly gentlemen rose from his swivel chair and planted both hands firmly on the desk. "Well, accident or not, someone's gonna pay!" He turned to glare at Sid Chandler who stood huddled near the wall. "What about you? You're the one who's supposed to be in charge of public relations. How did you let a thing like this get so out of hand?"

Chandler crept forward, his eyes shifting nervously. "It's like Roberts said. We never expected him to crack. We thought he was okay. The guy never gave any indication that he was gonna flip. He appeared totally rational."

"But a hundred-year-old heart transplant patient? Didn't you think you might have problems? How long has he been over in the Cove? Forty-eight years? Come on!" He tossed his head indignantly. "Even I can't help but feel sorry for the old man."

"Well, you see," Sid Chandler tried to explain. "We thought that if the public were able to view a patient like him, someone who has been able to survive that long. . . . well, it was supposed to be kind of an inspiration to others. You know, it could have alleviated their own fears. That there was nothing to worry about. That a mechanical heart could make you better than ever—stronger. I thought it would give the Institute more public acclaim."

"But it didn't work out that way, did it?" Armstrong roared. "Instead, a pathetic old man managed to pull the heartstrings of every American, making everyone feel as if he'd been victimized. I can't believe it." He sank back into the chair, and began rubbing the back of his neck, then looked up at them. "Did you see when he started to cry? It was horrible. And those hands! What happened to his hands? They looked deformed."

"The camera was supposed to stay off his hands," Chandler explained.

"But it didn't!" Armstrong shrieked. "Everyone heard him and saw him and felt sorry for him. And you know what? He was damn convincing. Now, we're the ones who look like the bad guys, and we're the ones who've been put on the defensive." He glanced over at the window. "Have you seen what's happening outside? I couldn't even get through the parking lot this morning. The place is surrounded with people carrying picket signs. Have you read any of them? They're calling us heartless. Damn!" He shook his head slowly as if he were finding it hard to believe. "The good name of the Northeastern Heart Institute has gone right down the toilet. And that's not all. My telephone's been ringing off the hook. Everyone wants answers, including the governor of the state. They want to know what's going on here. And the family members of all our other patients are just as distraught. They all think we're ghouls of some sort, wallowing in the suffering of others. They're talking about transferring their relatives. Do you know what that means? It means that our funds are threatened. And that means that my own job is threatened. If my job is on the line, where do you think yours are? How the hell can we maintain this place without adequate research grants? Now." He lowered his voice, riveting his eyes upon them. "What are you going to do about it?"

"The same thing we've always done," Dr. Roberts replied.

"Good." Otto Armstrong's face relaxed into a smile. "It's what you should've done before this situation was allowed to get so out of control." He folded his hands. "When can I expect the transfer?"

"I think we should give it a little time," Sid Chandler replied. "Otherwise, people might get suspicious."

"We don't have time!" Armstrong shouted at him. "No! I want something done today!"

"But that might be too obvious."

"No, it won't," Armstrong said dryly. "It won't because you and Roberts are going to put your heads together, and come up with a story that is convincing, something that'll tie it all together to make it all sound quite logical. Once everyone hears our version, they'll understand why Ernest Freeman said the things he said. And . . ." He eyed them fiercely. "The Northeastern Heart Institute will be off the hook."

Katherine Freeman sat stiffly in the rear seat of the cab as it wove its way through traffic. It was too warm, and she could feel the plastic seat sticking to her thighs as she crossed her shapely legs.

"So, what d'ya thinka that guy with the artificial heart?" The cab driver cocked his head so he could see her through the rear-view mirror. "Did ya see him on T.V. last night?"

Katherine squirmed in her seat. "Yes, I saw him."

"What d'ya think about the way he lost it? Think he meant all that stuff he said?"

"What purpose would he have in making it up?"

The cabby snorted. "I dunno. The guy's pretty old. Could've been senile."

Her eyes flashed defensively. "He wasn't senile."

"No?" He sighed. "Yeh, I didn't think so either." He paused while they waited at the red light. As soon as the light changed, the cab lurched forward and the driver resumed his conversation. "Those people at that hospital oughtta be shot. Bet they never thought he'd do a thing like that—saying that stuff. When he broke down, my own wife started to cry. Did ya see the way he looked—the expression on his face? And when he lifted up them hands. . . . I mean, I thought he looked pretty good 'til I saw them. I was talkin' to my sister-in-law. She's a nursing assistant over at the V.A. Anyway, she was tellin' me that people's hands git like that if they can't use 'em. Kin you imagine that? Livin' all them years without bein' able to use yer hands. Poor devil. When was the last time you think that old man was outdoors? I kin see why he went nuts. Locked inside all this time jest because of an artificial heart. Forty-eight years. Shit, I told my wife, 'Marge, don't you ever do that to me. If I git sick, jest let me go.' No sir. I don't wanta be put through any of that.''

They continued driving and the cabby stared out at the road muttering to himself. Katherine twisted uncomfortably in her seat. The smooth plastic was making the backs of her legs perspire, and she tried to position her dress so it wouldn't wrinkle.

It had taken her by surprise, discovering that the same Ernest P. Freeman who was the famous heart transplant patient was also her grandfather. Never in her wildest dreams would she have suspected that they'd be related. The first she'd ever heard of it was when Sid Chandler had called. She'd just gotten in from a twelve-mile hike, and was unpacking her bag, inspecting the sketches she'd been able to make, when the long distance call came through.

''Miss Freeman?'' he'd asked. ''Are you Miss Katherine Freeman?''

''Yes, I am.''

''Are you the grandchild of Ernest Freeman?''

''Why no. I think you must have the wrong number.''

''Perhaps, but would you mind telling me the name of your natural father?''

''Of course not. My father's name was Alex Freeman, but he's been dead for many years.''

There was a short pause, then the man continued. "Miss Freeman, it's possible that your father never informed either you or your mother that his own father was a patient at the Northeastern Heart Institute. You see, Miss Freeman, your grandfather is the Ernest Freeman who was once given an artificial heart. I'm sure you've probably heard of him."

"Yes, I have. But there must be some mistake. My mother never mentioned any of this to me."

"Like I said, it's possible that she didn't know. I understand your father died quite suddenly."

"That's right."

"Well you see? He probably never got the chance to tell your mother."

"I don't know. I mean, I'm not denying the fact that this man might be my grandfather, but you have to understand that I wouldn't want to be misled. Do you have any other proof? Something that I could see for myself?"

"Why don't I mail you copies of all the available documents? I'm sure they will satisfy any doubts you may have."

A few days later, the envelope arrived. After looking over the papers, she realized there had been no mistake. Her deceased father had definitely been the son of Ernest P. Freeman. Once she'd been convinced, she gladly accepted their offer to have her flown out for the show. She was anxious to meet him.

Even though she knew it was true, it wasn't easy accepting the fact that she'd had a living grandparent all these years. All the while, as she was making arrangements for the trip, she struggled with feelings of guilt. Had he known about her? Had he been waiting for the time when she would visit? Did he think she was deliberately trying to ignore him? What did he think? Or didn't he know? Well, she'd have to let him know what had happened, that it wasn't her fault, and that if she'd been aware that they were related, she certainly would've tried to communicate before this time.

It hadn't looked like a bad place—the area where he was staying. Perhaps it was a bit too quiet, and the uniform color and height of the artificial turf was obvious. Somehow it reminded her of the scenery one might expect to see on a movie set. Still, she had to admit she was viewing it with eyes accustomed to an unadulterated form of nature. Her surroundings in Sun Valley were wild and untouched. It would be normal for her to feel a slight revulsion over a world that had been molded by the hand of man—a place where nature's fine fingers had not been able to touch. But she'd passed it off as part of her own personal bias, and that anyone who chose a city life would obviously exist under conditions similar to these. Everyone had a right to form their own opinions, and this was how some people wanted to live.

He hadn't looked healthy. When she'd first laid eyes on her grandfather she suspected something was wrong. There was no color to his translucent skin, and his muscles were weak and atrophied. Even his eyes appeared watery, like a pair of sunken, muddy holes. She should've known that there was more to the story than they had led her to believe, but she wasn't ready to accept the fact that he might be experiencing a form of torture. Who could dare be so heartless? Instead, she rationalized that he was one hundred years old, and anything she was seeing was the product of age.

"So yer goin' there?" the cab driver interrupted her thoughts.

"Hm-m?"

"To the Institute?" The cab driver scowled into the mirror. "You got someone there? If you do, I'd start thinkin' about gittin' em out. No tellin' what might be happenin'."

She cleared her throat, and brushed a damp lock off her brow. "I'm not going there to visit anyone."

"You got other business, huh?"

"That's right," she replied. "I've got some business to take care of."

The cab turned into a long driveway that tapered its way to the entrance of the hospital. As they rolled along, a mob of intense people carrying boldly painted signs melted back, glaring through the windows to see who was arriving and whether or not they should decide to stage a demonstrative show. Nobody seemed to recognize her face from the television interview, being too caught up in the frenzy of their worthy cause.

After hastily slipping the cab driver his fee, she strolled briskly through the wide glass doors and directly to the receptionist's desk.

"Could you direct me to Mr. Armstrong's office?" she asked, using her most authoritative tone.

The polished lady looked up discriminately. "Do you have an oppointment?"

"No, I don't."

"Well, I can see if he's free, but he usually doesn't accept unsolicited calls." She reached for the phone, balancing it delicately on her shoulder before dialing. "Could I ask the nature of your visit?"

"It's regarding Ernest Freeman."

The receptionist frowned, easing the receiver back into its cradle. "I'm sorry. Mr. Armstrong isn't discussing the Freeman incident."

"But he must see me! I'm Katherine Freeman."

Her eyes widened, and without saying another word, she picked up the receiver again. "Hi. Listen Lois, Katherine Freeman is out here requesting to see Mr. Armstrong. Is it okay if I send her back?" There was an extended pause, then she hung up the phone and looked up. "Mr. Armstrong will see you, Miss Freeman. Just follow the corridor and turn left when you get to the elevators. You'll see a sign that says 'Personnel.' Go in and explain to the secretary who you are."

Katherine nodded, and started off in the direction the receptionist had indicated.

The moment she'd stepped through the door labled 'Personnel,' the secretary jumped up from behind her desk, and led her to another door with a broad bronze plaque announcing, 'Administrator.'

"Miss Freeman," a burly gentleman wearing a handsomely tailored suit said, smiling warmly and extending an arm as he moved forward to greet her. "Please." He motioned to one of the plush chairs. "Have a seat. Could I get you some coffee?"

"No, Mr. Armstrong. But you could get me back in to see my grandfather. Apparently, someone's placed some type of restriction on his visitors."

Otto Armstrong's smile faded. "Yes, that's right. You see, it would be going against medical advice for anyone to see him at this time." He folded his arms and wagged his head sadly. "It was tragic what happened. Something obviously snapped to cause his confusion."

"Confusion?" Katherine's face flushed with anger. "I don't believe he was confused."

"Well, you can't believe he was rational. What person in his right mind would dare to accuse the Northeastern Institute of acting so mercilessly? No. Our goal has always been a commitment to help others live—no matter what their handicaps. Your grandfather admitted he wanted to die. I ask you, Miss Freeman, could a claim like that be made by a rational man?"

"I want to talk to him. I'm his closest relative. If he's not in his right mind, I'd still have power of attorney. If he wants to leave, rational or not, I'll stand behind him."

Armstrong sighed. "Now, you're the one who's not thinking rationally. It's impossible to take your grandfather away from Winnow Cove. After all these years, he has no resistance to infection. His lungs require filtered air. He's on dialysis. He needs to keep up a regimen of synchronizing his heart. If you took him away, you'd be the one who was killing him. He'd be dead within a week."

"I don't care. If that's what he wants, so be it. No human being should be kept caged in like an animal."

"Look," Armstrong went on, placing his arms around her shoulders in a fatherly fashion. "You're basing your entire opinion on only one brief encounter with a man who had obviously become confused. You're conjuring up all kinds of unfounded fears without basing them on sound facts. How are you able to make any kind of logical judgment? You'd never even met the man before last night. Please don't be hasty. Work with us, and I can assure you we'll get to the bottom of this problem."

She wrenched her shoulder free, turning to face him. "I don't want to work with you. My mind's made up, and I won't be swayed by any smooth talk. And, if I'm not allowed to take my grandfather, I won't remain silent. I don't think I'm wrong, and neither do all those people outside carrying signs. If

I must, I'll get a court order to remove my grandfather from that place."

Otto Armstrong stiffened, and his face turned to stone. He turned coldly on his heel, strolling back to the desk where he began sifting through a stack of papers. "I didn't want it to come to this," he explained. "I had every intention of trying to work with you, but I can see you're being totally unreasonable. Miss Freeman, just where do you think you stand, legally speaking? Do you think we're fools? Your grandfather has never been held against his will. Before we ever agreed to take him on as a patient, he consented to our terms. We didn't make his choice. He did." He pulled several papers from the stack, and handed them over for her to read. "These are the original documents he signed. They're all in order. We had witnesses who attested to the fact that he was completely aware of what he was doing. No, Miss Freeman. When your grandfather signed these papers, he agreed to the terms, and there's not a court in the country that would back you up. Please, feel free to look through them, and then you can make up your mind as to who's right or wrong in this matter."

Ernie lay still. From his bed he could see the sun streaming through a crack in the drawn draperies, and he knew that it was daylight. They had kept him in bed ever since the interview incident. He glanced about. The television was gone, along with his radio. Nothing remained that could help fill in the gap of silence, and he found himself lying quietly in the shadows, listening. From the innermost depths of his chest he could hear the mournful lament of his mechanical heart. It had been a long time since he'd last been aware of its haunting melody, and now the click-clicking sounded especially menacing, urging him onward to an unexplainable height of panic.

He was glad he had spoken out; they deserved it. Just to have had the opportunity to witness their looks of surprise and fear, that he dared to turn against them publicly, gave him the ultimate satisfaction. But now they were getting back—keeping him confined to his room without even the companionship of a human voice. Sure, they'd said it was necessary because he wasn't feeling well, and that he didn't need external stimuli to aggravate his condition. But he knew better. This was really a subtle form of punishment.

It didn't matter. Katherine had understood his dilemma, and had the same fighting spirit as her father. The moment he'd seen her lovely face, his mind had been filled with a flood of old memories. Somehow, the face of his mother had been erased over the years, but seeing Katherine was enough to ignite a spark of recognition—recognition of purpose, giving him the courage to speak out against them boldly. Then, they'd taken her away, explaining that something terrible had happened, that he was sick. Had she believed their flimsy excuse, or had his words been convincing? And if she had believed him, why hadn't she yet returned?

The sound of muffled voices at the doorway caused him to pause in his thoughts and take notice. He watched as two men slipped silently through the door. Sid Chandler and Dr. Roberts made their way across the room, over to his bedside, and stared down at him without expression.

"How are you feeling today?" Dr. Roberts asked, clasping his hands beind his back and rocking on his heels.

"I . . . I'm fine," Ernie stammered, growing

suspicious as they continued to watch him cautiously.

"That's good." Roberts cleared his throat. "Very good."

There was a brief pause, and Ernie found himself tearing his eyes from them in order to glance nervously about.

"You know," Sid Chandler suddenly broke the silence. "What you did the other day was very very serious."

Ernie nodded his understanding.

"In the past, everyone at the Institute has tried to work with you. What you did was to turn the entire situation around, creating a public embarrassment."

"I . . . I'm sorry."

"No, Mr. Freeman," Chandler went on. "I don't think you are sorry. I think you knew exactly what you were doing." His face broke into a wry grin. "Let's be frank with one another, shall we? You were angry with us, isn't that right? Come on. There's no one listening now."

Ernie stared up into the public relations man's sneering face, feeling a familiar wave of indignation. "All right," he sputtered. "I'll tell you how I felt. I was angry, and you got what you deserved. People oughtta find out what you're doing."

Sid Chandler snickered. "Do you really think they believed you? Ha! You're nothing but a senile old man."

His words hit hard, and for a moment Ernie was too stunned to reply. Had everyone simply thought that he was crazy? He drew in his breath sharply. "Maybe I am a senile old man. It still doesn't give you the right to keep me locked up like a . . . a prisoner!"

"Is that what you think?" Dr. Roberts stepped

forward. "But we've never held you against your will." He pulled forth a thick stack of papers. "These are copies of the consent forms you once signed. Look at them. Isn't this your signature?"

Ernie struggled for his glasses, and when he had them on, craned his neck to see. Yes, these were the documents he'd once signed during a very desperate period in his life—the same papers Alex had warned him to thoroughly read.

"You see, Mr. Freeman. You aren't being held prisoner at the Northeastern Heart Institute; you belong to them. In exchange for your transplant, you willingly gave away all your rights. You're as much a possession of the Institute as that Biotron Pump. You became part of the research project. Why do you think you've never had to pay for our services? It's quite simple. We agreed to keep you alive and in the best possible health, to maintain you and look out for your well-being in exchange for only one small thing—yourself."

The color drained from Ernie's wrinkled face, and his hands began to tremble.

"Now," Sid Chandler continued. "Even though we are legally protected, it's still necessary to make several changes. Since you took such drastic measures against us, we're forced to do the same."

Horrified, Ernie watched the physician as his hands emerged with a loaded syringe.

"Try to relax," Dr. Roberts said soothingly. "This will help to make it easier." He sat next to the frail old man on the side of the bed, and injected the needle into his arm.

Ernie didn't move. Frozen to the spot and paralyzed with fear, he looked up helplessly at the two men. Now, he was at their complete mercy, and he could only wonder what they had planned.

The medicine was quick to act. Within a few short minutes the world around him had dissolved into a hazy blur. Two ambulance attendants appeared, pushing a narrow cart. With ease, they lifted him onto its firm surface, wrapping a warm blanket around his body and taking one loose end to flip over his face.

It was a floating sensation, having been drugged and moving through the apartment out to the front door. While the blanket served to block his view, it didn't prevent a gush of fresh air from penetrating the loose fibers and filling his nostrils with a strong scent of the outdoors. People were talking. He could hear their voices, and his first impulse was to try and get their attention in order to cry out for help. But the medication had left him weakened, and he didn't have enough strength to move.

He could hear the rear doors of the ambulance as they were snapped open—crisp and decisive, announcing their greeting in accepting him as the next passenger. Then the legs of the cart collapsed into a heap, and he could feel it being lifted up as he was placed neatly inside. The engine was started, and the vehicle began to move, driving away from the apartment where he had spent almost half his life. All he could do was lie beneath the heavy blanket in a stupor, wondering where he was being taken.

Winnow Cove consisted of a sprawling network of buildings more vast than anyone could've ever imagined. The ambulance wove its way down spiraling streets, deeper and deeper into the heart of the complex. Attractive apartments drifted by, but were soon replaced by cubicle buildings made of cold, concrete brick that sat on isolated lots with thick clusters of trees that kept them hidden. Gradually,

the forest thickened and even these structures
became scarce. The ambulance continued its
journey in solitude. Wind rustled through the foliage
and birds merrily chirped. Ernie strained to listen
beneath the covering over his face, unaware of his
destination.

It came as a surprise when the ambulance finally
stopped. He heard the engine grind to a halt, and the
bustling of the riders as they clambered out. A few
seconds later, the rear doors snapped open and his
cart was being pulled free. As it was settled on the
ground, someone finally flipped back the blanket
that had been covering his eyes. A burst of bright
sunlight rushed in, creating a temporary blindness.
The warm breeze played against his aged skin, and
he welcomed it, drinking in the rich air as if it were
an intoxicating beverage. He squinted and blinked,
trying hard to focus.

His eyes didn't adjust at first, but when they did
he found himself gazing up at the branches of the
towering trees. A lump rose in his throat, and he
fought to contain a rush of stinging tears. He had
forgotten their majestic beauty, and now as he
looked up at them, felt as if he were a stranger in a
new land. Before he could relish this thought
further, the cart was whisked away towards a broad
metal doorway that formed the entrance to the
concrete building that lay waiting in the distance.

"Where . . . are you . . . taking me?" he managed
to croak.

Dr. Roberts smiled down cordially. "To a place
where you'll be safe."

"Safe? What do'ya mean?" Ernie tried to lift his
head. "What is this place? Tell me!"

"Mr. Freeman." Sid Chandler came up beside the
cart. "Let's just say it's a place for others like you."

When they reached the door, a button was pressed, allowing them entrance. Ernie could hear the loud clunk of a heavy lock as it was released, and the creak of the labored hinges as the foreboding metal door swung wide open.

It couldn't be! Before they were able to pass across the threshold, they were greeted by a bone-chilling sound. Click-click; click-click; click-click. The inside of the building was alive with the hum of hundreds of beating hearts. Together, the metal valves created an eerie harmony, sounding like a swarm of angry bees. Click-click, click-click; click-click. The rhythmic chant echoed down the hallway, calling out to the new arrival who brought with him an addition to the chorus. Ernie listened in horror as his own mechanical heart blended in with the song.

He began to fight against the blankets that contained him, but a firm hand pushed him back against the cart. With eyes open wide in terror, he searched the dimly-lit corridor. "Where am I?" he cried out in panic.

"Mr. Freeman." It was Sid Chandler who replied. "Are you so vain as to believe that you had been the longest survivor? Listen. What you are hearing is the combination of all the artificial hearts that came before you."

"Are they alive?" he choked. "What about the people?"

"Of course they're alive. If they weren't, they wouldn't be here."

"But I thought I was the only one. You told me. I was the one who'd lived longer than anyone else."

"Well, we couldn't tell you the truth. You understand. How could we have continued keeping our patients in public view? After a period of time, they begin to change. It's not a pretty sight. No, it was best for everyone to believe that they had died. It was the only way. We had to continue our research on the Biotron series.''

''But I was the first one with a Biotron.''

''No, the Biotron 8000. There's a big difference. You forget that there were other models: the 1000, 2000, 3000 and so on.''

''You mean . . . you mean they're all here?''

''Don't be ridiculous. Not all of them. We have lost a few along the way. Couldn't be helped. They were bad risks to begin with.''

The cart moved down a tapered hallway, past dozens of closed doors. As they traveled further into the depths of the building, the clinking sound grew in intensity. Ernie twisted on the cart, trying to maintain his composure. They were mad! He couldn't be expected to stay here! He drew up his elbows, trying to pull himself to a sitting position, but it was a useless gesture. Giving in, he finally fell back against the surface of the cart, looking up pathetically at the set of expressionless faces. ''How long have they been here?'' he squeaked.

''I'm not sure,'' Sid Chandler replied. ''It was started before my time. But that's not important. What we're interested in is the long-term effects.''

''Not important?'' Ernie gasped. ''How can you do this?''

''Do what, Mr. Freeman? We're only following through with what each of you originally requested —to be kept alive.''

''You're crazy! Nobody in their right mind could come up with a thing like this!'' He struggled to set himself free, his face turning purple from the exertion.

''Please try to keep calm,'' Dr. Roberts warned him, shaking his head in disgust. ''It isn't as bad as you think. The rooms are quite nice. All of our patients are kept properly sedated. Time will pass by quickly. You'll see."

"You're nuts!" Ernie hissed. "There's no reason for any of this!"

"That's where you're wrong," Dr. Roberts explained. "And no matter what you might think, our intentions are not to cause anyone harm. What you are failing to see is the significance of what we're attempting. The hearts that we've developed must be guaranteed for a specific longevity. And the only way to tell how long they can last is by testing them to their limit. Someday, because of our research, we may be able to save people who are capable of changing the course of history. Just think how wonderful it would've been had the lives of men like Einstein been prolonged. To this very day, he could've been contributing to science. Someday, we will be able to use our knowledge in order to rescue brilliant men and women from a needless death. And it's only through patients like yourself that this goal will eventually be achieved. Mr. Freeman, it's a small price to pay when you consider the end results."

They came to a door that had been left invitingly open, and after making a sharp turn, they rolled the cart into the room. The first thing Ernie noticed about the area was a mountain of cardboard boxes resting in the corner, giving it the appearance of a miniature warehouse. His eyes darted over to the stack, and he instinctively sucked in his breath. They contained rolls and rolls of ticker tape.

"What's that for?" he asked, lifting a feeble hand in the direction of the pile.

"Those are the CSM graph papers we'll be using

on you.''

''But there are so many—enough . . . enough to last a thousand years.''

Dr. Roberts grinned and nodded. ''We certainly hope so. That would be the ideal. But of course, we'll have to be extremely careful in the way you're managed.''

''But someone'll find out. What're you gonna tell my granddaughter?''

Sid Chandler shrugged. ''The same thing we've told all the other families.''

Later that evening, Ernie lay quietly in the bed of his new room. There were no windows, no carpeting, no furniture; nothing to create the false impression of a home. At least the apartment had offered that simple luxury. This room was cold and sterile, and echoing through the corridors was the sound of the clicking mechanical hearts, crying out in unison from the bodies of anonymous prisoners. He reached for the remote control of the television set, turning up the volume in an attempt to smother the noise.

A female reporter had just started her portion of the news. ''This afternoon,'' she began. ''Ernest P. Freeman, the longest survivor of an artificial heart transplant, passed away.''

Ernie stared at the screen in disbelief, realizing that the scene had been filmed outside of his apartment in Winnow Cove. He continued watching as a cart was rolled out of the door and down the cement steps. It carried a body that was covered, wrapped securely inside a heavy blanket. It was his own body that had been drugged. So that was why they'd covered his face. The body lay motionless, and he thought back wishing he'd the strength to move. It had all been planned, but if he had moved, they'd have been exposed!

"As many of you are already aware, Mr. Freeman had launched into a verbal attack against the Northeastern Heart Institute the night before during a live interview. Apparently, he'd been in a compromised state. Dr. Roberts, his physician, has now commented on this unusual behavior."

The scene shifted to an office inside the hospital. Roberts sat poised at his desk, his face strained with anguish. The fake! Ernie screamed to himself. He was nothing but a fake!

"We knew that something was wrong, but we didn't know what it was that had caused the sudden confusion. Our only course of action was to confine him to restricted quarters under observation. Unfortunately, we were too late. A postmortem completed today confirmed the fact that Ernest Freeman was experiencing intercranial vasospasm. Blood was no longer being supplied to his brain, and he suffered a type of stroke."

The woman interrupted. "Isn't it true that Mr. Freeman had once suffered another such stroke?"

"Yes, that's correct; however it was due to an autonomic effect that caused a blood vessel inside of his head to burst. That incident had also been created by stress, and we have reason to believe that this latest response may have been the result of similar emotional strain."

The camera moved in on the anchorwoman. "Ernest P. Freeman has died today as the result of a massive stroke. He was the first artificial heart recipient to have reached a record-breaking one hundred years of age."

Ernie's hand began to quiver uncontrollably, and the remote control slipped through his fingers;

falling onto the floor. As it hit, the channels began to flip by, finally stopping at a number that had no station. The room was filled with static and the screen was swallowed up in a flurry of snow.

He continued staring at the television set, stunned. The world believed him dead! He would be kept alive inside this very room for as long as his body held up, and nobody would ever know. The snow of the screen swirled angrily, and somewhere in a forgotten corner of his mind, he could remember the day he had been shoveling—the day it had all begun. He thought back, recalling the words that had given him the strength to go on, the words of wisdom from a man he'd never thought had much sense. "Only the weak hafta depend on machines," his father had warned. Only the weak.

Suddenly, he was acutely aware of the steady clicking within his chest. It blended together with the mournful cry of all the other mechanical hearts. They were all the same—weak! They were all dependent on the same hideous machine to sustain them, and it was now that they were paying the price for their folly.

A picture of Doris flashed into his mind. Where was his wife at that moment? Had she known what would happen? Now she was gone, along with Alex and Shawn. When would he ever join them? When would he, at last, be ready?

With weary eyes, he gazed across the darkened room, fixing them upon the stacks of boxes containing ticker tape. As he stared at them his eyes filled with tears.

"Only the weak hafta depend on machines, Ernie ma boy. You 'member that, and don't let it ever happen ta you. Only the weak." He listened as the voice mocked him; words that had predicted his foolish fate.

But what else could he have done? What else did he have to rely on? With a trembling hand, he reached over to the nightstand for Doris' worn Bible. Drawing it up against his chest in the silence of the room, he bowed his head and began to weep.

11

Katherine Freeman was a streak of canary yellow, wearing a baggy jogging suit as she galloped through Roosevelt Park beneath the delicate pastels of dawn. As her stride lengthened and each foot alternately fell against the earth, the muscles of her long legs coiled together, forming ripples that absorbed the shock like a set of powerful springs. Her stomach was flat, and her buttocks had contracted into a hard ball. With arms swinging and head arched erectly in the breeze, she ran across the lawn as if being pursued by a host of invisible participants who were all part of the same race.

Running was her only release for tension, providing the proper outlet for pent-up emotions that might otherwise explode. It helped to fill her lungs with a rich source of oxygen that could be filtered through her bloodstream and act as a purifier.

Beneath her bosom, her heart was pounding, and she reminded herself that this served to strengthen it so that the fresh blood could be pumped to each individual body cell. And this oxygen-rich blood could then be supplied to her overworked brain, assisting her to think more clearly. That was why she ran. It helped her to think. And now it had served its purpose. Her mind was made up.

She slowed to a trot, and inhaled deeply. The grassy portion of the park had ended, forcing her to turn onto a gravel road. She followed the trail until it emerged into a busy intersection. She was out of the park and back in a world that was coming alive with its usual morning traffic. She continued jogging along the sidewalk until she reached the front of her hotel, then slowed to a walk as she entered the lobby.

Wiping the sweat from her brow, she strode purposefully across the luxurious carpet to the elevators. She pushed the button and waited, her face still flushed as her chest heaved in an attempt to catch her breath. When the door opened, several passengers strolled out, fresh from their morning showers. They nodded their heads politely, then unconsciously steered to one side, indicating their apprehension over her presence, and that her perspiring body might cause them also to become soiled. Katherine paid no attention, caught up in thoughts of her own.

When she arrived back in her room, she peeled off the sticky clothes and headed for the shower. Within a few seconds she was standing beneath a pulsating stream of warm water, and when she stepped out her decision was sealed.

Wrapping herself inside a towel, she walked over to the side of the bed and reached for the phone.

"Wendell?" she asked cheerfully. "This is Katherine."

"Katherine, where are you? I thought you were coming home today?"

"I'm sorry, honey. Something's come up. I've changed my mind."

"What do you mean? I need you here with me. The art fair's coming up, and you promised you'd be back."

She sighed. "I'm sorry, Wendell. But I've got to stay. Someone has to be here to look after my grandfather."

"What're you talking about? They said your grandfather was dead." He shifted the phone to his other hand. "Katherine, you don't have to fabricate any stories for me. If there's some other reason that you don't want to come back, just tell me. We've always been truthful with one another."

"I am being truthful. I don't believe what they said. I think my grandfather's alive."

"Alive?" he sputtered. "What purpose would they have in making a thing like that up? This is silly. Come home. There's still time to catch a flight." He paused, then lowered his voice intimately. "I miss you."

"I can't, sweetheart. I miss you, too. But I'm worried. I don't know why they're lying, but I have to find out."

"Do you have any proof?"

"No."

"Then what do you have?"

"Nothing. It just doesn't make any sense. First, he exposed them on national T.V., and the next thing you know, they're saying he's dead. It's just too . . . too convenient."

"Yeah, but they already explained all of that. He

was confused. He was sick. He didn't know what he was doing. It was probably all the excitement. For heaven's sake, Katherine, the man was a hundred years old. What did you expect?''

''I don't believe it. There was something about the way he looked. He was afraid. If they were so concerned, why would he have been frightened? I'm sorry, Wendell. I know I'm leaving you in a bind, but you'll have to get along without me for a while. I'll never feel right about any of this unless I know for sure.''

After a hasty goodbye, she hung up the receiver and pulled herself off the bed. It was getting late, and she had to get back to the Institute. There, she was certain, she'd find all the answers.

Dr. Roberts shared one of the smaller offices to the rear of the hospital. Katherine had found the address in the Yellow Pages, and now sat waiting for him inside its cramped foyer. The receptionist had positioned herself behind the sliding glass window, and would glance up and smile every so often, thinking it odd that the young woman never took her eyes off the door. She'd already explained that the doctor never arrived before ten, but the anxious woman had chosen to wait anyway. She hadn't moved from the spot in over an hour.

A few minutes before ten o'clock, the door opened and Dr. Roberts came sauntering through with a broad grin plastered on his smooth face. When he spotted Katherine, the smile faded, and he lowered his head, trying to rush past unnoticed.

''Dr. Roberts,'' Katherine called out, rising from her chair. ''Do you have a few minutes?''

He stopped in his tracks, pivoting on his heel. ''I really don't, Miss Freeman. You've caught me at an extremely busy time. If it's about your grandfather, there's nothing more I can say."

"But you never told me how he died."

Roberts shifted his weight uneasily. "I thought I'd already explained that. His death was due to vasospasm."

"I understand the technical explanation," she said, taking a step forward. "But I'd like to know the details. Was he awake at the end? Did he have anything to say?"

"No . . . no, he didn't," the physician stammered. "He had slipped into a coma. Look." He glanced about uncomfortably. "Why don't we go back to my office? This isn't the place to talk."

She followed him through the doorway, and down a short hall to a tiny room. When they were safely inside, he closed the door and indicated that she should take a seat.

"Now, what was it you wanted?" he asked, sinking behind the barrier of a squat desk.

"You were saying that he had slipped into a coma."

"That's right. He died quite peacefully."

"When?"

"When what? When did he die?"

"No. When did he slip into the coma?"

"I don't know. I wasn't there. It was sometime during the night."

"Did you think it was serious?"

"Of course I thought it was serious. Coma is always serious."

"Then he died at the hospital?"

"Why, no." Dr. Roberts' face flushed with embarrassment.

"But if you knew it was serious, why wasn't he transferred to the hospital?"

"There was nothing that could've been done. It was too late."

"So you just let him slip into a coma and die," she stated cynically. "Is that considered acceptable medical practice?"

"Look, Miss Freeman." He sprang from his seat with eyes flashing in rage. "If you have any questions regarding acceptable medical practice, I suggest you take it up with my Chief of Staff. Otherwise, I'd advise you to keep your opinions to yourself. We did everything possible over the past forty-eight years. Nobody should expect much more than that. It was time for him to go. He'd lived a long, fruitful life."

"You're right about one thing," she replied wryly. "It was long. I'm just wondering if you aren't planning on extending it for even a longer time."

"What are you trying to say?"

Her dark eyes bored into him, and she leaned forward. "I'm saying that I don't think he died. I believe he's still alive."

The physician rolled his eyes upward in an exaggerated grimace. "Is that a fact? Well, let me ask you this. If he were still alive, whose body did we take out of that building? And where do you think he'd be? I'm sure you're aware of the fact that he required a controlled environment."

"How do I know you didn't take him back there? He could've gone for a little ride, and then ended right back in the same place where he started. Who's to say? The television cameras aren't always guarding his apartment."

Dr. Roberts struggled to get out from behind the desk, then strode over to the door to push it open. "I think you'd better leave, Miss Freeman. There's no point in discussing this further. I know you're distraught, and I'm trying to take that into consideration, but if you don't get out I'll have to call one of the security guards to help you."

She withdrew from the office without further incident, mulling over the scene with the physician. He was lying. She could see it on his face. Years of special training had taught her to master the art of capturing images on canvas, and it was through the eyes of an artist that she had observed the telltale signs of deceit. They were subtle, but she hadn't missed the tense lines twisting around his mouth, nor the nervous twitch of his jaw, nor the way he couldn't look her in the eye. He was lying, all right, but it would be difficult to prove.

With determined strides, she headed for her rental car that sat waiting in the parking lot. Nothing would stand in the way of rescuing her gandfather. No matter what it took, she would find him. He was alive. She was certain. And the only way to prove it was to go back to Winnow Cove.

The sprawling network of buildings rested to one side of the vast hospital grounds and was surrounded by a high cyclone fence. There was only one entrance, and this was guarded by a miniature security station. When she pulled into the driveway, an officer stepped out.

"May I help you?" he asked gruffly.

Katherine rolled down her window and flashed a bright smile, displaying a set of perfectly matched teeth. "Why, yes. My name is Katherine Freeman. I was here a few nights ago for a television special." She shrugged helplessly. "I must've dropped my key chain. I've looked everywhere, and I just can't find it. I know I had it when I arrived. Would you mind if I go back in to take a look? I won't be long."

The security guard scowled. "I'm sorry, but visitors must have a special purpose."

"My purpose is specific," she replied, fluttering her thick lashes. Then her face fell in disappointment. "It had all my keys, even the ones to my apartment."

"Well," he muttered. "I suppose it wouldn't hurt for you to look. All right, but hurry."

He turned around smartly, and marched back into the small house. A few seconds later, the wooden arm that extended over the road was lifted, and she was allowed to pass through.

The apartment that sat on the corner of Vassal and Lyceum looked exactly the same. There was nothing to indicate that anything was occurring that might be suspicious. Katherine pulled over to the curb, watching and waiting.

Before long, a nurse wearing the standard electric blue came strolling down the walk. She stopped at the apartment, turning up to the front porch in order to use her key to enter. Katherine curiously observed her, deciding that there was still an inhabitant. Why else would a nurse's services be needed?

It was time to take a look. Opening the door to the car, she slid across the front seat and climbed out. With steady deliberation, she moved towards the apartment, taking a detour across the artificial turf, towards a side window. She stood on her toes, and pressing her forehead against the pane while shielding her eyes, she tried to see in. But the glass was specially treated, and it was impossible to look through.

After making a complete circle around the building, she arrived back at the front door. In a final attempt to unravel the mystery, she approached it, pressing her ear against its smooth surface to listen. There were voices, and she strained to hear what they were saying.

Just then, the door swung open, and she lost her balance which sent her stumbling forward.

The nurse glared at her angrily. "Who are you?"

Katherine brushed a lock of hair from her brow. "I was looking for Ernest Freeman."

The nurse folded her arms defiantly. "Mr. Freeman is no longer here. He passed away several days ago. Surely you must've heard. It was announced over all the television stations."

"But if that's true, why are you still here? Why would a nurse be needed in this apartment?"

"See here," the nurse growled. "That's none of your business. Now you get out of here before I call the police."

"Carol?" a voice called out faintly. "Carol, who's there?" A fragile lady with mousey hair and soft brown eyes crept up from behind the other woman. "May I help you?" she squeaked.

"I was looking for Ernest Freeman," Katherine explained. "He used to live here."

"Yes, I know." The woman lowered her eyes sadly. "They told us he'd lived in this very apartment for forty-eight years. At first I felt a little strange, taking over this place. But now I think of it more as a good luck charm. If he made it that long, perhaps my husband also will."

"Your husband?"

"I'm sorry." The frail woman extended a slender hand. "I didn't introduce myself. My name's Lois Presta. My husband is the first recipient of the Biotron 9000."

Northlawn Cemetery was untramodern, looking more like a peaceful park than a final resting place

241

for the deceased. Rolling hillsides were lined with
stately pines that swayed in the breeze, and handsome flower beds protruded in colorful mounds
from portions of the velvet lawn. There were no
headstones. Instead, flat slabs of engraved bronze
markers were embedded into the ground, and the
only way to identify the plots, at first glance, was by
the tall metal urns that jutted out above the neatly
clipped grass.

Katherine Freeman had found her way there, and
now stood at the bottom of a slope. Using her foot,
she brushed away the dried leaves that had fallen
over the face of one of the markers. She stared down
at the inscription which gave away the location of a
woman she'd never met—Doris Freeman, her grandmother.

The body of the person who lied buried beneath
the earth had once been part of her, carrying the
genetic code that had been passed along to a new
generation. The thought of this sent a shiver up and
down her spine, forcing her to face the reality of
their familial union. And in that moment, she found
herself wondering about the woman. What color
had her eyes been, and her hair? Had she been kind
or cruel? There had never been any pictures.
Nobody was left to tell—to fill in the gaps con-
cerning this half of her ancestry.

When she had visited her father's grave as a child,
her mother had been there to stand by and supply
her with fond memories. The stories had come alive
with the photographs they later shared. With the
information she'd been given, there was little that
was left to imagine, and her mind had been put at
ease. But here it was different. There were no tales,
no pictures, nothing to help her to relate to a person
she had never known, and that thought made her

feel desperately empty. An important part of her was missing.

It had always been that way, but she'd eventually learned to adjust to the fact that she wasn't like others who did know the details surrounding their families. However, it hadn't been easy, and she still remembered the first time she'd been faced with that painful moment of truth.

She was in the third grade. Miss Simms, a slender spinster with cold gray eyes, had announced that each of the young students would be learning how to construct a family tree. Instructions were given, and the children had rushed home excitedly, anxious to begin their project.

The first part of the genealogy was completed without difficulty. Her mother was helpful in supplying her with all the proper names to place in the appropriate boxes. That first sheet of paper had looked impressive, with all of the lines interlacing to form a complicated pyramid. But when it came to the second portion, the one that reflected her father's side, her mother was at a loss.

She could still recall the sheepish look on her mother's face as she'd shrugged her shoulders. "I just don't know, honey," she tried to explain. "Your father never told me anything about his family."

The child had lowered her eyes, staring down helplessly at the blank sheet of paper. "But what should I tell Miss Simms?"

"You'll have to tell her the truth, that we don't know."

"But what if they laugh at me?"

"They won't laugh at you. That's silly. Everyone will understand."

It was her mother who didn't understand. She couldn't go back to school announcing to all of her classmates that she had no information about one of her parents. What would they think? She would never be able to face them again. They'd make fun of her. What kind of child didn't know anything about her own father?

A week later, the assignment was due. The students sat perched behind their desks, proud of their accomplishments, except for little Katherine. Perhaps it was the way she squirmed in her seat, or the apprehension in her eyes that caused Miss Simms to take notice and call upon her.

"Katherine," the teacher's icy eyes bored into her, "why don't you begin? Come up here to the front, and we can all go over your family tree together."

The child's heart began to pound madly, and her throat suddenly felt dry. She leaned forward, using her chubby arms to conceal the blank portion of the paper.

"Katherine?" Miss Simms asked sharply. "Is there a problem?"

Her face turned a bright shade of pink, and she nodded.

"Do you mind telling us what it is?"

"I . . . I," she stammered, glancing at the neighboring desk where a boy had started to giggle. "I didn't get it done."

"But you had all week to work on this."

"I know. I forgot," she lied.

"You forgot? Well, I'm sorry, but forgetting assignments is not acceptable. If you don't have your family tree ready, I'll be forced into giving you a failing grade."

Katherine hung her head.

Miss Simms crossed her arms and frowned, then turned to another student. "Jamie, why don't we start with you? I'm sure you do have your assignment completed.''

The little girl had wanted to explain, but had been too humiliated. It was better to receive a failing mark than to have to listen to their cruel laughter. Not having a father at home was bad enough, but to know absolutely nothing about him was even worse. She couldn't let anyone find out.

That had been her first recollection of actually realizing that a significant portion of her life was missing, and even though she learned how to deal with it later by avoiding any reference to her father, the blank sheet of paper continued to haunt her. The day that Sid Chandler had called about her grandfather gave her a spark of hope that she would at last be supplied with the missing link. Seeing him, the day of the television interview, had ignited the spark and allowed it to burst into hungry flames that could only be quelled by finding all the pieces of the puzzle. There had been so much she'd wanted to ask, but before she'd been allowed this privilege, they'd taken her away and were now trying to convince her that her grandfather was dead.

She stared down at the bronze marker and trembled. This was all that remained of her grandmother. She would never know anything more than what had been written on the slab. If only her grandfather and she had been given a chance to talk, perhaps he would've told her about this woman. Had Doris Freeman known sorrow? Had she known emptiness? The dates that had been imprinted merely indicated the span of years that she'd walked the earth, but gave no information about her actual life. Had she suffered? Had she wanted to live—to remain with her husband? And now was she eager for him to join her, feeling alone until they could again be united?

Her eyes drifted over to the neighboring plot. Empty. It came as a surprise, causing her to become momentarily stunned. Why was this area empty? Because it had been the place reserved for the body of Doris' husband. That's why the small plot remained untouched in the heart of an overly crowded cemetery. If Ernest Freeman really were dead, why hadn't he been allowed to rest beside his wife? Was it because he had not yet been buried? And that would mean there would still be a body. How foolish of her to have not considered it before. That was what she needed for proof. Where was his body?

She arrived back at her hotel and returned to her room. She reached for the phone book, and thumbed through the pages. When she found what she was looking for, she reached for the phone to call.

"Coroner's office," a pert voice announced enthusiastically, as if she'd been waiting for a call all day.

"I wanted to know if it would be possible to speak with the County Coroner," Katherine asked.

"And what would this be regarding?"

"An autopsy."

"Could I have the name of the deceased?"

"Ernest P. Freeman."

There was the sound of rustling papers, and then the woman replied, "I'm sorry. Freeman is not a name that we have listed. Are you sure that he was taken here?"

"No, I'm not sure. That's why I wanted to speak to the Coroner."

"Perhaps I could help you."

"I don't think so. You see, Ernest Freeman was the artificial heart recipient who recently died. I'm his granddaughter, and I'd like to speak to the

Coroner about scheduling an autopsy."

"I see. But didn't his death occur at the North-eastern Heart Institute?"

"That's what they claim."

"Well, they're the ones who would be responsible for performing any post-mortem. I doubt whether our office could be of service."

"I'd still like to speak to the Coroner if it's at all possible. There are several questions I think he might be able to answer."

The woman hesitated, then sighed. "All right. I'll put you on hold and ring his office."

There was a click, and the sound of soothing music drifted out from the receiver. Katherine waited.

A few seconds later, the line clicked again and the throaty voice of a man addressed her. "Dave Mallory, may I help you?"

"Mr. Mallory?" Katherine asked. "Are you the Coroner?"

"I am."

She let out her breath in relief. "Oh good. Mr. Mallory . . ."

"Doctor Mallory," he corrected her.

"I'm sorry. Dr. Mallory, I wanted to know how I could get you to investigate the death of my grandfather."

He coughed. "Was it a sudden death?"

"Yes, it was."

"Where did his death occur?"

"In his apartment."

"I see. Was he taken to a hospital?"

"No, he wasn't. That's why it bothers me."

"Well, who was it that pronounced him dead?"

"Dr. Roberts, of the Northeastern Heart Institute."

"Then he was seen by a physician?"

"Yes."

"To tell you the truth, ma'am, I'm a little surprised. The Northeastern Heart Institute had never been found in violation of reporting sudden deaths. Frankly, I'm a bit puzzled. What was your grandfather's name?"

"Ernest P. Freeman."

He paused, then spoke out sharply. "Freeman? I hope you're not referring to that heart recipient."

"As a matter of fact, I am. Does that matter?"

"Of course it matters! He was a patient of the Institute for a good many years. I doubt whether his death could be considered sudden."

"He was there for forty-eight years, but I saw him the day before and I consider it very sudden."

"Yes but from what I understand, they've already completed a post-mortem. I think that if you have any questions, you should be speaking with them. I'm afraid our office can't help you. We deal with trying to find the causes of death. The cause of your grandfather's death is already known."

"But you don't understand. I think my grandfather was the victim of foul play. I'm not even sure that he is dead. I haven't even been allowed to view his body."

"And you say that you were his granddaughter?"

"That's right."

"Are there any other living relatives?"

"Just me."

"Did you ask to see his body?"

"No, I didn't."

"Well, why don't you try doing that?"

"Because I know they wouldn't let me."

"I find that hard to believe."

"It's true. They've been lying to me all along. I was just at the cemetery where my grandmother is buried. They never had him buried. They're trying to tell me that he's dead, but I can't believe them without seeing a body. And it's useless to ask them about it. I was down there today. I spoke with Dr. Roberts. He practically had me removed bodily." Her voice had been rising to a hysterical pitch, and now she suddenly halted, realizing what he must be thinking. She started over, lowering her tone in an attempt to sound rational. "Look, I'm not a kook. I just considered the whole thing strange. You must agree. They never let me see him when they claimed he had taken a turn for the worse, and now this. They tried to say that he'd lapsed into a coma, but they never even transferred him to the hospital. Everyone knows what he'd stated on T.V. I just think the whole story sounds fishy. Right after he tried to expose them, they'd announced that he'd died. If it were your grandfather, I'm sure you'd feel the same. I need more proof. Isn't it your job to investigate deaths that might be suspicious? They could be telling me anything, and I'd have to believe them. But not you. They would be forced into producing a body if it was by your request."

He drew in his breath, and let it out in a soft whistle. "If you feel this strongly about it, why don't you go to the police?"

"What could the police do?"

"They'd go in and investigate. File a report."

"But if they are right, I wouldn't need the police. I'd need someone to tell me how he died. That's why I need your help."

"Miss Freeman, are you aware of what you're implying? The Northeastern Heart Institute has an impeccable reputation."

"Please, Dr. Mallory. If only you'd give them a call. Ask to see his body. Find out how he actually died. It all sounds so odd."

"Well, you may be right about that. I suppose it does seem strange that he died so suddenly. . . . after creating such a commotion."

"Then you'll do it?"

"I didn't say that."

"But you must help. It's your responsibility."

"If we became involved unnecessarily, there could be a lawsuit."

"You're my only hope," she cried. "At least find out what they've done with his body. I'm his only living relative. I have a right to know."

"Look, I'll give them a call. Guess I can do that much."

"Oh, thank you, Dr. Mallory. Thank you so much."

"Give me your number, and I'll call you back just as soon as I've spoken with them. I don't agree with you, but I suppose you do have a right to view the body."

After hanging up the phone, she sank back against the pillow. At least she'd managed to convince him that something might not be right. It was only a thin thread, but it was more than she'd had to go on before. They might be able to push her around, but not a county official. Dr. Roberts would be backed into a corner. He'd have to come up with more than just his words.

The telephone rang, and she jumped, pulling herself to a sitting position. "Hello?"

"Miss Freeman, I just spoke with Mr. Armstrong, the hospital's administrator. I believe your accusations are unfounded. He's able to supply me with both his death certificate and a copy of the autopsy they performed. I'm sorry."

"But what about his body?"

''Perhaps if you'd called me earlier. At this point there's nothing I can do.''

''Why not? Why can't you check my grandfather's body?''

''Because they've already disposed of his body.''

''But it's not at the cemetery.''

''That's right. According to Mr. Armstrong, his body was cremated.''

12

All police stations were the same. Katherine decided this the moment she stepped inside the Ninth Precinct. Even though it was the middle of the day, and outside the sun was brilliantly beating down, the station was immune to cheer, protected by a gloomy coat of gray. Dusty lights hung from the high ceilings, casting yellow shadows across the room, and swarms of impish flies danced in through the open windows. There were rows of cluttered desks, and telephones that relentlessly continued to ring. All the somber officers displayed the same air of indifference as they answered the calls and sat filling out forms. The air reeked of the stale scent of papers mixed with cigars. She looked about, concluding that it wasn't really dirty, yet somehow not clean. It seemed to exist beneath the filmy exterior of tarnished lives.

She felt uncomfortable being there, and was disheartened when they told her to take a seat. Now, according to the round clock on the wall, she'd already sat waiting for over an hour, and was rapidly growing impatient.

A man came through the door, and she observed him as he shuffled up to the front desk. After several minutes, an officer got up to speak with him, and then he was also instructed to wait. The man didn't take a seat at first. Instead, he jammed his hands into his pockets and reluctantly strolled about until he arrived at the gum ball machine. Standing there, he fumbled for some change, then tossed a few pennies into the slot, giving the lever several quick thrusts. The gum came toppling out, and he popped it into his mouth before sauntering over to the bench where she was sitting, lowering himself with a deep sigh. She turned away from him, crossing her legs and folding her arms as if to create a barrier. She wondered if he were a criminal. He responded to this by also turning in the opposite direction, and in embarrassment she realized that he was undoubtedly thinking the same of her. Police stations had a way of putting everyone on the defensive, and she wished more than ever that she wasn't there.

There was no reason for her to feel self-conscious. She'd never done anything wrong. Perhaps her unfounded humiliation had been ingrained in her as a result of her mother. Sandra Freeman had raised her alone, without the support of a husband, and it was because of her mother that she'd been left permanently scarred. She'd been the first person to introduce her to the inside of a police station.

It was still clear, the night she'd received the call. For eighteen years she'd been deceived before having to admit the truth. The television had gone off the air, and she'd lain on the couch and dozed, until she was startled by the shrill ring of the telephone.

"Hello?" she'd mumbled into the receiver.

"Kath?" her mother asked anxiously. "Oh good, you're home. Listen Kath, I need your help. I've had a little trouble."

"Trouble? Where are you? What's happened?"

"It's nothing. I can't talk now, but don't worry. I wouldn't have bothered you, but I couldn't get a hold of Jack. Anyway, I need you to do something. Go into my bedroom and open the top drawer to my dresser. You'll find a white envelope. It's underneath my slips. There's some money in it. Bring it with you, and come down to Police Headquarters. Explain to one of the officers why you're there, and they'll be able to help you. Tell them you've come to pick me up—that you have my bail. Understand? Can you do that?"

"Sure . . . I guess."

Her bail? Why had her mother been arrested? What was going on? It should have occurred to her before that her mother had been changing. Perhaps an occasional doubt would surface, but she'd always managed to push it aside. At first she'd never thought of it as being drunk. After a few glasses of wine, she'd merely seem a bit more relaxed—cheerful. Sometimes she'd go out. Different dates would come to pick her up at the door, and she'd return later, stumbling about the apartment. Maybe she had had a bit too much to drink, but it wasn't right to question her mother's actions. It wasn't really a problem. She was still a good parent.

Sandra Freeman had once been quite beautiful. Katherine could remember that when she was still a child, she'd been proud of her mother's ivory skin and thick chestnut hair. Over the years, she'd relinquished this pride, watching as the face of the woman she loved grew puffy, and the sheen of her dark locks turned to straw. It was sad to witness the transformation that left the flawless woman nothing more than a disheveled figure of gelatinous flesh.

There were always different boyfriends. She'd seen them in the morning while they showered and shaved. Most of the time they were never introduced, and the child was curious as to why they never continued dating her mother. It would've been nice if one of these boyfriends had cared enough to become a husband and father. But her mother didn't seem to be searching for any permanent relationships.

Sandra Freeman had never gotten over the sudden death of her husband. It was impossible for her to love anyone else. From the time that Katherine was old enough to remember, they would pile into the car to take long drives. Inevitably they always arrived on Lexington Avenue, a place where clusters of towering office buildings competed for space. The car would slow to a crawl as they inched their way past, and Sandra would eagerly point a finger in the direction of a shiny skyscraper that stretched up to the clouds.

"That's where your Daddy and I used to work!" she'd exlaim. "Right there in that building on the sixth floor. You should've seen his office suite. It was incredible!" She'd giggle childishly while all the other cars in the back of them would honk their horns, her face wiped clean of the usual pain. Her eyes would be filled with a strange glimmer. "Did I ever tell you about him?" she'd ask the child for the hundredth time. "He could've had any woman. But he loved me." The glimmer would fade, being replaced by dewy tears. "I never thought he'd propose. I didn't think I was his type. But you know what he told me that night? He held me in his arms and said not to worry about it, that I was special. He told me he'd waited for a woman like me all his life." Then her face would crumple, and she'd sniff. "Can you believe that? He thought I was special," she'd whisper softly to herself. "Special enough to love."

The blare of the other cars would suddenly penetrate her sentimental trance, and she'd toss an angry glare in their direction. Stepping on the gas, she'd screech back out into the heart of traffic in order to return home. The office building would be left behind until their next visit, and her mother would return to the real world. As Katherine matured, the drives became less frequent and the office building vanished, being replaced by a struggle for life that ultimately ended at the police station.

She had walked into the dusky building that night, clutching the white envelope with eyes open wide with fright. Somehow she managed to find her way to the front desk.

"Sandra Freeman?" the officer asked gruffly as he thumbed through a roster of names. "Okay. You've got her bail?" Katherine handed him the envelope, and he counted the money. "Just take a seat over there," he said, pointing to a bench where several other people were huddled.

"Excuse me," she squeaked. "What are the charges?"

The officer glared up. "Huh?"

"Why was my mother arrested?"

His mouth fell open in surprise. "You're her daughter? She sent her own daughter down here?"

"What did she do?" Katherine firmly repeated.

His ruddy face twisted into a cruel sneer and he snickered. "Sweetheart, why don't you keep your mother home at night?"

"Why?"

"Because she's nothing but a damn drunk!" Everyone in the room turned to look as he started to laugh.

Katherine's knees turned to rubber, and at first she thought she might faint. With trembling legs she turned away so that he couldn't see her reddened face, then tried to make it over to the bench so that she could collapse. When she reached the seat all the other people turned away, shouting out their accusations with cold stares.

That's how police stations were. The people inside weren't capable of understanding. They drew their conclusions from what they selectively overheard, but that didn't make them right. How could they understand that love was more powerful? How could they accept the fact that nobody had the right to judge? She hated police stations. If her father hadn't died, this wouldn't have happened to her mother. She'd needed him, and he'd failed her. Somehow her mother's actions made her feel unclean. Perhaps if her father had shared more about his own family, it would've provided a missing link that they both could've clung to as a steady anchor, offering them more security. Her mother had to feel the same rejection, as if her father hadn't thought her worthy enough to explain the entire story. Even so, she was part of him. Perhaps that was why it meant so much to speak to her grandfather. She had to know that a part of her heritage was better. She had to find a way to prove her worth.

The sound of a subdued cough interrupted her thoughts. "Are you Kathleen Freeman?" A middle-aged man wearing a wrinkled suit hovered above the bench.

She nodded.

"Okay, why don't we go back to my office?"

She followed him down a long hallway to a cramped room.

"Have a seat," he said. "How can I help you?"

She folded her hands, managing a polite smile. "I'd like to know how I could get you to investigate the death of my grandfather."

"How did he die?"

"You've probably heard of him. His name was Ernest Freeman. He was an artificial heart recipient."

The detective's face broke out into a toothy grin, and he ran his hand across his head and chuckled. Somehow it reminded her of the officer she'd spoken to the night she'd gone to bail her mother out of jail. "You've got to be kidding," he commented wryly. "Not that old man who was on T.V. last week, the one who was a hundred years old?"

"That's right."

"Why should we investigate him? We all know what happened."

Her face colored slightly, and her nails bit into the palms of her hands. "I know what you probably think, but I'm asking that you not jump to any conclusions until you hear what I have to say."

"Look lady, we're busy people here. I don't have time for games. If you've got charges to press, we'll fill out a report. If not, you're wasting my time. Now what is it? And this better be good."

She measured her words carefully and began. "I know that they announced how he died. But even though they claimed he was dead, I was never allowed to see the body. They said he suffered a type of stroke. But I was with him the night before, and he wasn't even sick. I think it's suspicious. Everyone heard how he tried to expose them. It doesn't seem right that the very next day they'd claim he died. They're lying. If you want me to fill out the appropriate forms in order to press charges, I'm perfectly willing. They can't get away with this. I want an investigation as to his death.''

The detective slapped both palms on the table and rose. ''That's it,'' he stated. ''I've heard enough. Now look lady, I don't know what's gotten into your pretty head, but I suggest you come back down to reality. Do you know who you're accusing? The Northeastern Heart Institute has a good name. Who do you think you are, coming in here and making those kinds of claims? Now why don't you go on home, and we'll forget that you were ever here. Just be grateful your grandfather lived as long as he did. Not many people get those kinds of breaks.''

''But you don't . . . .''

''Goodbye, Miss Freeman. Have a nice day,'' the officer said as he led her out.

She left the police station with her head hung low, feeling the same way she'd felt after departing from the other building with her mother. Officers of the law would never change. Each of them shared the same cruel qualities. They were assuming, uncaring —cold.

The drive back to the hotel was dismal. Somehow she'd expected more from the police, that they'd take a valiant stand like knights on white horses who would come galloping to her rescue. She thought that they'd be able to size her up and know that she was telling the truth, that her character was good, that she had common sense. But after her side of the story had been told, they'd come to a different conclusion. It was the same as when the other officer had laughed at her that night. She had given them a second chance, but now she knew she would never trust them again.

Already, she was growing tired of having to return to an empty room in the hotel, making her feel like a transient with no permanent ties. Her quarters were impersonal, with no smiling faces to greet in order to lift her from a rapidly growing depression. As she turned the key in the lock, she found herself wishing that it could've been magically transformed into the front door of her apartment in Sun Valley, and that Wendell could be standing there waiting with a goblet of wine and a sympathetic ear. Instead, when the door swung open, she was faced with four cheerless walls. She could've been any of the other guests who had once passed through.

She slipped out of her dress and shoes, plodding wearily across the carpet. An insistent growl from the pit of her stomach reminded her that she was hungry, yet she couldn't bear the thought of eating another meal alone. In an impulsive gesture, she flipped on the television set, quickly checking each channel before deciding to turn it off. Then she fell onto the bed to think.

Wendell was probably furious with her for staying. It was already Thursday, and the Art Fair was about to begin. She could picture him frantically rushing about, trying to organize the event without her, and was consumed with guilt. It wouldn't help to call. She would be lucky if he'd ever speak to her again. But what would he say if he *really* understood her predicament? What would be his advice? One of his strongest attributes had always been his unbendable logic. How would Wendell have handled such a shabby rejection by an officer of the law? Would he have slinked his way back to the hotel as she had done, with his tail tucked between his legs? Of course not! Wendell was the type of man who didn't stop at the front desk. He'd push his way through up to the executive offices where all the rules were originally made. It was his attitude she needed, to refuse to relinquish hope until all of the higher avenues had been explored. It was then that she made her decision. The next day she would go to a more powerful source. She'd seek the help of an attorney.

Garth Madox's office foyer was decorated in a traditional style with expensively framed paintings and polished brass. The strong aroma of rich wood and fine upholstery blended together in fragrant harmony that boasted the wealth of its surroundings. The inside of the room was quiet, and nothing could be heard except for the piped-in music that drifted out through a speaker on the latticed wall.

Katherine sat on the edge of a wing chair tapping her fingers to the distant tune that balanced delicately in the air. When she caught herself chewing off the lipstick of her lower lip, as she always did when she was nervous, she stopped and opened her purse to check her makeup in order to reassure herself that she remained composed. No sooner had she tucked away the compact, when a matronly woman strutted through the door to announce that Mr. Madox was ready to be seen. Without thinking, she jumped up, spilling out the entire contents of her purse onto the floor. The secretary scowled as Katherine squatted down in embarrassment, trying to gracefully retrieve the contents.

Garth Madox was younger than she'd imagined, with a handsome smile and flamboyant air of confidence that could've won over the most objective jurors. He didn't get up when she entered, simply looked up cordially from his work and waved a hand in the direction of a chair.

"Miss Freeman," he said soothingly. "Please have a seat."

Obediently, she lowered herself with a subservient nod.

"Now what was it you were telling me on the phone about your grandfather? He was a patient at the Northeastern Heart Institute?"

"Yes," she replied, keeping her eyes steady as she looked directly at him. "They told me my grandfather had died, but were unable to produce a body."

He leaned toward her in interest with his elbows perched on the smooth desktop and his fingers intertwined. "Why don't you start at the beginning?" he suggested. "Tell me why your grandfather was there. What happened to him—exactly? Take your time, Miss Freeman. I want to get all the facts."

Grateful for his unhurried manner, she poured out her story with great deliberation.

"I see," he said when she had finished. "So you aren't sure of what actually happened to him?"

"No." She shrugged helplessly, then lowered her lashes in a feminine pout. "I know I probably sound like a kook, but I really believe something is wrong. I just can't believe their story. Maybe if I'd been shown his body . . . but now they're trying to tell me he was cremated, and the plot beside my grandmother is still empty. Well, it doesn't seem right." She smiled to herself and stiffened, realizing that she was beginning to sound as if she had flighty ideas, then calmly folded her hands in her lap, waiting for him to speak.

"First of all," he began. "I don't think you sound like a kook. You're obviously concerned, and for good reason. Now, you say that they were able to produce signed consents that gave them complete control?"

"That's right."

"Hm-m."

"But doesn't that mean they could've done anything with him?"

"Correct. Which makes me wonder why they went to all the trouble of concocting a story about his death."

"But don't you see?" she cried, suddenly losing control. "There were picketers, people who were angry and afraid. Patients were being removed from the hospital by the dozen. Everyone was thrown into panic. But when they announced that my grandfather was only confused, and then that he died, it all went back to normal. It was the solution to their problem."

"So what would you like from me?"

"To go there! Get a court order if you must. Charge them with a lawsuit!"

"Yes, I could bring about a suit, but that doesn't necessarily mean that I'd win. The Northeastern Heart Institute operates under the best legal counsel available. I doubt whether they'd have left themselves open, whether they're guilty or not. If you tried to prove wrongdoings and failed, it could be quite costly. All you'd have to do is ruffle their feathers enough by discrediting their reputation, and you could be faced with a countersuit for slander. Have you considered these consequences?"

"All I want to know is if my grandfather's still alive. It doesn't even matter any more how he died, just that he did. I must be positive that he's not being held prisoner inside that place."

"Yes, I understand all of that. I just don't think you have a strong enough case. I think if you were to go after them, it would be you who was most hurt. Miss Freeman, you sound like a sensible woman. Be reasonable. Forget about this and go home."

"Then you won't accept my case?"

"I don't think any attorney could accept your case in good conscience. With such flimsy evidence, you have no case."

She stared down at her folded hands, then looked up. "Thank you anyway."

"I'm sorry, Miss Freeman, and I do wish you the best of luck."

She left the building feeling more dejected than ever. Even though he'd been kind, she had seen through his disguise. All attorneys were the same. They never cared about the people they represented, only whether or not they could win a case.

Her mother's attorney had won. Bail was posted and she'd returned to court where Jack Nesbith convinced the judge to let her off the hook. His only job was to keep her from going to jail. It didn't matter that he'd released her back into a prison of alcohol where she would never be freed. Several days later, she would be back on a drunken binge where a worse fate awaited her.

It was foolish to have believed that an attorney would ever do more than simply juggle the law. Their sole function was to help untangle their clients by using loopholes, but the Northeastern Heart Institute was protected by a series of airtight legal knots.

Her grandfather's fate had also been sealed, and

there was nothing she could do about it. Whether he was alive or dead didn't seem to matter to anyone but herself, and that wasn't enough to help him. It was impossible to attack them alone.

She plodded along the sidewalk heading back to her car, then stopped as she happened to notice a sign. TED CUTSFORTH—PRIVATE DETECTIVE. It might be a long shot, but it was all she had left.

There was always a function for private detectives. That was how she'd been found. It was long after she'd moved to Colorado, away from her mother, trying to escape her jaded past. She had completed her education, and had set out to become active in the world of art, when the hired detective had surprised her with a visit.

He was an older man, not the type that was usually portrayed in movies, and he wore a drab brown suit and had lifeless eyes. An insurance company had sent him as a representative regarding a Will.

"My mother is dead?" she'd asked in agony. "How did it happen?"

"Well," he tried to stall. "I don't have a copy of the actual report."

"But surely you know how she died. Was she sick? Had she been in a hospital?"

"Not exactly."

"Then what? You must have some idea."

"She was found in the room of a motel."

"With a . . . a man?" Katherine swallowed a lump in her throat.

"No, she was alone. She wasn't found until after she'd been dead a while."

"But how did it happen?"

"Miss Freeman, I didn't want to be the one to tell you this, but I guess you leave me no other choice.

You see, Miss Freeman, your mother was found strangled.''

"She was murdered?" Katherine asked dumbfoundedly, sinking down onto a chair.

"Yes, but at least she provided for you. As a matter of fact, both your parents had. Our company will still be honoring her insurance policy, along with the one your father had left under the conditions that you finished college. It's all yours. I don't mind telling you it's quite a handsome sum. You'll never have to worry about working."

Katherine tried to push the scene aside as she opened the door to the storefront office. If the detective from the insurance company had found her when she'd wanted to cover her tracks, perhaps another would help to locate her grandfather. She walked up to a tall counter and rang the bell.

"Could I help you?" a wiry man asked, popping his head out from behind a closed door. "Jest a second. I'll be with you in a minute." The door eased shut, and he disappeared.

She turned on her heel and began to pace across the hardwood floor, wondering if she were only clutching at straws. She'd stay and talk with him, and whatever he suggested would be final.

Just then, the door flew open and an energetic man came rushing out. "Whew! What a day! If this keeps up, I'll have to hire a receptionist. Hi." He extended his lean hand. "My name's Ted."

He escorted her back into a shabby office with an ancient wooden desk, propping his feet up as they talked. When she had finished relaying her tale, he reached for a cigarette with a frown.

"I'll be honest with you," he started. "I could use a case like this. It could help with the finances."

"Then you don't think it's all my imagination?"

"I didn't say that. Who the hell knows? The only problem I have is messing around with such a powerhouse. When you play with fire, baby, you're gonna git burned. Know what I mean?"

"In other words, you're afraid of them."

"Not afraid. That's not it. I guess what I'm trying to say is that I don't think I could be of any help. I don't think I'd git anywhere. The whole thing would jest add up to a waste of time and money. Not for me. I'd git my fee. You could count on that. But yer the one who'd suffer with the expense."

It was odd that he'd come up with the same words the other detective had once said. The dull investigator had turned her down after she'd tried to convince him to find her mother's assailant, saying the same thing. It was useless, and would only be a waste of time and money.

"Thank you, Mr. Cutsforth. I appreciate your honesty."

"Now, if you needed me for something else . . ."

"No, that's quite all right. I don't live in this area, and I'll be returning home."

She finally understood. The only reason she hadn't been able to accept her grandfather's death was because of her mother. That was why she'd felt unnaturally sympathetic towards him. In certain respects, their situations had been similar. Both had been prisoners to a certain degree. Perhaps that's what she had seen in his eyes that night—the longing to escape from a terrible existence. Somehow they'd shared a similar fate—held captive for different reasons, yet crying to be set free. The look she'd seen in his eyes had been identical to the one she'd once seen in her mother's. That was why she'd thought it had been genuine.

She had never been allowed to see her mother's

body. By the time the private detective had sniffed her out, she had long since been buried. For years this had haunted her, and it had been difficult to accept the fact that she really had died. Doubts continued to linger that they might've been wrong. How did they know it was her for sure? Who was there to identify the body? She had only been projecting this unresolved guilt into a similar situation. Naturally she would want to see his body. She was fearful of making the same mistake.

But one couldn't go through life with these insecurities. Everything had to be placed in the proper perspective. The past was finished, and there was no way to change what had already happened. Now she had a life of her own—a good life with Wendell. All this time she'd thought that it would pacify her bruised ego by fitting together the pieces of a forgotten family tree, and that this would repair a shattered self-esteem. But she'd been wrong. She'd already accomplished all of this on her own. It was time to admit that one couldn't forever be chasing illusions. An individual was only as good as the name he made for himself. Discovering the facts surrounding her father's family, even had it been possible, wouldn't change her as a person.

She unlocked the door to her hotel room, and went to the closet to begin to pack. All of them couldn't have been deceived. Nobody had believed her because she hadn't been right. It was insane to have thought the Northeastern Heart Institute had done anything unethical. Her unfounded suspicions had only been based on her own guilt. Ernest P. Freeman was dead, and she would never be able to speak with him again. It was one of those things she'd learned to accept. Now it was time to go home. Wendell would forgive her when she explained.

There would still be time for the Art Fair.

Just then, the telephone rang. She paused for a moment, wondering who it could be, then reached for the receiver.

"Miss Freeman? Boy, am I glad I gotta hold of you! I've been trying to decide whether to call or not, but I just couldn't shake this feeling."

"Who is this?"

"Ness. Stewart Ness. Don't you remember me? I was the guy who was setting up the night of the television interview."

"I'm sorry. There were so many people."

"That's okay. It's not important. You'll remember me when you see me."

"I don't think I will be seeing you. I was just getting ready to return home."

"No! You can't do that. Not before we can talk."

"Talk about what? There's nothing to say."

"Maybe not, but there's still something I have to tell you." He hesitated before continuing. "Look, this may sound stupid, but I have a funny feeling about your grandfather and the place he was in."

"What do you mean?"

"I didn't want to discuss it over the phone. It'll probably sound far-fetched. I don't want you to think that I'm a nut."

"What is it, Mr. Ness?"

"Promise you won't hang up?"

"What is it?"

"Well you see, I have reason to believe that your grandfather never died. I think he's still alive."

She caught her breath, and sank onto the bed in a daze.

"Miss Freeman? Are you there?"

"Ye-es," she choked.

"Is anything wrong?"

A tear slipped down her cheek, and her lip began to quiver. "No, nothing's wrong. As a matter of fact, for the first time in days, something is right."

13

Katherine agreed to meet Stewart Ness at Magglio's, a quaint Italian restaurant located in the heart of town. When she entered, it was overcrowded, filled with dozens of customers who stood shoulder-to-shoulder behind a cloud of smoke. Over the steady roar of conversation, she asked the hostess if he had already arrived, and the woman checked her book, then motioned for her to follow as she led the way between rows of cramped tables that were decorated with red and white checked tablecloths and flickering candles.

She recognized him immediately as the loud man in her grandfather's apartment who'd been told to put out his cigarette. Seated behind the small table, he appeared much larger than the first time they'd met, and his wild Hawaiian shirt made him look like a billboard for a travel agency's ad. His hair was blonde, clipped unstylishly short for such a heavy face which served to accentuate the fleshiness of his lips. When he spotted her coming, he quickly finished shoveling in the lasagna, then looked up with twinkling eyes, and reached out to offer her a giant hand that was surprisingly gentle. After she'd taken a seat, he pushed his empty plate away, lit up a cigarette, and motioned for waitress to bring them drinks.

"Smoke?" he asked, tipping an open pack of cigarettes in her direction.

She shook her head.

"Nice crowd tonight," he commented, glancing about. "Are you hungry?"

"No."

The waitress arrived with their drinks, and Katherine watched as she placed a square paper napkin in front of each of them, then served them the brandy and water he'd ordered along with her glass of rosè.

When she'd finished, Stewart smiled up at her cordially and lifted his glass in order to take a thirsty gulp. "Sure you don't want to order?" he asked Katherine again. "They're noted for their veal parmesan."

"No thanks," she replied with indifference. "I'm a vegetarian."

He didn't try to hide his look of amusement. "Not one of those," he retorted humorously.

His comment had been offensive, and she stiffened, turning her head away to avoid a stream of smoke that was drifting into her eyes.

Stewart eyed the glass of wine. "Well, at least you drink."

"Only wine," she stated emphatically, continuing to hold her head off to one side.

He craned his neck in an exaggerated effort to study her face, that was deliberately pointed towards the back of the room, flaunting a grin of satisfaction. Katherine refused to acknowledge him, and he finally gave up, leaning back in his chair with a groan. "I didn't mean it that way," he apologized. "Maybe that's what I should become—a vegetarian. Might help me to lose a few pounds."

Katherine suddenly turned back to him, her eyes flashing impatiently. "Look, Mr. Ness. You said you had information that my grandfather might still be alive."

"Stew."

"What?"

"Call me Stew. All my friends call me Stew. Stew in a pot!" He reached down to pat his rotund belly, bursting into peals of laughter.

"That's not amusing," Katherine curtly replied, reaching for her purse to leave. Their meeting was obviously a farce.

Stew reached for her hand to stop her. "I'm sorry." He shrugged. "Thought you had more of a sense of humor."

She released her purse, and settled back into the chair as she waited for him to continue.

"Okay, let's stop the chit-chat and get down to business."

"Then you do have information about my grandfather?"

"Not really information. I told you on the phone. It's a feeling."

She stared at him with disgust, reaching for her purse again. "A feeling?" she muttered angrily. "You think I came down here for a feeling? I thought this was important."

"Now hold on," he growled, this time reaching for

275

her wrist to give it a slight tug, sending her flying forward into the rim of the table top. "When I have a feeling, it is important."

"How's that?"

He let go of her arm, smugly crossing his hands as if he were holding a loaded deck. "I get feelings," he explained. "Oh, I know everyone gets feelings, but mine are different. Call it a type of intuition. Anyway, sometimes I get a feeling I just can't shake. What I've learned to do is try with all my might to push it out of my mind. I go to bars to drink. Eat all my favorite foods. I read a good book, or watch T.V. Then, after a few days, if the feeling's still there, I know that it means something, that it's right."

"How delightful, but how does that tie in with my grandfather?"

"Because I have one of those feelings about him." He scratched his head. "I don't know why, but I think something's going on over there at that hospital. I think they're keeping him alive."

For the first time since she'd arrived, her face softened, and she nodded in agreement. "Yes, that's exactly how I felt. But what good does it do? I've been trying for days to prove that they're lying, and I haven't gotten anywhere."

"Maybe I can help."

"I don't see how, Mr. Ness."

"Stew."

"Okay . . . Stew." She smiled.

"Maybe you haven't thought of everything."

"Well, I've gone to the County Coroner, the police, a lawyer, a private detective. I've even tried reasoning with my grandfather's doctor. What else could I have done?"

"There's gotta be something else. Don't get me wrong. I think you were on the right track, but now it's time to get innovative.''

''Innovative?''

''Sure. If we're gonna outsmart them, we've gotta look for a mistake. There always has to be a constant, something they've done over and over again without realizing it could tip someone off.''

''Like what? I hardly know anything about the way they treated my grandfather. All I have to go on is what he said that night.''

''No, I'm not talking about your grandfather. We already know what's happened to him. I'm talking about the other heart recipients. Ones that they're also claiming have died.''

''And how are we supposed to find anything out about them? I can't even find my grandfather.''

''Not the recipients. Their families. If you had this feeling that he really hadn't died, maybe some of them felt that way, too.''

''Wait a minute,'' she said with a slight wave of the hand. ''Are you trying to say that they might have lied about the deaths of other patients? That my grandfather wasn't the only one?''

''Why not? What makes him so special? I'd venture to say that if they've done it to him, they've done it to others. That's what I mean about my feeling. There's something about that place that makes my blood curdle. All we have to do is find our constant, and we may just have them over a barrel.''

''If you don't mind my asking, why do you keep referring to 'we'? I mean, I know why I want to expose them. He was my grandfather. But what's in it for you?''

Stewart Ness drew up both hands as if he'd been caught in a crime. ''Yeh, I knew you'd get around to that sooner or later.''

Katherine scowled. ''Is it money? Are you

planning on getting paid?''

"In a sense."

"I thought so," she said, reaching into her purse for her checkbook. "How much?"

He motioned for her to put the book away. "Katherine," he said softly. "You don't mind if I call you Katherine?"

She shook her head.

"Katherine, how old do you think I am?"

"I don't know," she lied, but professional portrait painting had taught her to capture all the lines, and she knew that he was at least ten years older than herself.

"Then I'll tell you. I'm thirty-eight years old. In two years, I'll be hitting forty. And you know how long I've been with Channel 3?"

"How long?"

"Sixteen years! Sixteen years of putting up with all of their crap. For sixteen years I've been trotting behind pretty anchorwomen, helping to make them look good. But I was really trained to do their job. That's right. I didn't go into this business to be the scutt-boy. I had every intention of making it big for myself. Big?" He glanced down at his huge belly. "I'm big, all right. Maybe that's why they never wanta put a camera on me. I'm not one of their dashing television personalities. So instead, I have to run after all the people they've picked over me, even though I have more seniority. Geez! I hate it!" He paused for a moment to think, then leaned forward taking her slender hands in his. "But you know how I could get that to change real quick? If I were to crack a dynamic story about a place like the Northeastern Heart Institute, they'd be fallilng on their knees trying to lap up after me for a change. Yeh,

I'm gonna get paid what I deserve, but not with money."

She lowered her eyes. "I'm sorry."

He chuckled. "Don't be sorry. Hell, it's not your fault. Lady, you're gonna be my ticket to fame. If we can hunt down your grandfather and expose that place. . . . well, that's all I need."

"So where do we begin?"

"I'll pick you up at your hotel tomorrow."

"And then what?"

"Then, we'll go to the library—start going over old newspapers. We'll make a list of all the artificial heart recipients they claimed had died over the years."

At ten o'clock sharp the next morning, Stew met her in the hotel lobby. This time he wore a light blue cotton shirt that made him look like a small corner of the sky. They strolled out to his car that sat waiting in the center of a Taxi Zone, and climbed inside to begin their trip downtown.

"You're not from around here, huh?" he asked, glancing over at her from the corner of his eye as he continued driving.

"No. I live in a small community in Colorado."

"Colorado?" he asked, not hiding his apparent surprise. "Funny, but I always thought women from Colorado had those high altitude lungs." He smiled and glanced down at her flat chest.

She turned away from him, feeling the warmth creep into her neck. "Cute."

"Hey," he chuckled. "I was only kidding. Geez, but you're sensitive."

"Occupational hazard. It goes with creating fine works of art."

"Is that what you do? You're an artist?"

''That's right.''

''How about that? Guess you do look like one of those creative types. Do you do stuff like oil paintings?''

''Sure.''

''Are you good?''

''I think so.''

''Then how come I never heard of you?''

''Mr. Ness,'' she said threateningly.

''Stew,'' he replied with a playful laugh. ''You know, Kath, you've gotta learn not to take everything so seriously. Relax a little.''

She sank back against the seat of the car, realizing that he had used a name she'd last been called by her mother. For some reason he did make her feel comfortable.

In comparison to the noisy world outside, the inside of the library was like a tomb. They located a rack of old newspapers that had been mounted into frames, in a corner of the basement, and began going over the pages that had yellowed over the years. Katherine pulled a small notebook from her purse, and began jotting down any names that were tied into the artificial heart recipients who had died. After several hours, the list had grown to over one hundred people.

As Stewart turned the pages, she studied the articles with curious interest, being especially drawn to the ones about her grandfather. Gradually, they traveled back in time, until they reached stories that had been written during the days of his original surgery. She made him stop when they came across a front page picture that took up a forth of the sheet, her heart fluttering madly. As she looked down at the ancient newspaper, she realized she was staring

into the face of her grandmother, Doris Freeman.
The woman appeared tired as she stood beside the
wheelchair of her husband, but her exhaustion
didn't hide the expression of love in her eyes. She
had hair that was dark, but was beginning to gray,
and in some respects she resembled her own
mother. Is that what her father had seen in the
young woman, the reason why she'd been special?
She gazed at the picture. So this was how she had
looked, and she fought back the lump that had crept
into her throat. Before Stewart could turn the page,
she made him wait as she devoured the words that
were printed, and when she had finished, smiled
with satisfaction. The article had drawn them closer,
helping to fill in the blanks of a vacant family tree.

"Guess that's it," Stew said when they'd finally
finished. He checked the notebook as they left the
building. "I never thought there were that many.
We were lucky that they gave some addresses."

"What now?" she asked, trotting along after him.

"We make our calls."

"Yeh, but some of these addresses are over fifty
years old. I doubt whether the people are even alive."

"True, but we'll just have to start with the most
recent cases and go back as far as we can. All we
need are a few in order to find our constant. Take
this one for example. This lady died right before
your grandfather. There was a daughter. Lives in
Detroit. Come on. Let's give her a call."

Katherine followed him as he ducked into a drug-
store, heading towards a phone booth. She watched
as he slipped his change into the slot, and listened as
he spoke to the operator.

"It's ringing," he whispered, holding one hand
over the receiver.

She moved in closer to hear.

"Mrs. Radke?" Stew asked. "Are you the Mrs. Radke whose mother had once received an artificial heart?"

He paused and listened.

"Great! Mrs. Radke, this is Stewart Ness from Channel 3 T.V. We're in the area of the North-eastern Heart Institute. I was wondering if you'd mind answering a few questions?"

There was a short pause.

"Yes, well, we understand that your mother's death occurred quite suddenly."

Another pause.

"I understand. Of course you didn't expect it. Tell me, was she really happy at Winnow Cove?"

He listened.

"I see. Did she ever tell any of the nurses or doctors how she felt? Well, I suppose for her sake it's good that it's all over."

He waited and listened.

"Is that so? No, I didn't realize that. I'm sorry it worked out that way. Listen, thanks a lot, Mrs. Radke. Of course we'll let you know if we're ever doing another program. I'm sure you do have a lot to say. Have a good day. 'Bye."

He hung up the telephone and looked at Katherine. "Well, she felt the same way your grand-father did, like she was being held prisoner. But what would you expect? Still, she never really com-plained about it to the staff, as far as her daughter knows." He reached into the pocket of his shirt for a cigarette, flicking on his lighter and inhaling deeply, blowing out a puff of smoke that headed directly for her face, and not paying attention when she began to cough. "Poor lady. Never even got a chance to meet her own grandchildren. Pathetic. They were so desperate at the end that they thought the kids could at least see her at her own funeral, but there never was one."

Katherine stopped coughing and stared down at him. "What do you mean?"

"Guess they'd planned on a big hometown funeral, but it all fell through."

"Why?"

"Because they told her that they'd already disposed of the body. That it had been cremated."

Katherine reached down and grasped his hand in excitement. "Wait a minute. That's what they said about my grandfather. I was furious when they told me there wasn't a body."

Stew's eyes twinkled in delight. "You know what?" he asked. "We just may have found our constant."

The remainder of the day was spent in Stewart's apartment making telephone calls. Most of the time they came up with families who had moved away or had unlisted numbers. But when they did happen across a relative of a heart patient who was deceased, the answer was always the same. None of them had ever seen a body. By the end of the day, each of the names had been scratched off, and the floor around the phone was filled with wrinkled slips of paper that were crumpled into a pile.

"It's settled in my mind," Stew finally announced, propping his feet up on the coffee table with an exhausted sigh. "If they aren't alive, then what would they have done with the bodies?"

"I thought you said you had one of your special feelings that he is still alive."

"I do. And now I feel that way about the whole lot of them."

"Then what can we do?"

"The same thing I've always done. Let's get a few

drinks, eat a good meal, and if the feeling's still there tomorrow, we'll come up with a plan."

This time he chose a Greek restaurant. Stewart ordered a bottle of Retsina, and they watched as a voluptious belly dancer flitted from table to table. Katherine watched, embarrassed, when Stewart was picked to join her in the act, and relieved when her own spinach pie arrived. After the music died down and the half-naked girl had bounced away, Stew lit up another cigarette and filled her glass.

"Do you mind if I ask you something?" He eyed her over the tall goblet.

"What's that?" she coolly replied, irritated that he'd flirted with another woman in her presence, and feeling a little uninhibited by the wine.

"Why didn't you know anything about your grandfather?"

Her eyes flashed defensively. "Because my father never told my mother about him."

"Why?"

"Because he didn't get a chance. He died."

"I'm sorry." He paused to think, then looked up at her. "Still, I don't understand why he wouldn't have told her. Having a famous father isn't a thing a man keeps to himself."

"Maybe that's just it. My grandfather was famous. There were always interviews—stories about the family. You saw the articles today. Maybe that's what he didn't like. Maybe he was trying to protect her from prying eyes."

"So what are you saying? That he didn't want to say anything to his wife because he wanted to protect her? I don't see why."

"Maybe she was too sensitive. Maybe she would've crumpled beneath the stress of having to maintain a certain public image."

"Could be. I just can't imagine a woman who would need that type of protection. I mean, what's the worst that could've happened?"

"That she might've fallen apart. That she wouldn't be able to hold up emotionally."

"But he died. Didn't that affect her? Didn't she ever wonder about him? She had to be curious about his family."

"Of course it affected her. Maybe too much. She never really talked about it, but I knew that it bothered her. I could see how she began to change."

"What happened?"

Katherine smiled sadly. "Listen, it's not one of my fondest memories."

"So?"

"So, she never married again. She was young and he'd left her well off, but she never went back to work. She spent years locked inside the house. It was difficult to admit that she'd turned into an alcoholic."

"That's too bad."

"Yeh, well things like that do happen. I try not to be bitter. Guess there's always mixed emotions. I loved my mother, but I still hated her for what she'd become. I hated the different men who took advantage of her, and the times that she was arrested for anything from indecent exposure to vagrancy. Sometimes I hated my father, too. And through it all, I looked for my own excuses to leave. Whenever I was around her I never really felt clean." She tapped the stem of her glass. "I don't know why he never told her about my grandfather. They loved each other. I was sure of that. You'd think that with love, there would've been a bit more honesty. I've thought about it a lot, especially since the day they first came to tell me we were related.

At first I thought they had found the wrong person. There's lots of Freemans. Yeh, I'm sure she wondered about it. When he left her alone in the world, she went stumbling into the pit of spending the rest of her life as nothing more than a drunk.''

"Who's to say? My wife was worse than an alcoholic. She was a witch."

"Was?"

"I'm divorced."

"I'm sorry."

"Hell, don't apologize. It was the best thing that could've ever happened to me. Let's just say that when it came to the tree of love, I picked a real lemon." He began to laugh, and Katherine soon joined him. "What about you?" he asked, stopping in his laughter to glance down at her left hand. "You never been married?"

"No, but I have a boyfriend."

He shrugged. "That's the way it always goes. All the nice women are already taken. What does he do? Is he an artist, too?"

"No. He runs a kind of agency for other talented people. He helps them to sell their work."

"You mean to say that he makes money off of them? Enough to earn a decent living? Don't tell me you have a boyfriend who uses the talent of other people to make himself a profit?"

"You make it sound dirty. No, what he does is find buyers." She didn't conceal the fact that she'd been offended by his comment.

Stewart caught the irritation of her tone, and tried to make amends before she became angry. "Yeh, well I was gonna say that it wouldn't seem right, taking advantage of starving artists." The moment the words were out, he realized his mistake. She was more put off than ever.

"Don't worry, Mr. Ness," she replied in a frigid tone that was suddenly frighteningly aloof. "Wendell earns his fees. He's not the kind of man who would take advantage."

"Wendell?" Stew blurted, unable to control himself. "Suppose not. With a name like Wendell, I don't think he'd know enough to take advantage of anyone—including you."

Katherine became furious, ignoring his remark as she attacked her plate of food with fervor. The remainder of the meal was completed in silence, and when she had finished, asked if she could be taken home.

At first he was sorry. He hadn't wanted her to dislike him. It was just that he had a big mouth, an uncontrollable flaw in his nature that always served to create problems. He stared wistfully at the bottle of wine, hoping that she'd notice that it was still half full and decide to give him a second change. But it was too late for condolences, and when her forehead finally puckered into a displeased frown, he decided it was best if he took her back to the hotel in order to avoid further arguments. He needed her as badly as she needed him. They had to work as a team. With a pleasant motion of his hand, he called for the waitress and paid the bill before driving her home.

Katherine awoke the next morning, jarred from her sleep by the insistent ring of the telephone. Groggily, she reached for the receiver. "Yeh?" she mumbled.

"Kath?" Stew chirped. "It's still there."

She rubbed her eyes and stretched, wondering if he were playing some kind of an offbeat joke. "What's still there?"

"The feeling. The one about the bodies. I think they're all still alive."

Katherine pulled herself to a sitting position, realizing that he was serious, and that she was suddenly wide awake. "All of them? But that's insane!"

"I can't fight the feeling."

"So what should we do?"

"We've gotta find them."

"Find them? How can we do that?"

"By looking."

"Looking?"

"That's right. We're gonna have to go in there and find them. We have to get into that part of the hospital."

"We can't do that. They'll never let us in."

"I know. They're not gonna let us in. But we're gonna go in anyway. We'll sneak in—tonight."

14

Stewart parked his car on a desolate dirt road. Out-side it was too dark to see any of the details of their surroundings, including the depths of the forest that loomed threateningly off to one side. Against the night, a silent distraction materialized in the form of a flickering flashlight that suddenly burst forth in a brilliant beam, knifing its way through the shadows. Katherine's slight figure could be seen as she leaned across the seat, trying to see what it was that Stewart was studying. They sat together motionless, feeling outnumbered by a host of woodland crickets who boldly announced to the couple their exclusive terri-torial rights to their private domain.

"Where'd you get the map?" Katherine whispered, straining her eyes to see his face.

"The Department of City Works. This is an old blueprint they'd once used when they took out the original permit to lay the sewage lines. See?" He pointed a stubby finger. "These are all the apartments at the front where your grandfather used to live. And each of these," he moved his finger to different spots on the paper, "are individual buildings. For some reason they wanted them kept hidden. I always suspected they were there, but never knew for sure. Glad I gotta hold of this layout. Should've thought of asking Bobby Derne about it before. See this?" He ran his hand along the border of the sheet. "The entire area is surrounded by a fence. That one." He brought up the flashlight, pointing it through the window, sending a flood of light across the street onto the side of a towering cyclone fence. "This is it—the wall they put up to protect Winnow Cove."

"And you think my grandfather's in there?"

"Yup, along with all those other people."

She glanced at the fence, feeling somewhat intimidated. "How are we going to get in?"

He shrugged his hefty shoulders and sighed. "Guess we're gonna have to climb it."

Katherine clamped her lower lip between her teeth and began to chew nervously. Did he really know what he was doing? Could she trust him? What if they were caught? "You don't think they have it wired?" she finally inquired, not convinced that they were safe.

"Naw. I already checked that out. I don't think they would've wanted to attract any unnecessary attention. It would've meant a special permit. Naw. This fence wasn't put up to act as some kind of an impenetrable barrier, just a means to discourage trespassers."

"Are you sure we can get over?" She lowered her eyes in the direction of his obese abdomen.

She didn't notice the embarrassed shade of pink that crept into his ears, or the humiliating color that burned through his cheeks. "Of course," he taunted. "Why not?"

It was still difficult for her to conceal her reservations. "But what if we get caught? I don't know . . . maybe we should try something else first."

He stared at her in disbelief. Was she trying to back down? Did she think they should wait until they received an open invitation? "No," he stated, emphatically shaking his head. "Don't you remember? You said you already tried everything else. This is the only way." Before she could utter another objection he reached for the door handle. "Ready?"

All that was left to do was pull her thin jacket around her shoulders and follow, the matter having been settled.

With a decisive twist of the wrist, Stew opened the car door and climbed out. He scampered across the street with Katherine reluctantly following. When they reached the fence they stopped and stared up. Somehow it appeared much taller when viewed from below.

"You wanta go first?" Stew asked.

"No, that's okay."

"All right." He tucked the flashlight away in his back pocket, and grasped the webbing that made up the fence. With fingers clutching tightly and toes digging in, he began clawing his way to the top.

Katherine momentarily hesitated, then also pounced upon the fence to begin scaling it, trying not to notice how it swayed beneath their weight. She had just about reached the top when her head suddenly pushed against a thick cushion of fat, the jar surprising enough to cause her to temporarily lose her balance. It was Stew.

"I'm stuck," he grunted.

"Where?"

"I think it's my shirt."

"Okay, just a second."

Holding on tightly with one hand, and digging in her knees to keep from falling, she began snaking her fingers between the fence and his protruding belly.

"Hey, watch it!" He cringed and the fence rocked violently.

His doughy flesh was more sensitive than she'd first imagined, and she started over again, this time with a more delicate probe. Finally having located the place where his shirt was snagged, she worked on the material in order to set him free. All the while she could hear him muttering angry curses beneath his breath, and she couldn't tell whether he was resentful of her or simply digusted with himself. A final tug caused the material to give way, sending him reeling down against her as he lost his footing. She braced one shoulder up against his mountainous buttocks, trying to keep from falling as they teetered like two clowns in the center of a circus ring. Using her entire body weight she tried to push him over, with all her might, to the other side. With one giant heave he finally managed to swing himself over the top, but the mass of his rotund body was too much, and it set into motion a force that was uncontrollable and rapidly gaining in momentum. Barreling down the opposite side with fingers grasping the aluminum web, he found it impossible to stop. Thud! The earth shook as both feet squarely hit the ground. Once Katherine saw that he was safe, she pulled herself over and landed beside him. They couldn't speak, overcome by the spasmodic gasps that helped them catch their breath.

"Okay," Stew finally puffed, deliberately ignoring any reference to the rescue. In his most businesslike fashion he pulled out the flashlight, shining it down on the map in hopes that it would create a diversion. His ego was badly bruised. He had been at the mercy of a woman! "The first building is about fifty yards from here heading north. Come on."

At first she was hurt that he hadn't bothered offering any thanks, but decided it wasn't worth the effort to mention it. Without saying a word she obediently followed him across a small clearing, and they made their way through a wall of trees, slipping through the murky underbrush. They trudged along at a steady pace until they saw a faint glimmer of light.

"That's it," Stew said, stepping aside so she could also see. "Now stay right behind me," he warned, "and don't say a word. If anyone catches us now, we'll blow our chance."

Katherine nodded, trailing at his heels.

The building they'd come upon was a perfect rectangle made up of thick concrete bricks. A few cars were parked in the accompanying lot, but none of the caretakers could be seen in the vicinity. It was late, and everyone was probably inside. They ran across the street to the side of the structure, peering through an open window.

Inside, the building was brightly lit, and they found themselves looking into a large room. About a dozen elderly people wearing hospital gowns sat calmly in chairs. They didn't move, staring straight ahead as if they were in a deep trance.

"Who are they?" Katherine murmured.

"I don't know."

"Maybe it's a nursing home."

"Way back here? I doubt it."

"You think he's in there?"

"Naw. This building is used for something else."

"How do you know? They could be heart patients."

"Naw, the Institute wouldn't keep a bunch of heart recipients together. Think of all those germs."

Stew was right. None of the usual precautions had been taken.

Just then, a mask-like face popped up from behind the glass pane, staring directly into Katherine's eyes. Her hair was wild, looking as though it had never been combed, and her skin was shriveled with age. At first the woman didn't move, then her ancient face twisted in terror. Before either Katherine or Stew could react, her eyes lit up crazily and her mouth opened to reveal a dark toothless cavity. "Ay-y-y-y-ye!!!" she let out a bloodcurdling scream.

Immediately the room came to life. All the other statuesque patients responded by springing from their seats to join in with hysterical screams. The area soon became a mass of tangled bodies as the people ran wildly about, bumping into each other which made them shriek even louder. The woman at the window seemed to forget about the intruders, caught up in all the excitement. She spun around, joining her companions in the frenzy. Mad! The room had gone completely insane!

Katherine couldn't believe her eyes, stepping back to try and escape the inhuman sounds that penetrated the window. The scene had not ended. Just then, two men and a woman wearing electric blue burst through the door, flinging themselves into the mob in an attempt to get them to stop. The patients became more agitated then ever.

"Come on," Stew said, tugging at Katherine's sleeve. "Let's get outta here."

She pulled herself away, following him back across the street and into the woods.

Once they were out of view, Katherine leaned against the stout trunk of a tree, clasping her trembling hands together. "What happened?" she asked, dazed from the close encounter with raving maniacs. "It was like a bomb exploded in their heads."

"Yeh, and we were probably the ones who ignited the fuse by startling the old lady."

"But we didn't know she'd appear like that. She just popped up from under the window."

"Next time we'll have to be a little more careful. We could've been caught."

"Who were they?"

"I don't know."

"Why were they there?"

"Because they were nuts? Who knows? Come on," he said gruffly, taking her by the hand. "There's another building about a half mile up." He started in that direction.

For a moment Katherine lagged behind, wondering how he could so casually cast aside such an unnerving experience. He could've at least taken the time to discuss it. Perhaps if they would've mulled it over it would've put an end to the vague feeling of apprehension that had settled in the pit of her stomach like a rock. If they were crazy, how had they gotten that way? And how did this affect her grandfather? She shuddered. If they did find him, maybe it would be too late. But if he were still alive, and they had just begun to work on him, there still might be a chance. She leaped after Stew, filled with a new sense of urgency.

Together they plodded through the forest, tripping over fallen branches and brushing against prickly leaves. The dense foliage served to slow them down significantly, but gradually they made their way through the thicket. The sight of a distant light that glowed from another building caused them to halt, and they slowed to a crawl as they quietly crept forward.

The second building was identical to the first. A light from an open window shone out into the night. The two of them bent down, crawling carefully along one side of the structure to look inside.

This area was much smaller than the room they had left. Two beds jutted out from opposite corners making it look like a semi-private hospital room. An attendant was helping a man in a wheelchair prepare for sleep. Stewart and Katherine hovered in the shadows as they watched.

The attendant's dull expression gave away the fact that he considered his job routine. After hoisting the disabled man over to the side of the bed, he began calmly unbuttoning his shirt, slipping it down over his arms. Next came the trousers. The patient wriggled his hips cooperatively as they, too, were removed. The clothing was carefully folded and placed on a squat bedside table. Then the attendant started in with the man's underclothes, undressing him until he sat at the bedside in the nude. The attendant wasn't finished. Leaning forward without expression, he grasped the man's shoulder and began casually twisting his arm. The entire limb revolved in several complete circles until it had been screwed to the point where it could be detached at the shoulder. The limb was carefully layed on top of the stack of clothing. The other arm followed. When both arms had been unfastened, the patient fell back against the pillows so that the attendant could calmly set about removing each leg. When he had finished, all that remained of the man in the wheel-chair was a head and torso!

Neither the man nor the attendant seemed to think it unusual. The sight of the limbs lying there did not appear to be disturbing. Without a word, a sacklike shirt was produced that was neatly pulled over his head. Then the attendant lifted up the fragment of a body, like a bulging bag of potatoes, and tucked it beneath the covers. After he had finished, he strolled casually over to the other bed.

"I'm already in for the night," the other man said, looking up from his pillow with a satisfied grin.

"You sure?" the attendant asked. "Let's see." He pulled back the blanket, revealing a body that was exactly the same. No limbs. Only an amputated torso. "Good," he said blandly. "You guys get some sleep. See you tomorrow." With that, he turned off the light and closed the door.

Katherine let out her breath in a shrill whistle. "My God!"

"Yeh," Stewart replied, his own voice wavering. "I know."

"How did they get that way?"

"Probably a birth defect. There were little stubs where it looked as though limbs had started to grow."

"I don't know why I found it so grotesque," Katherine tried to explain. "Lots of people are born without appendanges. When I was taking anatomy, I saw my share. There was something peculiar about them, though. Maybe it was that they appeared so apathetic, as if they didn't care. And I guess I really didn't expect those limbs to be removed. Stew, I've sketched nude human bodies hundreds of times, and I would've sworn that those arms and legs were real. It came as a shock." She chuckled nervously.

"Maybe it was just the lighting. Do you think they're doing some kind of research on more realistic prosthesis? Is that why those men are here?"

"I don't know, Kath." He scratched his head. "I wish I did. It doesn't make any sense. Why keep them out here unless . . . unless you didn't want anyone to know about them?" His eyes lit up. "And the only reason you might not want anyone to know about people with birth defects is because of the way they may have acquired them."

"What do you mean?"

"I mean, how did they get that way? Why are people born without appendages? Drugs? Still, if it were drugs they would have a family. And if they had relatives, they wouldn't be kept way out here. I just don't know."

"I doubt if we'll ever find out," Katherine replied distantly. "Just the same, I feel sorry for them."

"Don't feel sorry for them. Feel sorry for all the new victims, the ones who may be created if the people at the Institute aren't stopped."

She tilted her head, curious about his statement. "You're convinced that they did something to make them that way?"

Stewart nodded. "Call it another of my feelings." He pulled himself up, and began walking back towards the woods. "Come on," he called over his shoulder. "We'd better go on."

Steward remained silent as he led the way to the next building on the map. His huge body plowed through the underbrush like a determined bulldozer, not noticing any of the scraping branches because he was lost in thought. Crazy people in one building and deformities in another. It didn't make sense. Why keep them out here? All hospitals housed similar wards. Those types of patients weren't unnusual. It certainly wasn't enough information to prove a case. So far, there was nothing abnormal taking place within the secret buildings inside Winnow Cove. Still, he had a feeling. They were close on the trail of something, and he could sense that a gristly tale was yet to unfold.

As they trudged along, the wind picked up, sending an icy breeze through their thin summer clothing. Katherine shivered.

"Cold?" Stew asked, realizing that he'd been shutting her out.

"A little." She managed a brave smile. "I don't mind. It's these damn mosquitos I really can't stand." She reached up to give her shoulder a swat. "How long do we have to keep walking through these woods?"

"I don't 'think it would be wise to try pararding down the road. We are trespassers. You don't want to get caught, do you?"

"No," she snorted, brushing away another insect that had perched on her face. "Are we almost there?"

He craned his neck to see. "Just about. Think I saw a light."

By the time they reached the next building, they were both showing visible signs of fatigue. Katherine's feet ached, and she was certain that she'd twisted an ankle. Stewart had it much worse, his flabby body unaccustomed to such demanding physical stress. Each heavy step was accompanied with a shallow pant as they moved along, and every few minutes he would reach up to sweep away another beaded cluster of perspiration from his flushed brow.

"This one looks a little different," he remarked when they'd crept up upon the building to view it from the opposite side of the road. "No windows. Do you see any windows?"

"No."

"They must not want anyone accidentally looking inside."

"Then how're we going to know who's in there?"

"We'll have to go in and look."

"Inside?"

"Yup."

"How?"

"They've gotta have a service entrance. Nobody ever keeps those locked. Let's go see."

She followed him across the street to one side of the concrete wall, staying directly behind him as he encircled the building.

"This is it," he announced, placing his hand against a thick metal door. "Stay right with me."

Cautiously, he gave the heavy handle a squeeze, easing it open to check if anyone stood waiting on the other side. It was okay. He pushed it open even wider, and slipped through. Katherine remained glued to his heels.

They entered a long hallway that was dimly lit with two exit signs that cast a firey glow, sending reddish shadows across the tiled floor. Stew crept steadily down the corridor, surprisingly light on his feet. When he reached the first door, he paused to peek inside.

"What do you see?" Katherine whispered over his shoulder.

"Sh-h-h-h!" he hissed, reaching for his flashlight. The beam of light helped to lead the way as he entered. Katherine fell behind, and once they were inside he closed the door.

The air inside the room was filled with the stench of animals. Stew flashed the beam of light further into the room, revealing a series of tall metal cages.

"Research animals?" Katherine asked.

"Don't know." He inched his way across the floor to the first cage, and shone the light in.

Without warning, a dark figure sprang out from a corner of the cage, and hurled itself against the bar with a guttural cry.

"Grr-arr-rgh!!!"

Stewart and Katherine clambered back to escape its reach. The light had flashed up long enough to disclose a pair of angry red eyes.

For a moment they were paralyzed with fear, listening as the animal grunted furiously. Then with a mad burst of energy, they raced for the door, flinging it open and rushing down the hallway without stopping until they were safely outside. When they reached the familiar woods, they fell to the ground gasping.

"What was it?" Katherine cried.

"Some kind of animal."

"But it almost looked human."

"I know."

"Then what could it have been?"

"I think," Stew choked, carefully formulating his response so that it wouldn't sound too incredible. "I think they must be doing some kind of animal experimentation on humans. . . . or vice versa. I don't know. Geez! I never saw anything like it!"

"Stew?" Katherine suddenly asked tearfully. "I don't think I can go on. There's something evil about this place. I'm afraid."

"But we can't quit now. We must go on." He reached for her hand to give it a comforting squeeze, and she found herself crumpling into his arms.

"There's nothing to be afraid of," he whispered gently. "It's okay. Come on."

The moon had risen like a luminous white ball that cast eerie shadows into the night. Together they struggled along, fighting the sharp branches that jutted out into their path. Stewart kept a firm hand around Katherine's quivering shoulder as he led her onward.

When the next building emerged, she cowered back in fear. "I can't," she whispered fiercely. "I don't want to go in there."

"But what if this is the place where they have your grandfather?"

"I don't care."

"Yes, you do," he replied so sharply that it gave her a start. "Why the hell else are we here?"

She didn't stop him as he pulled her forward.

"Come on," he said, trying to sound reassuring. "I'm here. Nothing's gonna happen."

This structure was similar to the other in that it didn't have any windows. They were forced to make their entrance from a rear service door. There was the same narrow corridor with an identical set of closed doors that brought back a painful picture of the room they had just left. Stew made his way to the first door and hesitated before turning the knob.

"No," Katherine whimpered.

Her plea supplied him with the masculine pride he needed to go forward, and he gallantly threw back his head and slowly opened the door. Katherine waited as he stepped into the room, holding her breath until he returned a few seconds later.

"It's okay," he said with a grin. "See for yourself."

He held the door open so she could peer inside. Test tubes. The walls and counters were filled with a

302

various assortment of test tubes. Each of the glass containers held a type of pinkish medium. It was harmless, and she felt a rush of relief.

The first thing she noticed about the second room was a bright fluorescent hue that streamed out from the crack as soon as they opened the door. They glanced at one another and shrugged, curious to discover what it was that was causing the color. The sight that waited them came as a shocking jolt.

It was a huge room, as massive as a deep auditorium. Ultraviolet lights glowed down from futuristic fixtures implanted in the ceiling, and it was from these that the odd color emerged. High in the air, a network of thick plastic tubing was suspended. Woo-oosh-sh . . . Woo-oosh-sh . . . Woo-oosh-sh. It was filled with pulsating blood. The tubing snaked its way down to rows and rows of glass incubators. Sealed safely within their clear containers lay hundreds of tiny infants—naked and exposed.

They stared at the scene transfixed. Stew was the one who finally took a step forward to view one of the babies more closely. Katherine followed behind, then clasped her hand over her mouth to hold back a muffled scream. It wasn't a totally developed baby, being in the earlier stages of uterine development. They were gazing down at a human embryo! She buried her face against Stewart's shoulder as he continued with the gruesome tour. The scene was horrible. Every so often Katherine would glance up, only to find the sights unbearable. Most of the infants were deformed. Some had developed a layer of crusty scar tissue as the result of the intense lights. By the time they had completed a circle of the room, Katherine's cheeks were covered with rivers of tears.

"How could they?" she cried out in anguish once

they were safely outside. "How could they do that to those innocent babies?"

"Kath," Stewart replied tenderly, gathering her in his arms as she wept. "Who knows?"

"But why?" she asked, her eyes filled with pain. "What purpose could they have?"

"Research, I suppose. It looked as though they were deliberately exposing them to a form of radiation."

"Oh, my God!" she sobbed, burying her face in her hands. "But where are their mothers? To whom do they belong?"

"Nobody," Stew replied. "Didn't you see? They hadn't yet reached maturity. The incubators were set up to simulate a mother's uterus. That tubing that hung down from the ceiling was acting like a gigantic umbilical cord. And those test tubes we saw in the other room. . . . well, that's probably where they were all conceived."

"It's cruel!" she choked. "They're nothing but barbarians! Maybe that's how those others became freaks. No wonder they've kept them hidden. It wasn't drugs after all!"

Stew didn't respond. He couldn't. Everything she had said seemed true. He stood beside her as she continued to weep.

"I guess I don't understand," she suddenly blurted. "Maybe I'm stupid, but why would anyone do such a thing?"

"I don't know," he mumbled. "Nuclear war. Maybe they believe it's a way to someday save the human race. Hell, who knows? So many atrocities are done in the name of research."

Now he understood. This was why they were forced to hide their victims in the depths of a forbidden forest. Yes. They were involved with research. They were consumed with the most devious forms of experimentation imaginable— research on human specimens. His feeling had been correct, and once he exposed them the entire world would loathe them as much as he did.

"We'd better go on," he reminded her once she had stopped crying. "There's another building, according to the map."

She took a step back, brushing a damp lock off her brow. Maybe this would be the place where she'd find her grandfather. It no longer mattered to her if she were caught. She'd come for one purpose, and now her mission seethed through her veins like burning lava. They were ghouls, and he was still being held tight within their grip. Her purpose was to set him free! She bit down on her lower lip, following Stewart as he plodded onward.

It wasn't long before they reached the last building. Like the others, it had no windows. Stew made his entrance through the rear service door for one final time.

They hadn't expected the sound. It seemed to leap out at them from every crack and crevice once they were inside. At first they were stunned, feeling as though they'd made a terrible mistake, stumbling through the door of a Swiss clock factory. They didn't associate the rhythmic clicking with anything human, at first. It was more a curious noise that had caught them by surprise as they stood by motionlessly and listened.

Click-click . . . Click-click . . . Click-click . . . Click-click.

Then they knew. The sound they were hearing came from an army of mechanical hearts.

Katherine took a step forward, her own heart pounding out an eager response. This building was more horrible than any of the others. It represented an assault against life itself. From behind the orchestra of mechanical sounds loomed a chilling silence—the type that was reserved for the depths of tombs. Within these walls the tables had been ironically turned, and what they were hearing was the most mournful lament for all mankind.

Click-click . . . Click-click . . . Click-click . . . Click-click.

It was a prison they had entered where the inmates shared one terrible commonality. At one time the desire for life had been fought for so savagely that science had been called upon to help, and now it was science which had taken them captive. In the end, they were forced to linger with only one new request. The weary beats of their artificial hearts called out to anyone willing to listen to their plea. They cried out for assistance; they begged for forgiveness; they were asking to be given back the most precious of all gifts.

Click-click . . . Click-click . . . Click-click . . . Click-click.

They were asking for the final peace that could only come through eternal sleep.

15

Stewart stood in the center of yet another long hallway, but this time there were no great secrets lurking behind the closed doors, for he already knew the search had ended. They had found what they had been looking for. His sole purpose now was to find Ernest Freeman, and bring him back out into the world so that everyone could see how the Northeastern Heart Institute had lied about his death. From there he would tell the rest of his stories about the other buildings—the other *research projects.* Hopefully, it would be enough to make the authorities launch an investigation. The plan was simple. Only one problem remained—locating Katherine's grandfather.

Because of the heart patients, this building was different, and even though it looked the same as the others from the outside, the inside was distinctive.

Besides the peculiar sound of the clicking hearts—to which he found himself growing accustomed in the same manner a blue collar worker grows accustomed to the continual noise of machinery—a queer odor filled the air. Not an unpleasant smell, it was more of an annatural scent that lacked any identifiable characteristics—a bland, nothing odor that came from an atmosphere that had been filtered to the point of absolute sterility.

They had come in through a basement, cool and dark, and he took Katherine by the hand in search of a stairwell that would take them to the main level.

Katherine didn't object. She no longer cared, for the experience of the night had already taken its toll. At one time she'd lived in a safe world, a peaceful place where the only great tragedy might come in an unexpected snowstorm that left the inhabitants of Sun Valley stranded for a few days, or not having the proper equipment to complete a work of art. She'd deliberately locked herself away, knowing full well that she was not the type of person who could tolerate severe stress. All of this had been changed when she'd first been told about her grandfather, and now the realization that he'd been locked away for so many years, the frantic days that had followed as she'd tried to convince others that he was still alive, and all the unspeakable sights that she'd witnessed within the desolate buildings had been too much to bear, causing her delicate psyche to crumble. She no longer cared about dealing with reality, and from the emotionless expression that had frozen on her face, the way she stared straight ahead without even bothering to blink, it was clear that she'd slipped into a mild form of shock. Instead of facing the nightmare head on, she'd allowed herself the luxury of submerging into a world she knew best, a fantasy world where she could more comfortably wage her mental battles free from the threat of the pressures of life. As she walked along behind Stew, she set up an impenetrable psychological barrier that made her appear almost catatonic.

There is beauty in the world, she tried to tell herself. It still exists. Colors are beautiful, and what is even more lovely are hundreds of colors blending together to form a picture. Painting. How she wished she were painting at that moment—creating a world where she alone had control. All of the ugly blemishes of life could be smothered by an intricate work of art.

From behind her subconscious wall she could still hear the nagging cry of the artificial hearts. Her barrier was not strong enough. How would one attempt to paint this picture, she asked herself? Different tones of gray for the sullenness; blues to reflect sorrow? No bright colors could be used for those should indicate hope and cheer, and there was none of that in this place. Yes, a lifelike portrait of Winnow Cove would be best captured in black, and this thought filled her with a desperate depression where she fought the urge to sit down and weep.

Black was the most dismal of all shades. It was the tone she'd used most after the death of her mother. Wendell was the first to notice her obsession with it.

"Don't you ever paint anything happy?" he'd asked one day while gazing over her shoulder as she worked.

"Happy?" she'd asked. "Sorry, but I don't see the world as a very happy place, and I only paint what I see."

"Do you think that's fair?"

"Why should it be fair?"

"Because whatever an artist creates will have an effect on others. Why should you deliberately portray more sorrow when you have the capability of bestowing a little cheer? Sure, misery exists, but that doesn't mean that anyone wants to look at it."

He was right, and from that moment on she decided to change her depressing style, giving to others only the beauty they wanted to see. The response was positive. She found that it was easier to sell her works, for people felt better looking at life through rose-colored glasses in the same way that they felt better viewing an attractive apartment complex that concealed horrors within. That was why places like Winnow Cove could successfully survive. Nobody wanted to see the real inner picture—the one that was painted in black.

"Kath?" Stew was calling out and shaking her shoulder.

It was impossible for him to penetrate her mental fortress. She giggled. How foolish of him for trying. Why didn't he just go away?

"Kath?" he hissed between clenched teeth. "What the hell's wrong with you?"

Her eyes began to focus and she found herself staring into his concerned face. Go away, she shouted to herself! Go away and leave me alone! I won't be part of your world any more. I'm tired of painting in black.

"Kath!" he pulled her towards him, shaking her shoulders violently. "Damn you! Don't fall apart now! I need you!"

A tear fell from her eye, and she blinked. "Stew?"

"Kath." A look of relief washed across his face. "Are you okay?"

"I . . . I don't know," she stammered.

"What's wrong?"

Wrong? He asked what was wrong after all they'd seen? She hung her head. "Why . . . why nothing." He'd never understand.

"You sure?"

"Yeh, I'm okay now."

Stewart studied her, wondering if she were being truthful.

"I really am okay," she said, brushing away a lock of hair that had fallen across one eye. "Guess I was a little shook, but now I'm all right."

Satisfied that she really had pulled herself together, he opened the door to the stairwell that led upward. The sound of the clicking hearts grew in intensity as they ascended, and he forgot about the scare with Katherine, concentrating more on what they would find. How many were there in this building? Who had been the first? And after all these years, how old would the victims be? Perhaps there were more surprises in store on the main level.

They reached the top of the stairs, and he pushed the door open a crack to see what was on the other side. It was another long corridor with brightly waxed floors and sparkling walls that gave it the appearance of a small hospital. Two nurses wearing the standard electric blue uniforms of the Institute padded along in their dazzling white shoes, quietly conversing. Stew allowed the door to ease shut as they passed.

"I really do hate to leave," the younger nurse was saying. "I like the hours. The work is easy. And everyone on the staff has been kind."

"Then why'd you put in for the transfer?" the older nurse asked in a voice as coarse as sandpaper.

"I don't know. Guess they're beginning to get to me—the patients. Oh, I don't mind the ones who are comatose; it's the ones who are still awake that I can't stand. They ask too many questions . . . and they complain. According to them we can't do anything right. I'm tired of it. It's not my fault that they're here. I didn't make that decision. I don't see why they have to take it out on us.''

''You have to learn to ignore them,'' the older nurse explained. ''It's just that they find it difficult to accept this way of life. You're not the one who should feel guilty, in spite of what they might say. This was by their choosing. If they didn't want to become part of the research project, they should've decided that before signing the papers. Instead, all they could think about was getting their artificial hearts. No, I don't feel sympathetic in the least—no matter what they try and say!''

The voices faded off, and Stewart opened the door an inch to see if they had gone. So that was how the employees managed to keep their sanity, explaining the horror of their acts away by blaming it on the patients. But how did they explain away the other 'projects,' the tests that were being conducted on all those unborn babies in the other building? What papers had the infants signed? Who gave their permission? They were sick! In order to work here they had to be sick. He turned and motioned for Katherine to follow as he slipped down the hall.

''Wait,'' Stew suddenly whispered, drawing back. There was the sound of distant voices.

Clinging closely to the wall, he made his way down to the far end and craned his neck around the corner.

''Looks like a nurse's station,'' he muttered softly. ''We'll have to sneak past in order to get to the rooms. Looks like they're all sitting behind the desk. I don't think they'll be able to see us from below. Come on.'' He fell to his knees, creeping down the hallway on all fours. Katherine followed.

"I think," a woman was saying in a loud nasal tone, unaware of the pair who were passing beneath. "I think that if they keep saying they want to die, we should call their bluff. Tell them we're going to take back their hearts, and see what they have to say about that."

The station burst into laughter, and a man spoke up. "Not a bad idea. 314B is a prime example. Every time I get near the man he motions for me to pull the plug on his ventilator. Shoot! What's wrong with him? I keep telling him that it wouldn't matter. It's not the respirator that keeps him going. It's his Biotron. But he just can't accept that. Drives me crazy! Next time he tries that on me, I'm gonna scare the shit outa him. I'll tell him we're taking him back to surgery to give him back his old heart." He chuckled snidely. "Can't wait to see his face!"

Stew felt his pulse rise in anger. They were all the same—not an ounce of human compassion among the lot of them. How had they grown so callous? Perhaps it was this insensitivity that had first alerted him to the fact that something was wrong—the feeling he just couldn't shake. That night when they'd requested that the camera be kept off Ernie's hands was when he had first realized there was something uncanny about the hospital, as if they couldn't imagine that the old man had any feelings. It had come as a tremendous disappointment, for, like everyone else who lived in the area, he had once considered the Northeastern Heart Institute a type of medical giant, heroically striving for the betterment of mankind. He could still remember the first time he'd been sent on an assignment to set up an interview with the Chief of Staff. He'd been new to the station at that time, and had considered it a great honor to be called upon to meet such a distinguished man.

"I'd be pleased to appear on your program," the stately physician replied from behind his massive oak desk. "I'm sure you're aware that the Institute was originally founded for the purpose of research and development of heart disease, but if we were to generate enough interest and gain more community support, I'm sure we could acquire enough funding to move on into different areas. That's my dream."

"Maybe our program will help," Stew had said, wanting more than anything to be able to help him in attaining his goal. There was something powerful about him that was quite impressive. Becoming an ally of a man like this seemed right, as if you'd joined a type of majestic ethical team that was waging a valiant war against disease. As he'd walked out of that office later, he felt proud, and was anxious to make the television program a success. If they needed more funding, he would try in any possible way to help.

So the program was a success, and they did receive more private donations and grants. New buildings were developed, and the Northeastern Heart Institute had grown. They were able to expand their services to include more than just hearts. The regal Chief of Staff would live to see his dream come true, and as a result more secret buildings could be hidden inside the woods filled with all the new *research projects* that could somehow benefit the human race. It was just the helpless subjects of the research who wouldn't benefit; but everyone, including the rest of the staff, would never believe that they had done anything wrong. Why should they? It was in the name of *research!* And now he felt ashamed that he'd ever been in a position to assist them in their growth.

They made it safely past the station without being found out, and now knew they were in the final stages of their journey. They stood at the foot of another long corridor, facing dozens of closed doors. From behind the doors came the clicking of the mechanical hearts, and they didn't sound quite so weary now; they sounded angry and desperate, as if they knew someone was listening who might care enough to respond to their urgent plea. For a moment they stood there reverently, not certain if they were ready for this final curtain to be drawn in a play that had already proved itself hideous.

"Look," Stew explained. "We're gonna have to check all these rooms if we wanta find him. Why don't you take all the doors on the left, and I'll take the ones on the right?"

"I'd rather not," Katherine said, trying to sound apologetic. "I don't know what I'd do if I found him and . . . ." She couldn't go on, frightened by the picture that flashed through her mind.

"It's okay," Stew replied, deciding that she was probably right after recalling what had happened earlier. "You just keep watch then. I'll be right back." He ducked into the first room and was gone for only a few seconds before the door opened again and he staggered out. His face was white.

"What is it?" Katherine asked, reaching out so that he could balance himself.

"Kath," he choked, bringing up his hand to wipe a moist brow. "It was better that you didn't see."

"You mean it was . . . ?" Her voice cracked under the strain.

"No. It wasn't him. It was . . . it was someone else." He leaned against the wall to steady himself, closing his eyes. Immediately, the vision of the shell of a human being he had just left sprang back into his mind, and his eyes popped open in horror. The bastards! The dirty fiends! Sure, he was going to be the big man, finding an unbelievable story that would make him rich and famous. But he hadn't planned on anything like this! Every man had dreams, just as the Chief of Staff had once admitted. Dreams of wealth and success and eternal youth. Maybe that was how the man in the room had been destroyed, searching for his own dream of living forever.

Katherine didn't say a word. There was nothing to say that could erase the agony on his face. All she could do was to stand by helplessly and wait for him to regain his composure, thankful that it was he who had gone inside rather than she.

There remained more doors; other rooms still had to be checked. Stew decided there was no point in putting it off any longer. He took a deep breath and continued.

After the shock of that first room, none of the others seemed quite as bad, like taking the first plunge into cold water. But even as the water remained cold, and it was only the fact that your body could acquire a tolerance, so it was with each of the rooms he entered and left. As he moved down the hallway, opening each of the doors and going inside and coming back out again, he was paying an expensive price. The expression on his face told the story, and there was no need for Katherine to ask.

They moved slowly along, checking each room one by one. Stewart's face became even more pale and withdrawn, reflecting a severe emotional fatigue. He had put himself through this because he had believed. Katherine thought back to the scene in the police station, and how the detective hadn't been convinced that the Institute could do anything wrong. She thought back to the attorney who was afraid that he couldn't win his case. She pictured the fear in the private detective's eyes when he talked about playing with fire. Now they were the ones who had played with fire, stepping into an inferno that was worse than anything they could've imagined. Stew had been the only one who had been willing to believe. If it hadn't been for him, she would've gone home and they wouldn't have discovered the hundreds of tiny babies or the men with their deformities or the people who had been driven insane. They wouldn't have discovered that the accusations they'd made about the Institute were true; worse than true, it proved that they were medical monsters feeding off human prey. Stew had believed, and because he believed it showed he cared, which was more than she could say about anyone else. Because of it she felt a close bond grow between them that would never be broken.

His face was darkened when he came out of the next room, and Katherine took this opportunity to reach out for him with a fondness he didn't expect. "Thank you," she said softly.

He looked at her questioningly.

"I just wanted you to know," she continued, "how much this means to me; that you weren't like all the others; that you cared—that you've been a friend."

Her words filled him with warmth, and the darkness of his face magically brightened. He had thought that the story was his only motivation, but now he realized that being able to help her was a greater reward. With a revitalized spring to his step, he headed towards the next door and strutted inside.

He didn't return as quickly this time. The

moments dragged on and she began to feel uneasy. What had happened? She took a step forward, wondering if she should go in to check. Something must've happened. It shouldn't take this long. Then the door eased open and he stepped out into the hall, taking her by the arm and leading her to the other side so that they could speak.

"Kath," he said. "I think I've found him."

She clutched his hand excitedly. "What do you mean, you think? Don't you know? Did you ask him?"

"It sure looks like him, and I did try to ask. It's just that I couldn't get anything out of him. He seems confused. He keeps babbling about something . . . flowers and Doris and something about being ready."

"Doris?" Katherine cried softly. "Then it is him! Doris was my grandmother!"

He was alive! Somehow, even though she'd dared not admit it before, she hadn't really known for sure. Everything she'd done had only been based on a hunch, but now that she was standing outside the room of the man whom everyone had tried to convince her was dead, she realized that this was also what she'd wanted to believe. The purpose of her hunt was to know for sure that he had died. It was the same need that kept her awake at night for years after her mother's death. All this while the only thing she'd been fighting for was to put her mind at rest, and now she didn't know what to think. She was bewildered, confused because she had been right. He was alive after all!

And because he was alive, she found herself swimming in a sea of thoughts as each of the blanks was filled in. The tale had suddenly developed into a true story that was unbelievably cruel. Because he was alive it meant that he really had been hauled away mercilessly. While once he had cried out to the world for help because they were holding him prisoner inside an apartment; now they had taken him away to a place like this where a far worse penalty had awaited. Any of the anger she felt up to this point was swallowed up by a consuming rage. She despised them! She wanted to burst into the room, and throw her arms around her grandfather's frail shoulders, telling him that from this point on, everything would be okay. She longed to rush through the closed doorway, but she couldn't. For some reason her feet felt glued to the floor, and she found herself frozen with a sudden apprehension over what she could say—speechless.

"Well?" Stewart nudged her shoulder. "Aren't you gonna go inside? Isn't that what you were looking for?"

She took a step forward, her knees having turned to rubber, then reached for the door with a trembling hand.

It was a dark room, alarmingly cool, like stepping into a tiny cellar where forgotten articles had become mildewed and decayed. What was decaying in here? The menacing sounds of the other hearts were blotted out, smothered by the gentle clicking that the lone heart in the room produced. She paused to listen, wondering why it hadn't sounded this loud when they'd first met at the apartment. Then it occurred to her why there had been a change. It was because his chest had been covered with more flesh at that time, and the thinner the wall had become, the louder the clicking of the heart. So that was why the building was filled with such a clear beating. The patients didn't have enough flesh left to contain the sound, the walls of their chests having grown dangerously thin!

Gradually, her eyes began to adjust to the dim light, and she began studying the surroundings as she inched herself further inside. There were boxes, dozens and dozens of large boxes that had been loosely stacked upon one another, looking as though they'd been the huge toy building blocks of a child. Next to the stack of boxes was an odd looking machine that very closely resembled the kind she'd seen in hospitals that were used to test hearts. An EKG machine; yes that's what they called it, yet this one looked somewhat different. Close to the machine sat a tall metal gooseneck lamp that glowed down onto one side of a narrow hospital bed. She stepped forward in an attempt to see, and discovered that the lamp was positioned to shine directly upon a boney hip where there was exposed a deep, raw sore. Moving quietly forward, she searched for its owner.

Bending forward to study the figure in the bed, she sucked in her breath. It was Ernest Freeman! His body appeared surprisingly frail, nestled upon the high hospital bed like a shriveled skeleton. His bald head rested on the pillow, and he was lying on his side so that the lamp could focus its light on his hip in an attempt to heal the gaping sore. She recognized his face even though his crepe paper eyelids were sealed shut, and his cheekbones had become more deeply sunken.

"Who's . . . there?" he suddenly croaked, the pale lids fluttering open to reveal a pair of hollow, reddened eyes.

"Grandfather?" Katherine squeaked.

"Gran . . . father," the old man croaked. "Is this a . . . new game? Now ya try . . . ya try an' call me grand . . . father? Git outa her! Git outa here, ya damned bitch! Ya don't have the right ta call me yer grand . . . father!''

For a moment she was taken back. Had he known it was really her, or did he think he was speaking to one of the nurses? She stepped closer, reaching for his glasses.

"I told ya ta git outa here!" he screeched, pulling her hand away when she tried to perch the glasses on his nose. "Not git outa here an' leave me alone before I scratch our yer eyes!"

"Grandfather," she tried again. "It's me. It's Katherine."

"Katherine?" the old man whispered. "My mother's name was Katherine. Nobody knew that 'cept me."

"But I'm your granddaughter. I'm Alex's daughter. Don't you remember? I came for the television interview. Please, let me put your glasses on so you can see."

She picked up the glasses and nestled them across his nose. This time he lay still, deciding not to fight. Once they were in place, she bent down so that he could study her face. "Grandfather," she said with a warm smile. "See? It is me."

The old man squinted, then turned his head away. "Alex's daughter? Alex . . . Alex is dead."

"Yes he is, but I'm still here. Remember? I came for the television interview? We were on T.V."

"Television . . . yes . . . then they took me away." He brought up his withered hands, and buried his face in them as he began to cry. "They took me away! Said I was dead!" Suddenly he stopped crying, and looked at her fiercely. "But I'm not dead. I'm alive. They're still keeping me alive."

She bowed her head solemnly. "Yes, I know." Then she reached down to gently pat his shoulder.

"But I'm here now. We're going to take you away."

"Away? Away from here? But I can't leave . . . I'm sick."

"Yes you can. I'll help."

"Katherine," he repeated softly, seeming to savor the name. "My granddaughter." And for the first time there was a flicker of recognition. "You're Alex's girl."

"That's right. And now I'm here to take you away. You don't have to stay in this place any longer."

"No, it's too late."

"It's not too late! Grandfather, don't you want to leave?"

He sighed. "Sit down, Katherine. Sit down and talk."

"But there isn't time right now. We can talk later —once you're safe."

"Nobody ever wants to talk." He wagged his head in defeat.

For a moment she was silent, milling over his words. Even if there wasn't much time, if this is what he wanted, it seemed right to honor his request. She gazed at him lovingly. This was one of the empty spaces on a forgotten family tree. "All right," she finally agreed, pulling up a chair. "We can talk."

He closed his eyes and nodded. "Thank you."

She sat in the chair waiting for him to begin.

After several moments of silence, his eyes fluttered open. "How did you find me?"

"It wasn't easy," she replied, feeling a rush of relief now that he'd come to his senses.

"There were . . . there were so many things . . . so many things I wanted to tell you that night. But I lost my head. And they took me away. I never . . . I never

322

thought I'd see you again." He paused for a moment and scowled. "They're scoundrels, the whole lot of them. You don't know what they're doing. I'm not alone."

"Yes, I know."

"You know," he went on. "I didn't think I had any family left. When I first heard about you . . . well, I thought it was another one of their lies. Suppose I don't deserve to have any family. Never was much of a family man. Never thought it was important . . . until. . . ."

"I understand," she said. "It's hard for me to believe, too. I never knew anything about my father's side of the family."

"So now you know." He looked at her wistfully. "Did you ever know your father?"

"No. All I knew was what my mother told me."

Ernie's wrinkled face softened, and he stared into space. "He was a stubborn young man. Nothing was good enough for him. Somehow, I never felt as though I lived up to his high expectations. He had big ideas. I put him through college. Never had much schooling myself, but Alex wanted to go to college, so I scraped together enough money to send him." He didn't wait for her to respond, anxious to continue speaking now that he'd finally found a listener. "I had a business once. Wasn't much, but gave us enough to get by." His aged eyes sharpened. "Your father wouldn't have anything to do with it. Guess it wasn't good enough for him. Funny, but he always made me feel as if I wasn't good enough, either. That's a strange way to feel about your own son. When I decided to have this heart put in, well it was supposed to prove to him that I could do something right. Imagine he's sitting there laughing at me right now. I didn't even do that right."

"I don't think that's true. I'll bet he was very proud of you."

"No. You didn't know him, but I did. That's why he kept me a secret. He never even told your mother. I've thought about that." He paused to think. "I can remember the last time I saw him. Told me he was getting married." Ernie smiled to himself. "After all those years, he was finally taking my advice. And you know, he looked happy. A little tired, but happy. Then I found out that he had died —of a heart attack." His bald head tilted to one side. "Tell me, what was your mother like? Is she still . . . alive?"

"No, she's dead." Katherine stopped to think back, picturing her mother the way she remembered her as a child—before the alcohol—the way she must've looked at the time her father had met her. "She was a wonderful woman. Looked very much like your own wife, my grandmother Doris."

"Doris?" Ernie's bloodshot eyes turned misty. "Doris was a good woman. Always wanted to have a nice garden. She had this thing about nature. Liked spending time outdoors. I still can picture her in her favorite dress. It was green."

Katherine smiled, suddenly understanding where she'd acquired her own love for nature, and feeling much closer to the name on the cemetery marker.

"I put her through hell," he continued. "Alex could see what was happening, but I was too blind." He pursed his dry lips. "There's so little time—so little time to spend with the people you love."

She sat in the chair and listened, knowing that the words he was speaking were genuine.

"I lay here," he went on, "and I think. I think of all the mistakes I've made in this miserable lifetime

—all the people I've hurt along the way. Doris, Shawn, and I know I caused your father his share of pain. That's why he wanted to forget about me. That's why he never told your mother."

"I don't think so," Katherine objected. "I think my father loved you very much. Maybe he didn't say anything because he didn't want you to feel hurt." She leaned forward, taking his shriveled hand in hers. "Nobody's life is perfect. You said that I didn't know your son, and that's true. But in the same respect, you didn't know my mother. She was a very sensitive person, not the kind who could easily adapt to stress. I think you underestimate my father. Love can make a big difference. Sometimes, even though people make mistakes, love teaches them to forgive."

His eyes welled with tears. "Then you don't think he was ashamed . . . ashamed of me?"

"No grandfather. Time just ran out."

"Time," he groaned. "What do any of us really know about time?" He took a deep breath, staring straight ahead as if he could visualize a world she wasn't capable of perceiving—the same expression she'd seen on the faces of artists at a moment of great inspiration.

"You know what?" he suddenly asked. "You know what I want most?"

She waited for him to reveal the answer.

"All I want now is to be able to go home."

At first she was puzzled. Surely he knew a request like that was impossible. Too many years had gone by in which he'd been kept a possession of the Institute. "But grandfather, you don't understand," she stammered. "Your home is no longer there."

His eyes narrowed, and he gazed back at her with profound wisdom. "Katherine, my dear, it's you who don't understand. My home will always be there. Home is with the people you love—with your family. And now I'm ready to join them. Can you see what I'm trying to say? I'm finally ready to go home.''

It was then that she understood. A thought flashed through her head, the accusation once made by the hospital administrator. He had claimed that if Ernest Freeman were removed from his artificial environment he would most certainly die, and that would mean that she had willingly taken part in an act of murder. When he'd made that statement, she'd felt uneasy, not knowing if what she was contemplating was right. But now she did know. It was impossible to murder this man. The people of the Institute had killed his spirit many years before. Now, the most merciful thing to do was to allow him to die—to let him join the ones he loved. Any doubts that may have lingered were erased, and she felt confident in her decision.

Before she could reply, the door suddenly burst open and Stewart came scrambling in, his face filled with fear. ''Kath!'' he cried. ''We've gotta get outa here! Someone's coming!''

16

Katherine was stunned. Stewart's hurried announcement came like a blow to the head, leaving her tumbling in a sea of panic and indecisiveness where she remained frozen to the chair, unable to move. She never really believed she'd ever have to confront one of them.

"Come on!" Stew growled, grabbing her by the arm to pull her away.

Her eyes darted back to her grandfather.

No! Ernie seemed to scream in desperation. Don't go away! If you do, I'll never see you again. "Katherine," he finally choked, for it was all that he could manage. He tried to pull himself up, but his limbs were too weak, and he fell back against the pillows like a dried heap of bones. "Katherine! Don't leave me! Please!"

She stared down at the helpless old man, not

knowing what to do, then glanced up at Stewart. "Can't we take him?"

"We'll come back later. But if we don't get outa here now, we're gonna get caught!"

Ernie extended a withered hand. No!

"Come on!" Stew insisted.

Feeling hopelessly torn, she slowly pulled herself up. "I'll be back, grandfather," she whispered, leaning over to plant a fond kiss of farewell on his wrinkled forehead. "I promise."

Stewart gave her arm one more tug, and succeeded in pulling her away from the bedside and over to the doorway.

Ernie watched them leave. If only time hadn't stolen from him the vitality he'd once possessed; if only he'd have been stronger, then they would've taken him—he could've gone with them. He pulled back the thin arm that was still stretched out in their direction, and closed his eyes to erase the vision of the last remaining remnant of his family as she vanished. "Goodbye," he muttered softly to himself.

Their escape was short-lived, interrupted before they'd made it as far as the hallway. The door to the room flew open, and a burly nurse, who was so large she made Stew look tiny in comparison, stood towering on the threshold. When she saw them her mouth fell open in surprise. "Who're you?" she snapped. "What is this?"

Stewart didn't reply, instead he tried to push his way past the set of mountainous hips. But she barred the way with her massive body, refusing to let him through.

They watched as her eyes flashed angrily, and her face puckered into a frown. "I know what this is!" she stated emphatically. "Why this is a security violation!" With a flick of her hamlike arms, she shoved him aside and reached for a small red button that sat posted on the wall. Once it had been pressed, she spun around with a shrill cry. "Security Code! Security Code!" A wailing alarm blared through every speaker in the building, and a thunder of footsteps could be hear racing in their direction. "Security Code! Room 321! Security Code, in here!" the obese nurse continued to shriek, her voice sounding more piercing than the siren. Katherine and Stew stood by defenseless, knowing that to run at this point would be futile.

Before they had time to formulate a new plan, the room was swarming with an army of nurses and attendants all wearing the standard uniforms of electric blue that made them look like a colorful military regiment. They spotted the intruders, and immediately pushed them back against the wall to pin them down so that they could be captured.

Stewart glared at them, his eyes wild with indignant fury. If they were coming as a ruthless gang who didn't take the time to ask questions, then he wasn't going down without a fight! With that he braced his huge body, and letting out a courageous cry, flung himself against the oncoming mob. The staff was caught off guard and went stumbling backwards, falling on top of each other like a row of painted dominos, their arms and legs violently thrashing.

"Security Code! Security Code!" the chunky nurse in the corner continued to scream.

Katherine, being unable to tolerate the incessant noise any longer, whirled around and flew at the woman to clasp her hand over the blaring mouth. The nurse, amazed at Katherine's sudden show of valor, reached up in an attempt to pry away the

Linda Brieno

clenching fingers, and the two went tumbling to the
floor in a frantic scuffle.

Having recovered from the initial shock of Stew's
onslaught, the crowd of employees began pulling
themselves apart for a second attack. This time Stew
ran towards the stack of boxes nestled in the corner,
and began hurling them at the assailants one by one.
As each box hit the floor, rolls and rolls of ticker tape
spilled out at their feet, and as the employees
continued coming they slipped across the wide
ribbons of red and white graph paper. When they
reached Stew's flailing arms, each of them grabbed
at them until they were pulled up painfully against
his perspiring back. With three on each arm he
continued to struggle valiantly, but the battle was
over and eventually he was forced to give up. Over
in the corner, Katherine had also lost her fight. The
gigantic nurse had overpowered her willowy foe,
and now held a lock of Katherine's thick hair in her
chubby fist. With a shove, she sent Katherine flying
across the floor over to where Stew was standing.

"Okay," one of the guards addressed the pair,
panting breathlessly. "Who the hell are you, and
what are you doing in this room?"

Stew sneered at him, then leaned forward to spit
in his face.

"Damn you!" the irate man cursed, rearing back
on his heels. "Okay. Have it your own way. Come
on." He grabbed Stew by the scruff of the neck, and
pushed him ahead through the doorway. "Let's go!"

They were about to make their exit when a
tortured voice cried from the bed. "Katherine!" It
was Ernie.

Katherine tried to turn towards him, but there
were too many pairs of hands that were holding her
fast. "Grandfather," she called out in response, but

330

before anything more could be said they'd hauled her away.

"So you had to come in here and start stirring up trouble," Otto Armstrong was saying as he stood in the cramped office where Stew and Katherine had been bound to a pair of wooden chairs. It was the engineer's room on the lower level, and wasn't equipped for the number of guests who now occupied the area. Armstrong paced back and forth in the small space allotted. "You were trespassing. Not only that, but you're guilty of *breaking and entering*." He stopped pacing long enough to scowl down at them ferociously. "You had no business coming on this property!" he shouted. "No business at all!" He turned on his heel, sputtering to himself. "Damned if I don't get called in the middle of the night because of two idiots who think they have the right to just traipse in here and try to take one of our patients."

"We did have business here," Katherine objected, squirming against the ropes so she could see him as he walked about. "My grandfather was here. You told me he was dead, but he was here all along. You lied!"

"You had no business being here," Armstrong repeated. "The papers were signed. He belongs to us! Both of you have broken the law."

"So what're you gonna do about it?" Stew asked. "Have us arrested? Just try it. It'll help to speed up the process. The authorities should've investigated this place a long time ago."

The hospital administrator paused, cocking his head to one side in apparent confusion. "I don't know what you're talking about."

"The hell you don't!" Stew strained at the rope that was holding him tightly in the chair. "You think

we didn't see what was in all those other buildings?
You think we don't know what you're doing?"

Dr. Roberts stepped forward, insulted by such an
unfounded claim. "Mr. Ness," he explained. "Each
of the buildings in Winnow Cove is designed for a
specific purpose. There are intensive medical
research projects taking place. Of course, as a lay
person, I wouldn't expect you to understand. But
that certainly doesn't mean we must justify our
actions for someone like you."

"All I understand is what I saw," Stew boldly
retorted. "There are human beings in there, and
you're testing them like animals; worse than
animals! Why I wouldn't treat a dog like that.
They're being tortured!"

"Like I said," Roberts went on, crossing his arms
defensively. "Since you obviously have no medical
background, it's impossible for you to understand
why these programs are crucial."

"Maybe I don't know what you have as a
purpose," Stew argued. "Maybe I'm not trained in
the field of medicine. But I am skilled in communi-
cations. I'm trained to understand the public, and I
can tell you right now that the average person would
feel just as revolted as I am. What you're doing is
sick, and when people find out about this you'll see
who understands."

"Mr. Ness," Otto Armstrong smiled down con-
descendingly. "You're no threat to us."

"No? Then who would be a threat? Certainly not a
bunch of helpless unborn babies that you're turning
into freaks. And the people who work for you? I'm
sure they're no threat, you have them so pathetically
programmed they can't even think for themselves.
Who is a threat to you? Was it Ernest Freeman when
he went on national television and tried to expose

you for what you were? Is that why it was necessary to announce that he'd died, when all along you planned on keeping him alive in this hell-hole with all these other poor creatures? By the way, how many are there? I only saw a few. How many other families have been deceived? I'm sure they'll be utterly amazed when they find out. Is that a threat to you? Is it?'' His face had turned purple with rage.

"And just how do you suppose that they'll ever find out?" Sid Chandler, who was seated on one corner of the desk, asked.

Stew looked over at him, then caught the full gist of his question. "Hey, wait a minute!" he replied, twisting his wrists in the ropes to try and set himself free. "What do you plan on doing with us?"

"It's really rather unfortunate that you found it necessary to interfere at this time," Armstrong said with a sympathetic shrug. "Long before we were prepared to have our results published. I'm afraid that if word were to get out prematurely, the results of our testing could be greatly jeopardized."

"What do you plan on doing?" Stew repeated.

Otto Armstrong nodded to Dr. Roberts to continue.

"The human body is simply fascinating," Roberts said with a kindly smile. "Sometimes problems arise that we're able to correct, and sometimes conditions surface where we find ourselves in circumstances we know nothing about. Even here at the Northeastern Heart Institute, the finest medical research facility in the world, we don't have all the answers. For instance, how does a team of physicians set about reversing the effects of severe head injury after the fatal fall of a young woman, or how could anyone hope to counteract the results of a massive heart attack in an obese, middle-aged male?

We may know a lot about the human body, but we don't know enough to work miracles."

"You can do those things to us?" Katherine asked.

"Of course. We may not be able to work miracles in order to reverse these problems, but we do know how to cause them."

The picture was becoming clear. Katherine looked at them in horror. Why was it that her father had died of a heart attack so soon after visiting her grandfather? "You did this to my father!" she screamed. "You killed him!" She struggled against the rope, then fell back against the wooden chair in tears.

Dr. Roberts looked down at her coldly. "It had to be. He would've interfered with our research program. Besides, that was a long time ago and the men who were responsible are no longer here."

She closed her eyes, feeling the full extent of her hatred seep through her body. Her mother's lonely existence—the alchohol—going through life without ever knowing her father. They did this to her! Their cruelty knew no limits.

"So, what about us?" Stew asked, curious as to what they had planned.

"Wouldn't it be tragic," Sid Chandler jumped off the desk, and walked over to where they were seated. "Wouldn't it be tragic if for some odd reason the granddaughter of one of our former artificial heart recipients convinced a low grade reporter to trespass on our premises one night? And just as they were making their way over the fence, the young woman lost her balance and fell? Naturally, a fall like that would result in severe cerebral edema that would cause a profound coma and death. And the reporter, suddenly alone and fearful of getting caught and losing his job, tried dragging her away, but the strain of his own excessive weight, along with a natural coronary artery disease, caused him to suffer an acute myocardiac infarction—a heart attack that also resulted in his death? I think it's a rather heartbreaking story. Too bad it couldn't have been prevented."

"You'll never get away with it," Stew growled.

"No? We'll keep that for posterity as your famous last words." Sid chuckled, then looked over at the physician. "Dr. Roberts, would you kindly call one of your attendants to help them get ready? It's almost morning, and we still have to take a short drive."

Ernie lay in the darkened room, forlornly staring at his surroundings. He was angry. They had not only tampered with his life, but they were threatening his grandchild. Why? What had any of them ever done to cause them to react in such a way? She would never return, no matter what she'd promised —just like all the others. He knew. Now, the solution to his problem was left entirely up to him. If only he'd been stronger, he would've been able to join them in their fight—if only he'd still been a man.

But he wasn't a man. His surroundings lent proof that they'd succeeded in reducing him to a mere fragment of humanity. All that he'd become was reflected by the cell-like room that was worse than any prison, for it was actually a sterile laboratory where he was kept alive as their specimen.

Alive? Was he really alive—living? How could one consider it living when the world had been limited to four bare walls, and when the extent of a journey took place within the confines of a hospital bed when he was rolled from side to side? Was it living to have a heat lamp as your only sun, or to stare up at the tiled ceiling and know that it was your only sky? Was life meant to be controlled by a piece of machinery and continued to click within your chest, or by a thing called the ticker tape machine?

The ticker tape machine. His weary eyes beheld the mechanical monster as it slept in the corner, ready to be awakened at any time. This was the real culprit, the electrifying drill sergeant that kept his heart marching along at a predetermined cadence. New faces would always be there to operate the device; new hands would adjust the dials; but it was the ticker tape that was guilty of the crime—condemning him to everlasting life. He might hate the mechanical heart and loathe the ones responsible for its design, but it would always be the ticker tape that he despised the most.

How foolish he'd once been when he'd thought there was nothing else on which to rely. Doris had always disagreed. She claimed the real answer came within a book—the Bible. Now her Bible was the only visible proof that she had once walked the earth. The underlined passages had been her last words of warning. And he'd read them. Not at first, but as time went by he'd turned to the pages where he found peace in the written words. Doris had been right all along. Within her torn and ragged Bible, Ernie found the promise of a better life—if he believed.

And death? What was so terrible about death in comparison to this hell on earth? What prize had he fought so hard to win? To be locked inside a human laboratory—imprisoned within a body that was nothing more than a corroding shell?

Once there had been a great canyon, and he hadn't been allowed to cross over to the other side. Now he understood that the canyon represented a false hope in man, and that his first mistake had been in believing it was man on whom he should rely. There had also been a brilliant light that illuminated love and peace. To be without this light was to exist in utter darkness, and God was that light. Yes, he needed all this time to set his priorities—to get his house in order. And when the time was right—when he was finally ready, God would call him home.

He lay on the bed feeling the mechanical heart as it thumped inside his chest, and he listened to the rhythmic clicking as it echoed its lament. The heart was only a fabrication of what God had first created, and because it was created by man it could never be perfect. There was a difference. There was a flaw.

What was the great difference between the products of men and what God had created? What made a man unique when compared to a machine? Hadn't man been created in God's image? What did that really mean? There must be a fine line that separated the two, and he lay alone in his silent room trying to think. Suddenly he knew the answer! It was his ability to do just that—to think! God had equipped each and every person with a mind of their own, and it was in having this freedom to think for yourself that protected you from ever having to be chained!

ONLY THE WEAK HAFTA DEPEND ON MACHINES. Isn't that what his father had once said? BUT—if the human mind were capable of creating such monstrosities, then couldn't the human mind find a way in which one could be destroyed?

He looked at the lamp that still shown down from where it had been pushed during the scuffle. After studying the lamp he glanced over at the ticker tape machine. Now he understood. He was a man, a creation of God, and because of this he could think for himself. And because of that he knew what he must do.

With all the strength that he could muster, he clawed his way over to the side of the bed. The pain was excruciating, but he gritted his teeth and continued moving slowly across the mattress. When he successfully reached the edge, he swung his contracted legs towards the floor, fighting to control a wave of dizziness. For a moment he paused, then reached down for the light cord that dangled at his knees. Slowly. Slowly. He inched the shiny metal lamp closer, until he could grasp its skinny neck between his claw-like fingers. Using the pole as a brace he climbed to his feet, leaning against it to keep himself steady. Beneath the weight of his frail body, he could hear the brittle bones of his hip crackle, but he continued to draw himself up until he was standing. It had been many years since he had last stood alone, and even though his slight figure was stooped forward and his legs were only capable of managing a rigid squat, he was still overcome with a sense of power. For the first time in years he was viewing the ticker tape machine from a higher position.

He reached for the lamp. This was his final hour. MAN WILL NEVER BE CONTROLLED BY A MACHINE. MAN WILL ALWAYS BE STRONGER. With the smooth metal in his hands, he began to lift the lamp off the floor, elevating it higher—higher—until it was trembling overhead in the air. Then with all of his might, all the strength of mankind throughout the ages—that primitive strength that was endowed by God to be summoned by the human mind—he braced his stringy muscles and swung! The metal lamp came crashing down against the plastic cover of the ticker tape machine, shattering its surface and exposing all its internal mechanisms in a shower of colorful sparks. The sparks didn't contain themselves, leaping out like a bursting firecracker and sending a jolt of electricity through the metal lamp and up into Ernie's shriveled hands. For a moment his body remained erect, overcome by this new source of power. And in that moment he smiled. In that fraction of a second, one fragment of time, he had the satisfaction of knowing—Man had conquered. It had always been this easy. Death had, at long last, come. Then his singed body crumpled to the floor in a heap.

The sparks had not only destroyed the machine, but served to ignite the many rolls of ticker tape that lay scattered upon the floor. In an instant the room had burst into flames. An alarm began to sound, and at the same time the lapping fire had made its way over to an oxygen inlet. The intense heat licked its way into the air system, and was followed by a series of explosions. Traveling along at an incredible pace, the fire made its way through the walls, consuming anything in its path. The employees at the end of the hall, who sat in the nurse's station, dropped what they were doing and began to run. Shoving each other aside, they raced to the door in order to find safety outside.

When the alarm sounded down in the cramped engineer's office on the ground level, none of the occupants guessed that it was of any significance. A drill. Testing the system. Perhaps smoke from an exhaust vent. Anything ordinary could've triggered the alarm. There was no need to worry. But when they heard the explosions and felt the structure shake, they realized that it was serious. Within seconds they were engulfed in smoke.

"Fire!" Otto Armstrong shouted.

"Oh, my God! We've gotta get out!" Sid Chandler raced for the door.

Dr. Roberts hesitated. "What about the patients?" he asked. "What about our research?"

"Are you nuts? It's too late for that," Armstrong replied, snatching up his briefcase and scrambling out. "The building's on fire! Save yourself!"

Billowy clouds of smoke streamed in through the heating ducts. Katherine and Stew, still tied to the chairs, looked at each other anxiously. Rocking and twisting their bodies, they tried to get free as the smoke around them thickened.

"Help!" Katherine screamed. "Someone help us!"

Stew joined her. "Help!"

"He-el-el-lp!!!" they shouted together, hoping that someone might hear.

Just then, an underweight attendant came running down the hallway, bursting his way into the room. But when he saw who was calling for help, he took a step back and turned to leave.

"Untie us!" Stew demanded.

"I . . . I can't," the man stammered. "They put you here."

"My God, man! Have you no compassion?" Stewart began to cough. "Don't leave us here to die!"

The attendant faltered, pausing to wipe the smoke from his eyes.

"Just cut the ropes," Stew pleaded. "Nobody'll ever know."

Glancing nervously over his shoulder, the man checked to see if anyone was watching. Then he rushed over to them with a bandage scissors, quickly cutting the ties.

"Thank you," Katherine gasped. "Thank you so much."

The attendant said nothing, turning on his heel to run off before Katherine could say anything else.

"Come on!" Stew shouted over the boom of another explosion. Plaster came crashing in around their heads. "This place is gonna go up at any minute. We've gotta get out!" He pulled her by the arm to lead her away.

"But my grandfather," she tried to explain. "What about my grandfather?"

"If they don't have him out by now, there's nothing we can do."

"But we can't just leave him!" Katherine cried. "I promised!"

"It's too late!" Stew bellowed, dragging her out the door.

She followed him as he made his way to the service exit. "Grandfather!" she called out, turning around for the last time. Stew opened the door, and pulled her to safety. "Grandfather," she sobbed once they were outdoors, her face streaming with tears as she stared back at the burning building.

The structure continued to burn into the early hours of dawn, when the horizon began to lighten and the rising sun made its first appearance as a hazy orange ball. Katherine and Stewart stood by solemnly, choosing not to speak. Words could never explain the emptiness as they watched the hungry flames devour the concrete building—destroying it completely.

The fire department arrived. Hoses were connected, and men in rubber raincoats wearing high boots dashed about the area. But it was too late. Dark smoke continued to pour angrily out of every crack and crevice, and a portion of the roof collapsed, sending a new display of multicolored flames shooting up into the sky.

They watched the scene together, wondering why this particular fire seemed so strange. When the wind suddenly shifted, the air was filled with the stench of charred bodies, and Katherine realized what it was. People had been left inside—patients who knew they were being burned to death. Yet they never uttered a sound; they never called out for help—almost as if they didn't want to be saved, as if they wanted to die. As the fire gutted its way through the building, the only sounds that could be heard were the shouts from the firefighters and a lonely wind as it howled through the empty hallways.

"Ness?" a distinguished looking gentleman called out through the window of his car.

Stewart turned to Katherine with a shrug. "Guess this is it. I'll be right back."

She didn't turn around, listening as he trudged across the gravel. Somehow she hoped that her grandfather had died a peaceful death. Keeping her eyes on the building, she waited for Stewart's return.

"Well?" she asked when he had joined her again.

"They want the story," he said, too exhausted to attempt a smile.

"And?"

"And they're promising me a raise, along with a permanent spot."

"Not bad." Katherine nodded her approval.

"No. They said that if this story mushrooms, it won't be the end. They'll need a good investigative reporter." He stuffed his hands in his pockets wishing he could sound a bit more cheerful. After all, he had achieved his goal. "Guess this is the end," he finally muttered.

"The end?" She looked up at him. "What do you mean?"

"Suppose we won't be seeing each other again. You'll be going back."

She lowered her eyes. "Wendell will be waiting."

"Yeh, Wendell."

"But I do want to thank you for your help."

"Think nothing of it."

They were silent for a moment, concentrating on the fire. A heavy beam of conrete fell with a crash, and burning embers scattered across the ground.

"What do you think happened?" Katherine suddenly blurted.

"You mean the fire?"

"Yes. We were so close to . . . to . . . you know."

"I don't know." He reached up to swat at a mosquito. "Guess we were just lucky."

"What about the people in the other buildings? What's going to happen to them?"

"Well, the dynamic trio was caught trying to make it out the main gate. The police took them away. Most of the patients will be evacuated. It'll take time to go through all the files."

"And the babies?"

"The babies are safe. Fortunately, these buildings were placed far enough apart. The fire didn't spread. They've got a team of state obstetricians in there right now. I don't know what they'll do about them. Even though they're not fully developoed, they're still human. Nobody could simply shut off their life supply. Of course, they did turn off those lights."

She studied the building. "What about the people

in there?''

''Suppose they'll dig through the remains. Try and get a positive ID on the victims. See how the fire was started.''

''Then, they're all dead?''

''Yeh, I don't think anyone gave much thought as to how to get 'em out.''

''And my grandfather?''

''He probably went fast. They already know that the fire was started in his wing.''

''I never thought it would end like this.''

''Neither did I. I suppose those patients in there never thought so either. All of them were somehow sucked into becoming the playthings of science.'' He shook his head. ''Research. Scientific advancement. Just doesn't seem right. It doesn't seem natural. Wonder how far the world's gonna go before this will all stop? It's a good lesson. There's no reward in trying to live forever. People should think about that.''

''Do you think that was a lesson my grandfather eventually learned?''

''Could be. I had a feeling about him the first time we met—like he was tired, but something was missing. It almost seemed as if he still wasn't ready to go.'' He jammed his hands in his pockets. ''But it was just a feeling.''

''I think he was ready. When I talked to him he mentioned something I didn't understand at first. He said that all he wanted was to go home. The only problem was that I don't think he knew the way.''

A chilly morning breeze gushed over them, and Katherine pulled her jacket tighter.

''Stew?'' she asked.

''Yeh?''

"I don't have to go back right away. The Art Fair's almost over, and Wendell can get along without me. Maybe we can talk. Besides, I don't know if I'm really ready."

"Ready for what?"

"To add any more limbs to a dying family tree, or find out that I may have picked a lemon."

He looked down at her and smiled.

Later that afternoon, a fireman waded through the smoldering debris. He heard something and paused. Digging his foot into the ashen cinders, he made a discovery. Reaching down, he pulled out a charred contraption that resembled a human heart. He called out to his partner to come take a look, and they stared down at the device in amazement. The mechanical heart, badly burned and completely un-attached, continued to beat. As he held it in his hand, they listened—to the rhythmic clicking.

"They were right what they said about this place," the firefighter dryly commented. "How many more do you think we'll find?"

"Hard to tell." The other fireman glanced about nervously, then turned back to the machine. Taking a sooty finger, he prodded at one of the valves. "Can you imagine those guys inventing a thing like this? Must've known what they were doing."

"Yeh, but they'll get what they deserve. I don't see how they thought they'd ever get away with it."

"Maybe," the first fireman replied, tilting his head to one side as he continued to listen to the steady beat. "But it might not have been such a bad idea."

"What're you talking about?"

He sighed wistfully, then drew the artificial heart up to his own stout chest as if trying it on for size. "With a ticker like this, who would ever want to die? It could become the world's next pacemaker."

THE END

MORE BLOOD-CHILLERS
FROM LEISURE BOOKS

2329-6	**EVIL STALKS THE NIGHT**	$3.50 US, $3.95 Can
2319-9	**LATE AT NIGHT**	$3.95 US, $4.50 Can
2309-1	**EVIL DREAMS**	$3.95 US, $4.50 Can
2300-8	**THE SECRET OF AMITYVILLE**	$3.50 US, $3.95 Can
2275-3	**FANGS**	$3.95 US, $4.50 Can
2269-9	**NIGHT OF THE WOLF**	$3.25
2265-6	**KISS NOT THE CHILD**	$3.75 US, $4.50 Can
2256-7	**CREATURE**	$3.75 US, $4.50 Can
2246-x	**DEATHBRINGER**	$3.75 US, $4.50 Can
2235-4	**SHIVERS**	$3.75 US, $4.50 Can
2225-7	**UNTO THE ALTAR**	$3.75 US, $4.50 Can
2220-6	**THE RIVARD HOUSE**	$3.25
2195-1	**BRAIN WATCH**	$3.50 US, $4.25 Can
2185-4	**BLOOD OFFERINGS**	$3.75 US, $4.50 Can
2152-8	**SISTER SATAN**	$3.75 US, $4.50 Can
2121-8	**UNDERTOW**	$3.75 US, $4.50 Can
2112-9	**SPAWN OF HELL**	$3.75 US, $4.50 Can

Spellbinding Medical Thrillers
From Leisure Books

THE ANATOMY LESSON   2344-x
Marshall Goldberg, M.D. $3.95 US, $4.50 CAN

NATURAL KILLERS   2339-3
Marshall Goldberg, M.D. $3.95 US, $4.50 CAN

INOCULATE   2333-4
Neil F. Bayne $3.50 US, $3.95 CAN

DISPOSABLE PEOPLE   2278-8
Marshall Goldberg, M.D. and Kenneth Kay $3.50 US
                                          $3.95 CAN

PAN   2238-9
J. Birney Dibble, M.D. $2.95

ELECTRIFYING HORROR
AND OCCULT

2343-1	**THE WERELING**	$3.50 US, $3.95 Can
2341-5	**THE ONI**	$3.95 US, $4.50 Can
2334-2	**PREMONITION**	$3.50 US, $3.95 Can
2331-8	**RESURREXIT**	$3.95 US, $4.50 Can
2302-4	**WORSHIP THE NIGHT**	$3.95 US, $3.95 Can
2289-3	**THE WITCHING**	$3.50 US, $3.95 Can
2281-8	**THE FREAK**	$2.50 US, $2.95 Can
2251-6	**THE HOUSE**	$2.50
2206-0	**CHILD OF DEMONS**	$3.75 US, $4.50 Can
2142-0	**THE FELLOWSHIP**	$3.75 US, $4.50 Can

A COMPUTER WIZARD HACKS INTO A NETWORK OF HIGH-TECH TERROR!

SAFETY CATCH

When his attractive neighbor suddenly disappears and the police are stumped, computer wizard David Cursore decides to do his own electronic sleuthing. With the help of a gorgeous red-haired reporter assigned to interview him for a national magazine, Cursore begins to trace the missing woman's movements by hacking into credit card and bank computers. Their investigation puts them on the trail of an unknown killer—but not even the most sophisticated technology can penetrate the twisted recesses of this particular madman's mind.

Grappling with the nation's computer network, Cursore races against time to extract the truth from its memory banks before "The Shadow" tops blackmail and extortion with the most bizarre mass murder plot ever devised.

2301-6 $3.95 US, $4.95 Can

Make the Most of Your Leisure Time with
LEISURE BOOKS

Please send me the following titles:

Quantity	Book Number	Price
_____	_____	_____
_____	_____	_____
_____	_____	_____
_____	_____	_____
_____	_____	_____

If out of stock on any of the above titles, please send me the alternate title(s) listed below:

_____	_____	_____
_____	_____	_____
_____	_____	_____
_____	_____	_____

Postage & Handling _____

Total Enclosed $ _____

☐ Please send me a free catalog.

NAME _____
(please print)

ADDRESS _____

CITY _____ STATE _____ ZIP _____

Please include $1.00 shipping and handling for the first book ordered and 25¢ for each book thereafter in the same order. All orders are shipped within approximately 4 weeks via postal service book rate. PAYMENT MUST ACCOMPANY ALL ORDERS.*

*Canadian orders must be paid in US dollars payable through a New York banking facility.

Mail coupon to: **Dorchester Publishing Co., Inc.
6 East 39 Street, Suite 900
New York, NY 10016
Att: ORDER DEPT.**